THE GUIDE

To Jarrolyn, Nov. 2007

THE GUIDE

by

Grant and Mary Workman

Hope you enjoy the story,

Mary and Grant

Copyright © 1996 by Grant and Mary Workman

All rights reserved. No part of this book may be reproduced, stored in a retrieval system, or transmitted by any means, electronic, mechanical, photocopying, recording, or otherwise, without written permission from the author.

ISBN 1-58500-279-8

ABOUT THE BOOK

In the Guide, you meet a different breed of vampire. In a world in which becoming a vampire isn't a matter of being bitten, of a demonic encounter or some curse buried in myth and lost lore but a matter of your genetic code, your DNA.

In this world, there is a society where vampire humans and non-vampire humans work together to guide the whole of mankind into an understanding and acceptance of one another. Most non-vampires don't know of the vampires' peaceful co-existence. Of course, not all vampires are members of the Guide and share the Guide's views and values. The newest member of the Guide, Eddie Laidlaw, is about to find that out.

CHAPTER 1

Eddie Laidlaw shook his head to clear the fuzz that was supposed to be his mind. He was cold and the room was dark. Eddie could tell he was in bed, but it wasn't his bed. He had a waterbed, and this was a firm mattress. The bed sheets were thin material, and there was no comforter or blanket that he could find by feeling around.

"You are awake sooner than I had expected," a voice said from somewhere in the dark room.

"Who's there?" Eddie demanded, sitting up in the bed. His head started spinning instantly and he had to lie back down. As he felt like he was going to be sick. Someone grabbed his shoulders and steadied his shaking.

"You are too weak to move." It was the voice from the dark.

Eddie forced himself to look at the person holding him. He couldn't see them too well, mostly just a shape. It was a woman though, but he knew that from the voice.

"Be still. You have no reason to worry. You are safe." The woman's voice was soft, calming, and almost hypnotic. "Sleep, we will talk when you are stronger." Eddie Laidlaw dropped into a restless sleep almost before she finished speaking.

The woman gently stroked Eddie's ruffled brown hair. As she looked down on the sleeping form beside her she thought back to her first morning after joining the Guide. She wondered if she would be able to make it easier for him than it had been for her. She hoped she could, but only time would tell. He would still sleep for hours, and Rachel could see no reason for her not to do the same. She would know if he awoke. Rachel walked to a chair not too far from the bed and relaxed.

Eddie woke up with a start. He didn't know how long he'd been sleeping, but it felt like it had been a long time. His disorientation was similar to the first waking, but not as bad. He remembered going out to Mick's night club with his buddies and drinking heavily, but he didn't remember leaving, or know where he was right now. A hotel, that was simple and easy, but what hotel and where? The furnishings were nice--it wasn't a fleabag, anyway. Eddie sat up and felt his stomach turn, he thought he might throw up, but was able to force himself not to. The room wasn't dark this time. There was a light on next to the bed and some sunlight coming in around the edges of the heavy curtains. The light was enough to see someone sleeping in a chair not far from the bed. The sleeper was female, but that was all he could tell except that she looked--no that was wrong--she felt familiar. Still, he was sure he didn't know her. Eddie moved to the edge of the bed. Something was telling him it was time to go, and Eddie had made a habit of listening to that little something most of the time. Too bad he hadn't listened to that little something last night. He sure felt like hell right now.

"You are still very weak. It would be better for you to lay back. Rest, even if you don't sleep."

Eddie looked to the woman. She did not stir. "Who are you?" His voice was heavy from his throat being dry.

"A friend. My name is Rachel." The woman rose from her chair. Although there was light, it was stronger on the opposite side of the bed, leaving Rachel mostly in the shadows. Eddie couldn't tell much about her. She was dressed in a black skirt and top, with a black waistcoat over the top. "If you insist on staying up, let me get you something to drink. I'm sure you must be thirsty." Turning her back to Eddie, Rachel walked to a small refrigerator in the room, knelt, and opened it. "It will replace some of your strength."

Eddie did feel weak and thirsty, but he wondered how she knew. He heard a soft puncture sound like a hole being made in a milk carton. Then there was the sound of liquid pouring.

Rachel stood up, closing the refrigerator as she turned to Eddie. As she neared, Eddie could see her better and he did recognize her.

"I saw you in the bar last night, didn't I?" He wasn't asking her. "You looked out of place there." He looked around the room. Classy--elegant almost. "Hope you got the bucks for this place, lady."

"Rachel," she reminded him, and smiled. "Drink this." Rachel handed Eddie the glass. Orange juice filled the glass to the rim.

He took a drink and tried to hand it back to her. "There's something in this besides O.J."

"It will help you get your strength back, drink it up, Eddie." She pushed it back towards him.

Eddie looked at her then put the glass on the floor next to the bed. "I don't know you. I'll pass."

"If harming you were part of my plans, don't you think I would have done so while you slept?"

"I don't know. Maybe you get your kicks from drugging people. You see, I've been drunk before, and this hangover doesn't feel like a normal drunk."

"Well, Eddie, you did have quite a bit to drink, but I might have worn you out a bit more, myself."

Eddie forced himself to his feet. He wobbled and Rachel reached out to steady him. Eddie brushed her hands off. He tilted, but didn't fall. After a second or two, he was still and standing straight.

"You seem to be able to care for yourself now. I'll be on my way." Rachel went to a table in the room and retrieved her purse from it.

"Wait," Eddie called out. He wasn't sure why. "How can I reach you?" The question surprised Eddie more than it did Rachel.

"I'll be in touch, Mr. Laidlaw." Rachel opened the door and stepped out into the afternoon sunlight. "And Eddie, the room is on my credit card, you can stay as long as you like. I set that up with the hotel yesterday." Rachel pulled sunglasses from her waistcoat pocket, slipped them on, and walked away, not closing the door.

Eddie sat on the bed watching this woman walk away. Her words echoed in his head a minute before he thought about them. Yesterday! Eddie hurried across the bed to the phone on the nightstand, forcing the last bit of nausea away. He grabbed the receiver and punched the "0" button.

"Front Desk, how may I help you?" a woman's voice asked.

"I need an outside line."

"Of course, sir." There was an audible click, and she then came back on the line. "Just dial nine and the number you wish to call. Will that be all, sir?"

"What time is it?"

"Almost three, sir."

"Thanks." Eddie pushed the disconnect button of the phone, released it, then started dialing.

After a couple of rings the other phone was answered. A woman's voice came on the line. "Hello."

"Debra, let me talk to Frank. It's Eddie."

"Frank's at work, Eddie, where you're supposed to be, I think." Eddie could hear a touch of anger from her.

"Work?" Eddie asked sounding confused. "Isn't it Sunday?"

"Eddie, it's Monday. Are you all right?" Concern laced Debra's voice.

"Monday," Eddie repeated, almost not loud enough to hear.

"Are you all right?" she asked again.

"I just seem to have lost track of time. Yeah, I'm fine."

"You know, the guys were worried about you when you left with that woman Friday night, but I guess you're okay. You need to call Marsha, too. She was worried when she couldn't reach you."

"Marsha's always worried about something." Eddie's sarcasm came through the phone. He thought about all the times Marsha was after him to be careful about what he was involved in and who he ran with.

"She's your older sister, and the only family you have besides Frank and me. Don't tell me about her nagging you." All concern was gone from Debra's voice.

"I gotta go. Tell Frank I'll drop in tonight. I don't know exactly when." Eddie hesitated before hanging up. "Debra, call Marsha for me. Tell her I'm fine." Eddie didn't wait for a reply, putting the receiver back in the cradle.

Talking to a familiar voice had calmed him. His head was clear now, his thoughts not jumbled by nightmare-filled sleep and thoughts of a woman he didn't know. Eddie stood in the middle of the room looking around. Looking for what, he did not know. It was a spacious room with a queen size bed. There was a table with two chairs, a dresser for clothes, a nightstand, and a desk with a chair. At the back of the room was a door. It was open, letting Eddie see the bathroom. A shower came to mind at the sight of the bathroom. Eddie went to the still open front door, closed and locked it, then headed for the bathroom.

He stood in the shower for a long time, trying to let the water wash-up some of the memories of the weekend. Eddie remembered going to Mick's night club with the guys. A drink or two after work, on Fridays, was a tradition with them. He remembered going there, and he remembered seeing Rachel at the club, but he sure didn't remember talking to her or leaving with her.

The other hole in his memory was an injury to his left side. When he'd undressed to get in the shower, Eddie found a wound just below his rib cage. A puncture, from the look of it, about the size of a pencil, but it didn't appear to be deep. It seemed to be healing fine. It would have been nice to know how it happened, though. His shower didn't seem to be helping to clear his memories of the weekend, so Eddie turned the water off.

When he was dressed, he located his wallet and apartment keys. The keys and wallet were on the table Eddie had seen Rachel retrieve her purse from as she left. To Eddie's surprise and pleasure, he found a note wrapped around ten fifty dollar bills under his wallet. He read the note.

DEAR EDDIE,

GOOD MORNING SLEEPY. THE MONEY IS FOR TRAVELING EXPENSES TO SEE YOU GET HOME SAFELY. I HAD A VERY NICE TIME WITH YOU, BUT I'M SURE YOU'LL JUST HAVE TO TAKE MY WORD ON THAT, WON'T YOU. THERE'S A PARTY IN ABOUT A MONTH, SO I'LL BE IN TOUCH.
RACHEL

P.S. WELCOME TO THE GUIDE

Eddie read the note over and over again. It made no sense to him but five hundred dollars made up for that. He stuffed the money into his jeans pocket and left the hotel.

CHAPTER 2

"So you have absolutely no memory of leaving Friday night with this woman, until this afternoon?" Marsha repeated Eddie's statement.

"Just like I told all of you." Eddie looked from Frank to Debra to Marsha. "Only thing I remember was waking up once, and she was there. I can't even tell you when that was. Then I woke up this afternoon. I don't even remember leaving with her, or even talking to her."

"Well, you did, pal. You were drinking like you intended to drain the club dry. She and you were close all night." Frank related the events of Friday night to Eddie.

"Maybe we should take you for a blood test, Eddie."

"A blood test? For what?" Eddie was not going to the hospital over a one-night stand.

"Yeah, a blood test," Frank agreed, a serious look on his face. Then Frank burst into laughter. "For the marriage license."

Eddie laughed with him.

Even Debra giggled under her breath.

Marsha didn't find the joke as funny. "No, not for marriage, but to see what she gave you. It sounds like you were drugged. She might have slipped something in your drink. And you did say the orange juice tasted funny."

Eddie could see Marsha was serious about the blood test idea, though he didn't see the need for it. If Rachel had drugged him, it was done with, now. And next time, assuming there was a next time, he'd know to watch himself. "I don't think we need any tests. Besides, I feel fine now."

"You lost a day and a half of memories to this woman. Not to mention money. You were scheduled to work Sunday and today, of course. And your rent is already past due. What are you going to do about that?" Marsha knew she would loan him the money, again, but he'd regret making her go into her savings for it. "I'm not able to help you this month, not without going into my savings, and you know how I feel about that."

"I got rent covered, Marsha, so don't worry," Eddie assured her.

"Eddie, I've heard that--"

Eddie cut her off before she could finish. "I know I've told you that before. Well, you're hearing it again. But this time I do have it handled. I saw Mrs. Waverly already." Eddie pulled his rent receipt out of his shirt pocket.

Marsha looked at the receipt in disbelief. "How? You were short Friday. That's why you were working Sunday."

"That's not important. What is important is that I'm covered for another month." Eddie grinned at Frank. Frank knew the grin meant he'd find out later.

The rest of the afternoon and on into the early evening, the four people talked about the lost days, speculating as to what had taken place. Eddie didn't mention the puncture. He knew Marsha would drag him down to the hospital to have him checked top to bottom. He didn't need that, and the wound was healing just fine.

By ten o'clock, Debra was declaring the evening over. She pointed out that they all had to go to work in the morning. Frank hadn't mentioned it, but Debra told Eddie that Frank would not be covering for him any more at the warehouse. Debra also told Eddie that she wasn't going to let Frank lose his job because of him. Eddie wouldn't let that happen either, but he had pushed their boss at work to the limits.

"I'll be at work tomorrow. And, yes, on time," Eddie promised them emphatically. Debra and Frank walked Eddie and Marsha out to Marsha's car.

"Get in, Eddie, and I'll give you a lift home," Marsha told Eddie as she started the car.

"It's only a couple of blocks, Sis. I'll walk it. Thanks."

"You sure?"

Eddie nodded.

Marsha put the car in gear. "I'll see you at the hospital tomorrow, Debra," Marsha told her as she pulled away. Debra looked to Frank and Eddie and could see that they were waiting for her to go back inside.

"Men talk," Frank told her.

"Little kids talk is more like it." Debra smirked, and headed into the house.

"So what have you forgotten to tell the others?" Frank asked with a grin. Frank was older than Eddie by almost twenty years. They had met through Debra and Marsha, who worked together at Saint John's Hospital. The two men had hit it off at once, and when Eddie needed a job, Frank talked to his boss at the warehouse where he worked and had gotten Eddie hired.

"Not much, I wish I could remember more--like how I got this." Eddie pulled his shirt up, revealing the injury.

"My god, Eddie, what happened?" Frank started then stopped himself. "Stupid question." Frank touched the healing injury. Eddie flinched slightly. "It's red."

"It's kind of tender, but I think it's healing okay," Eddie told Frank.

"We'll let Debra decide that," Frank told him.

"I ain't tellin' her. She'll tell Marsha."

"She won't tell Marsha if I ask her not to. But if you don't march your butt in that house for her to look at it, I'll tell Marsha." Frank glared at Eddie with a look Eddie knew too well. Frank had taken on the role of big brother, best friend, and when needed, father.

Eddie could tell Frank wasn't kidding around, so he headed back to the house.

Debra wasn't pleased with him either, but promised not to say anything to Marsha. She also was none too gentle about scrubbing Eddie's puncture wound clean. She scrubbed it with a brush until it bled and cleaned it with alcohol, cursing Eddie for not letting her take him to the emergency room, where she had the proper equipment to work with. After she finished and chewed him out about not saying something sooner, Frank drove Eddie home. Frank told Eddie he would pick him up for work in the morning.

Eddie's sleep that night was filled with visions of places he didn't know, and of Rachel. He woke not feeling rested. He shoveled down a breakfast of eggs, bacon, toast, almost a full pot of coffee, and a candy bar. None of it seemed to hit the spot. His ride picked him up on time, and to Frank's delight, Eddie was ready to go.

The next week and a half flew by. Frank and Eddie skipped the club that Friday night. Instead, they took Debra and Marsha out to dinner and a movie. The week had been calm and the weekend was relaxing, but Eddie was still having strange dreams. He was only remembering little bits and pieces of the dreams. Mainly, it was dreams of Rachel. He hadn't been able to remember anything specific. His dreams were usually that way-- vague and unreal.

Eddie and Frank walked into work Thursday morning and joined the rest of the work crew, waiting for the foreman to give out the assignments he needed done that day. The crews knew for the most part what supplies and crates needed loading for delivery, but they waited for the boss anyway.

"Well, it's the weekend again. We going to see you two at Mick's this weekend?" Joe asked.

"Don't know yet," Frank replied.

"Probably," answered Eddie, giving Frank a quick look. Eddie didn't want to spend another weekend, quite so soon, with his sister, having her tell him he needed to plan his life and set some goals. He liked his life just fine.

Barn Haynes, the crew's foreman, joined the group. He was a tall man in his sixties. His once black hair was mostly gray now, but his body was still powerfully built. Lots of changes had taken place in this man since he started in this warehouse as a skinny, wise ass, Italian kid. With the stub of his cigar held firmly between his teeth, he said, "Laidlaw, truck two is loaded, manifest is in the drivers seat. Go."

"But Mr. Haynes, I'm not one of the drivers," Eddie informed the foreman.

Haynes turned to Eddie and poked him in the chest with a forefinger that was a cross between a steel I-beam and a jackhammer. "You're what I tell you you are. If I want your opinion on the matter, I'll tell you what it is. Now get." Haynes considered the matter closed. He turned his attention to handing out the rest of the assignments.

Eddie thought about smacking Haynes upside his head for

the finger in the chest. Then Eddie thought about a guy that used to work at the warehouse. A big guy, bigger than Eddie, had swung his fist at Haynes. That guy got the ass kicking of his life from Barn. Walking away, headed out to his truck, Eddie decided his decision was the sane one.

Eddie pulled the manifest from the driver's seat and headed to the back of the truck to check the cargo. That's what Eddie was doing when he got the feeling he was being watched. He turned around to find Barn standing there.

"Mr. Haynes," Eddie said, acknowledging his presence, wondering why Barn had stopped by the truck.

"Laidlaw, I think you should know something about me. I grew up working in this place, and I've seen a lot a people come and go. You're not a stupid kid, and when you're here you do good work, but if you ever talk back to me again in front of the crew, I'll tear your head off. It wouldn't be personal. Hell, Laidlaw, I kind of like you. You remind me of my kid brother in some ways. But the point is I learned this job from the bottom up, I've seen foremen get pushed around by punk kids, and I've seen foremen make punk kids into hard working men. I don't get pushed around. If you got anything to say to me, now's the time." Barn Haynes stood there, like some kind of brick wall, with a face of stone.

Eddie stayed quiet but stared right back at him. After a minute, Barn smiled.

"Okay then, just do what you're told around here and we'll get along fine." Haynes turned and walked away. Before Eddie could get his mind back on checking cargo, Frank jumped up in the truck with him.

"You just get the 'I've been here forever' speech? The one about 'I'll tear your head off next time' thing?"

"He gives it to everyone, I take it," Eddie stated.

"Just to jokers."

"Not to worry then?"

"He'll beat the hell out of you if you challenge him, Eddie."

"Beat me up and fire me?"

"No. You fight him and lose, and you got the guts to report back to work, he'll respect you. He'll still expect you to obey his orders, though." Frank got out of the truck and let Eddie get back to work. After checking the cargo Eddie left to make his deliveries.

The day went fairly smoothly. All of the drops were made on time and Eddie got back to the warehouse five minutes ahead of schedule. That's when his day fell apart. Eddie parked the truck and jumped down from the cab. Barn was on top of him almost before his feet touched the ground.

"What the hell's wrong with you?" Haynes yelled at the top of his lungs. "It was an easy route. All you had to do was unload the stuff, get a signature for the delivery, and leave." Barn pulled Eddie along to his office by the collar of his shirt. Inside the office, Barn pushed Eddie into a chair. "Come on, give me an answer."

"What? I didn't do anything." Eddie had no idea about what Barn was upset about.

"I've been getting calls all day about you. Did you make any deliveries without pulling an attitude on the customers?"

"I don't know what you're talking about?" Eddie tried to tell Barn the truth.

"Don't be lying to me. One customer I could overlook, but everyone on your list called in about the rude delivery driver. What's the problem? Did my little talk this morning not sink in, or did it piss you off?"

"But--" Eddie started to argue.

"No buts, orders from the owner. He got some calls today as well. You're fired. Clear out your locker, Laidlaw. I'll give Frank your last check tomorrow."

Eddie looked at the stone face of the foreman and knew arguing would be pointless. He had been fired, and he really wasn't sure for what. He got to his feet and walked as far as the door.

"For what it's worth, Mr. Haynes, I was nice to these people. I didn't do anything to them." Eddie walked away from the office.

"Frank!" Barn called out of the office door. Frank came in, and Barn closed the door. "You know what I just did." It wasn't a question.

"Yeah, Barn, I know."

"It was from the owner, not my idea."

"There wasn't any way around it?"

"He didn't want to hear it. 'Fire him' was the extent of our conversation."

"Why tell me?" Frank asked.

"You're assistant foreman for one. You're his friend for another. I've seen people get set up to be fired before, and I'm telling you that someone just went to a lot of trouble to fire that guy. I don't think he did anything, but I didn't have a choice in firing him. Tell him to keep his nose clean, Frank, and tell him to come see me in a month. Let this work itself out and I'll hire him back. You tell him, Frank."

Frank nodded and left the office. He'd get Eddie out of there and tell him over dinner.

Eddie didn't have a lot to collect from his locker. The tennis shoes that he wore to work before changing into his work boots for the day. And he kept a jacket in the locker as well. That was about it. Eddie tied the shoelaces together and tossed them over one shoulder, and his jacket over them. Frank walked into the locker room as Eddie was turning toward the door to leave.

"Come on, Eddie, we need to talk. I'll drive you home."

"I didn't do anything, Frank. I swear I didn't."

"I know, so does Barn, but he had his orders. We got lots to talk about. Come on."

"I'm going to walk, Frank--try to think this day over."

Frank saw the resolve on Eddie's face and nodded. "You be at my house at seven thirty for dinner and we'll talk then. Be there, it's important."

"I'll be there. Besides, I'm not in the position to turn down a free meal." Eddie smiled slightly at his friend's concern.

"I didn't say it was free," Frank pointed out, and then grinned. He walked Eddie out of the warehouse before he returned to work.

Eddie looked up the street and started his walk home. It wasn't that far, really. He would have to take one bus, but it would give him time to think. What Eddie found himself thinking about was the feeling that someone was watching him.

CHAPTER 3

Rachel Westchester stood in a side street near Eddie's apartment. Here, she could see the front of the building and the windows of his apartment. More importantly, she could watch without being seen. Eddie should be getting home anytime now. His job at the warehouse was through, she had seen to that. Rachel thought back to the weekend she'd spent with Eddie.

It was a strange feeling, the mind touch, as blooded members of the Guide called it. A mental tug drawing one person to another. Comparable, she thought, of two people brushing against one another in a crowded room. For the briefest instant, they were strangers, then not, then separate again. It seemed funny that this touch was the method by which many people had been recruited to Guide Membership. Many of those new members had worked out well with the one they'd mind touched, like Eddie had reached out to Rachel, but some did not. Rachel felt confident deep in her heart that she and Eddie would have no trouble between them. The party coming up would tell for sure if they would clash when it was time, when Eddie was ready.

Rachel suspected that wouldn't be a problem with Eddie, and the party would tell if she were right. Sebastian had told her that there were to be four new members at the party, including Laidlaw, four that he knew of, anyway. Of course, there was always the possibility of more. Rachel forced her thoughts from the past as she saw Eddie coming up the street.

Eddie was moving slowly and only half watching where he was going. He didn't see the two young men until they grabbed him. Rachel had seen them but had not thought about them being thieves. Eddie went down easily under the unexpected assault. The two men were throwing blow after blow, not wanting to have to fight their victim.

Rachel watched for half a second and then moved forward to help. The first mugger never saw her. One minute he was pounding away at Eddie, the next two hammer blows were slamming into his spine, centered between his shoulder blades.

He hardly screamed. The force of the blows took his breath away and sent him flying over the top of Eddie. Eddie didn't notice. He was mostly unconscious. The second mugger looked up as his partner pitched forward. He found Rachel's fist waiting. She hit him twice before he could even think. He fell back next to his partner and lay there. Rachel looked down at Eddie. He would have a few bruises for a day or two, but he would be fine. She got Eddie's keys out of his pocket, picked him up, and took him upstairs to his apartment.

Eddie woke to find himself in his own bed. He jumped as the attack returned to his thoughts. Questions popped into his mind. How did he get here? What had happened to the muggers? How long had be been unconscious, or had he been unconscious? Eddie caught a whiff of something in the air, something familiar, and he heard the front door in the living room open. With his head and his back hurting from the pounding, Eddie forced himself to roll off of the bed feeling every ache as he did. He stepped into the living room just in time to see the front door close. Eddie tried to race to the door, against the protests of his injured body. Not noticing the door was locked until he tried to open it, he lost several seconds fumbling with the locks. A few seconds later, Eddie jerked the door open.

At the far end of the hall, Eddie saw Rachel in the elevator. She saw him as well. Rachel winked, smiled, and blew him a kiss. The elevator doors slid closed.

"Wait!" Eddie yelled, charging the elevator. He reached the doors running full bore and pounded on them with his fist. "Come back!" He realized the familiar scent he'd smelled was her perfume. Eddie ran half way back up the hall to the door marked, "STAIRS." He raced down the two flights of stairs, missing most of the steps, and tore into the lobby of his apartment building. He ran past the desk to the elevator doors, which chimed before they opened. Eddie had her. The doors opened and Eddie stepped inside of the doorway. The elevator was empty. "Shit!" he cursed, returning to the front desk. "Albert, did you see which direction the woman who just came out of the elevator went?" Eddie pointed to the street entrance doors.

"What woman?"

"She just came through here, Albert. This is the only door from the elevator. Good looking, dark hair, wearing a tan skirt and white top?"

"Believe me, Eddie, if something even close to attractive came through here, I'd have seen it." Albert tugged on his gray beard. "When you get to be my age, lookin' is about all you can do."

"Thanks, Albert." Eddie punched the elevator button, waited, and climbed in as the doors opened. The elevator headed up, taking a confused Eddie with it.

In the lobby, Rachel stood up from behind Albert's security desk. She looked to the elevator, then to Albert.

"Thanks, Albert. You're such a dear." She walked around to the front of the desk and handed him a hundred dollar bill.

"Any time I can help," Albert said, taking the money.

Rachel left the apartment building and returned to her spot in the side street. As she left, she thought about how she would have liked to stay, but this wasn't the time. Rachel watched the windows of the apartment and leaned against the side of the building she had made her observation point.

After several hours, Eddie exited his apartment building. Rachel watched, unobserved, and followed him at a discreet distance. His waking up so soon after his attack had told her his senses were getting sharper, even if he didn't know it. She would have to be more cautious from now on. For the minute she was his guardian, if not his confidante. She followed him to his friend's house. Eddie spent much of his time there when not at work and not at his own apartment. Since he had been fired due to the Guide's intervention, work was one less place for him to be. During the hours that Frank was at work, Rachel was betting that Eddie wouldn't be around Frank's house.

After Eddie reached Frank's house and it was clear to Rachel that he would likely be there for a while, Rachel decided it was time to slip away back to her hotel room. She needed a change of clothes with night coming on. Her white blouse would soon be a beacon to someone with better than average night vision.

Rachel walked away, thinking about when her improved senses started manifesting themselves. The Guide had come to her late, and she had been victimized by her country and nearly killed, all in the name of science and religion. Rachel wanted to let those early memories fade, but she had vowed not to, not ever. Rachel saw herself in her mind's eye. She watched as the scalpel was drawn along her forearm. She remembered pleading with the surgeons around her, to no avail. She wasn't a person to their cold eyes, only a piece of meat. She screamed and they cut deeper.

But they got theirs in the end. The heavy wooden door to the lab got torn from its frame and the iron hinges snapped like a twig. Rachel was barely coherent at this time, but she clearly remembered her Guardian standing in the shattered doorway, with long white hair laying around and down his shoulders, and the beastly roar. The surgeons and their religious counterparts turned pale, as their worst demonic fears filled them. She remembered clearly, somehow knowing she was safe, as this savage, brutal man, ravaged the scientists. Rachel fell into a deep sleep as the blood soaked man untied her and lifted her into his strong arms. He talked calmly as he carried her away and brought her into the arms of the Guide. She knew things would be different.

Rachel had changed clothes. She wore flat black jeans and a flat black sweater, with a black tote bag over one shoulder. She climbed into the tree not far from Frank's house. From there, she rested and watched. There was nothing more to do at this time but watch. The sun was down and had given way to a handful of stars and a sliver of a moon. Rachel knew that the darkness had more eyes than the day. She thought of Sebastian. He was always telling her that beasts of the dark didn't need shades, so they saw better than the beasts of the light.

"That's a real disappointment Eddie. You let me down. I never figured you for the type to let a woman fight your battles for you." Frank laughed after Eddie told him and Debra of his afternoon.

"You're sure you're all right?" Debra asked.

"Positive. But I wouldn't have been if it wasn't for Rachel."

"All kidding aside, Eddie, maybe there's something you haven't thought about. Maybe the two thugs only stunned you for a reason. Like that's what they got paid to do. Have you considered that?" Frank leaned forward from his place on the couch.

"By who?" Eddie asked. Instantly, he knew what his two friends were suggesting. "Why would Rachel do that, then let me see her?"

"You only just caught sight of her. Maybe being seen wasn't part of the plan," Debra told him.

"Maybe it was," Frank added. "To make you trust her."

Eddie thought about their suggestions. He knew they were only trying to help him figure some of this mess out, trying to help.

"If they didn't work for her, then she stopped two thugs, carried you by herself around to the back of the apartment building and up to your apartment, alone." Frank thought for a moment. "Or she paid them, they nailed you, took you upstairs, and left before you woke up. She waited until you started waking up, let you see her, and then left. They couldn't have used the front door or security at the front desk would have seen them, and her."

"Yeah, but the apartment's back door has a security door," Eddie reminded them.

"She had your keys, Eddie. Which means you might want to consider changing your door locks, just to be safe."

"Why don't you stay here tonight? Try to rest, relax and forget about this day."

"Thanks, Debra."

"Call Marsha so she knows where to reach you," Frank added.

Eddie nodded. "I'm bushed, I'm going to crash. I'll call Marsha, then I'll see you two in the morning."

Frank and Debra watched Eddie leave the living room and head upstairs to the guest room that was his when he stayed over.

"What do you think is going on?" Debra asked Frank after Eddie had left them.

"I don't know, but I wish I did," he replied. "I'd like some way to check this Rachel person out."

"I know Marsh wants to know what her game is." Debra wrapped both hands around Frank's upper arm, feeling better at just the contact with his muscled body. She leaned herself against his right shoulder and sighed.

"We'll just have to wait on this and hope for the best." Frank reached to his wife's shoulder with his free hand and pulled her tightly to his chest.

Outside, Rachel watched as the house lights went out one by one. The room Eddie was in was the last light to go dark. Rachel could see Eddie standing in the open window of the dark room. He just stood there, staring out at the night.

"Eddie," Rachel whispered on the breeze. She was deep in the branches of the tree. She had hardly breathed his name. Eddie looked straight to her tree. She had not expected his reaction.

"Why do you hide from me?" he inquired.

"I do not," Rachel replied. "I am here."

"But you are not here."

"I can not be, not now. Go to bed, Eddie. You'll feel better in the morning. Sleep and dream."

"I doubt it. I don't sleep well lately. And dreams are not relaxing."

"What do you dream of, Eddie?"

"You."

Rachel smiled warmly, not that Eddie could see.

"Go to bed and dream of me. Some dreams can come true. Eddie, know that I am here and I will keep you safe."

Eddie stood there another minute. Safe from what? He wished he had the courage to go to the tree. Instead, Eddie turned to his bed and pulled the covers up around himself. It didn't help. He couldn't shake the chill.

In the morning, Eddie wondered if his conversation with the tree had been really a dream or just real and he was insane. But he felt good this morning, and wasn't going to let a little insanity change that. Frank was already off for work when Eddie made it downstairs. Debra was just walking out the door.

"Morning, sleepyhead. Afraid you'll have to feed yourself, getting up this late."

"Hell of a way to treat a house guest. You should have been bringing me breakfast in bed."

"Poor boy." She started to close the kitchen door, then stopped and looked back at Eddie. "How did you sleep Eddie?" This was the concerned friend and nurse asking.

"Best I've slept in a month. Really."

"You know you're welcome to stay as long as you want or need to."

"Thanks."

Debra nodded and left.

Eddie set about making breakfast.

CHAPTER 4

For Eddie, the next two weeks went by like a snail's race. He was beginning to think things had returned to normal. He hadn't seen Rachel or had the feeling that he was being watched. Eddie told Frank about the conversation with the tree the one night, and Frank convinced Eddie that he must have been dreaming. Marsha insisted that Eddie consider seeing a professional about his obsession with this Rachel woman. Eddie obliged her and went to a doctor Marsha knew at the hospital. After laying out the past month of his life to the doctor, the doctor had no cure for what wasn't even an aliment. Eddie decided that was good enough to quiet Marsha. He did promise to call the doctor's office and make a second appointment, though. After leaving the office, Eddie threw the doctor's card away.

It was Friday and Frank was going to swing in to pick Eddie up after work. They were headed to Mick's night club to have a drink with the crew. It would be their first trip to Mick's since Eddie had been fired.

"Good news, Eddie," Frank said as Eddie got into his car. "Barn told me to tell you to report to work Monday. He thinks enough time has gone by that your name on the pay roster would probably be overlooked."

"I'll change my damn name to have a job again," Eddie told Frank, making the two men laugh. They drove over to Mick's and headed inside. The rest of the guys from work were already there. Eddie and Frank melted into the group and got lost in conversations. As the evening progressed, the group of warehouse workers drank more and slipped into a jubilant tone. This atmosphere of lighthearted banter covered everyone except Eddie and Frank. Frank watched Eddie with worried eyes as his young friend appeared agitated and nervous. Soon, his jumpiness turned to open hostility. Before much longer Eddie stormed out of the club. Frank started after him, but by the time he made it outside, Eddie was nowhere to be seen.

Eddie ran without thinking. He didn't know why he was running or where he was running to, but he knew he had to keep moving. Get away, far away. He ran blindly from one street to the next. At one point, Eddie ran out in front of an on-coming car. He jumped and got his feet up at the last second. His momentum twisted him in the air. He landed hard on his back, denting the hood from the impact. The driver, in total shock, couldn't react to Eddie's coming off of the hood and punching him in the face. Eddie ran as the driver held his bleeding nose, his eyes blurred by tears of pain.

Eddie finally stopped running, collapsing to his knees in an alley. His breathing was labored. To him, it felt like his lungs had just shut down. He couldn't catch his breath and strange scents filled the air. Many different smells assaulted him, but one overrode the rest with ease.

"Well, what do we have here?" a cautious voice said from behind.

"Don't know, let's check it out," said a second older, more raspy voice.

Eddie twisted to see two men in uniforms walking up the alley toward him. The desire to run forced Eddie to his feet.

"Hey, buddy, you all right? Come back here," yelled the first police officer. The two cops quickened their pace after Eddie as he moved faster away from them. Running irrationally, he turned a corner of the alley, to find a dead end. A second after Eddie entered the alley the two cops also rounded the corner. Eddie looked around frantically for an escape, but found none.

"Easy does it, friend. You take some bad stuff or what?" The second cop spoke in as calm a tone as he could manage.

"It's all right, officers. I'll see to Eddie." Rachel walked around from behind them before they knew she was there. "Eddie, calm down. You need to come with me now." Rachel raised her empty hands, palms toward Eddie as she approached. "I will take you home. You can rest there. This will seem different when you have rested. Come, Eddie." Rachel worked to keep her voice level and soft to sooth Eddie.

"Who are you?" asked the first officer.

"A friend." Rachel directed her comment to the wild eyes of Eddie Laidlaw. She knew well the feeling he was experiencing, the thoughts he was thinking. "You two may go. He'll settle down more quickly if I'm alone with him." Rachel didn't think this would work, just asking the police to leave but it was worth a try and a prayer.

"Look, lady, this guy doesn't look so hot. Looks like he's strung out on something. We can't, and aren't, going to just leave. He could hurt you for one thing, or someone else if he gets past you," replied the second, older cop. "If you are his friend, you can come with us to the station house and calm him down there."

Rachel didn't want to break eye contact with Eddie so she walked backwards toward the officers.

"Perhaps you're right. That may work better."

"Damn straight it will," replied the first officer. The two men approached Eddie slowly, not wanting to spook him. Eddie looked ready to bolt, and had nowhere to run except through them. They locked their attention on him. That was a mistake. Rachel hit one officer, then the other, without taking her eyes off of Eddie. As the officers fell, Eddie started to race past them. Rachel grabbed Eddie, the two of them tripping over one of the unconscious officers.

"Eddie, it's me, Rachel. It's okay, I'll help you, I promise. Calm down, Eddie." Rachel pleaded with him as she wrestled to get a better hold on him. He was thrashing around, trying to get free, trying to run. Eddie didn't want to calm down. He had to get away.

"No," he screamed at Rachel. It was the only word that would come to mind. "No," he repeated, only this time it wasn't a scream. It was a plea and Eddie broke into tears. Quivering in Rachel's arms, Eddie sat there crying. He didn't know why, but he couldn't seem to stop. He pressed his face hard against Rachel's shoulder. Rachel's voice softly cooed in his ear as he tried to block out the visions he kept seeing. The thoughts that were rising up from his mind were almost animalistic and brutal. There was the pain in his gut like his stomach was on fire.

Rachel held Eddie several minutes, but knew they couldn't

stay there. For one thing, the two officers would wake up before too long. She hadn't hit them particularly hard. Rachel took firm hold of Eddie's shoulders and got to her feet. She pulled Eddie to his, and started walking out of the alley.

Eddie was calmer now, almost comatose. Rachel guided him several blocks away, where it would be safer, then found a phone booth and called for a taxi. They were picked up quickly and whisked away. Eddie didn't seem to notice what was happening around him. The taxi ride to the airport and boarding a waiting private jet happened dream-like for him. His thoughts were wandering through events in his life. The night he and Marsh's parents died came to him over and over. His first love, his first fist fight, nothing came into focus for a time, and when it did he wished his mind were still wandering.

Sitting in his seat, Eddie realized that his life was changing. Looking around slowly didn't shake the misty feeling, like going from one dream to another. He noticed blood on his shirt at the point of his injury from his last encounter with Rachel. He must have torn the healing cut back open.

Rachel stood back, watching him for a time. She was behind him. Eddie could feel her presence without seeing her. He knew when she approached him and looked to her as Rachel sat down next to him. "Where are we going?"

"To a party. Remember I told you that we would be going in about a month? Well, we're going." Rachel's voice was soft and warm, and Eddie wanted to let it wash over him, but he kept seeing the look of savagery on her face as she knocked out the two cops. What really scared him was that he had total recall about the night club and arguing with his friends and running from Mick's. Eddie remembered the car and its driver. Even the confrontation with the cops had not scared him. And there was a vision of Rachel, with blood on her hands, standing over him. What stood out above all the events of the night was that through it all, he had no control of himself. That scared him to the bone.

"I don't recall you saying we had to fly there." Eddie turned back to looking out the airplane window. There was nothing to see but ocean for miles.

"I didn't mention where the party was to be held. For that

you have my apology. Will that do? Will that even help?"

"No, it won't help." Eddie looked back to Rachel. "What did you do to me that first weekend?"

"I know, to you, it must seem that I did something to you, but that isn't the case. The loss of memory from that weekend was my doing, but not by choice. It would be hard to explain right now. Even with all that has happened, you can trust me."

"I'm just supposed to trust you, with all the half explained stories and mystery around you?" He wanted to get angry with her, to scream and yell. But the truth was, he just didn't have the energy to get mad.

"I'll make you a promise, Eddie. Come Monday, I will tell you anything you want to know that hasn't made itself clear by then, but in the meantime, no questions. I really don't like putting you off, and you wouldn't accept anything I could tell you. Will you promise me one thing?"

Eddie waited, not committing to anything.

"Will you promise me that you will try to relax? As hard as that thought might be, I think you will enjoy the weekend."

Before he could reply, the jet's public address system came on.

"Ms. Westchester, we'll be landing shortly. I've called in and the tower wants to inform you that a car will be waiting for your party. I've activated the seat belt signs as well." The P.A. clicked off abruptly.

Eddie never undid his belt, but he watched as Rachel snapped her belt into place. He looked her up and down, and as she noticed this scrutiny, she flashed a smile.

"Do I pass inspection, my friend?"

Eddie took hold of Rachel's chin with an iron grip, from years of working with his hands. He knew he was applying a great deal of pressure. Rachel didn't pull away or flinch. He held her firmly then kissed her. "I will know everything on Monday, or I might twist your pretty head off." Eddie released his grip.

"Monday it is, My Lord Laidlaw," Rachel agreed. "Eddie, a word of warning--not really warning, but more just a point of concern." It was clear from her expression that Rachel was unsure of what to say and how to say it. "The best way to put this is that you will see many things you won't understand, some of which I will explain. Some of those explanations will not help one bit. You know very little about the Guide or its membership, and that is my doing. I've told you very little. I will be telling you more."

"Monday," Eddie said in a displeased, hateful tone of voice.

Rachel's smile spoke of secrets to be told and of a slight weariness too. "Something else, my young friend, you will want to keep in mind. Right now you are Guide in name alone, an outsider to some of the Guide. Some of the members have short tempers, even shorter with outsiders. I am your Guardian and Mentor until you no longer require one. I will teach you the rules of the Guide and protect you as needed. It goes with the job. It would be advisable to talk to me more respectfully. When we are alone, as now, I will overlook it. In the company of others, I cannot, and I will not. On the Island, if I tell you to do something, don't argue or talk back, just do it. You can cause us both a great deal of pain if you don't." Rachel stopped talking for a second to let her words sink in, and then continued. "I tell myself that you did not ask for this and I remember my feelings when first I was inducted into the Guide. We are not evil people Eddie, please try to keep that in mind. The night that I came to you at the bar, I did not know who I was looking for. Guide members are selected in a way I will not describe just now. What I will tell you is that in the Guide it is called a mind-touch. That is what drew me to you. It was not, and is not, random selection by members. The Guide does not control who will be mind-touched to whom."

Eddie looked at her. "Gotta love you Guide members. I get what I would call kidnapped. In one breath, I get promised protection, and with the next you promise injury if I don't respect you. Didn't anybody ever tell you respect is earned?" He did not point this out to her in a cruel and mean manner. He simply stated the fact like a man at the end of his rope. "You tell me nothing, you kidnap me, and you threaten me. If you're one of the nice Guides, your friends must be a real treat."

"Eddie--" Rachel started. She was handling this badly and

she knew it, but she wasn't sure how else it should be done. It would be a new life for him, soon.

"Just leave me alone. Do what you will, but leave me in peace until you do whatever it is you intend to do to me."

"You really aren't alone." Rachel laid her hand on his. Eddie's reaction was only to pull his hand free and return to staring blankly out the window.

The jet slowed to a stop and the flight crew swung open the passenger door. Two men on the ground wheeled a stairway to the open door letting Eddie and Rachel exit. Eddie noticed two jeeps. One, the farthest away, had two men in it and a small trailer attached. The second jeep started up and drove over to meet the new arrivals. Eddie watched the big man that got out of the jeep. He had white-gray hair that he wore pulled back and braided. The braid lay across the front of his left shoulder. He had a mustache and goatee, neatly trimmed. The definition of his body would make most body builders envious. He also had a gentle, warm smile, and wrapped Rachel up in a hug when they reached him. The man spoke to Rachel in a language Eddie didn't understand or recognize.

"English," Rachel said, stopping the conversation. Rachel turned to Eddie. "This is my friend, Eddie. And this, Eddie, was and is my Mentor."

"You look unhappy my friend," the man said to Eddie, reaching out to shake his hand.

"Well, so far that hasn't been a real important matter to anybody."

The man looked to Rachel, then back to Eddie. "I have spent far too many evenings listening to someone crying about the confusion and unpleasant emotions of a certain young man to be hearing what I'm hearing. I strongly suggest you sharpen your skills of observation or expand that tiny bit of gray matter you call a mind."

"Perhaps, Eddie, I should have told you that Sebastian doesn't mince words."

"I'm far too old for that foolishness." Sebastian laughed.

"And I should tell you, Sebastian, that Eddie knows very little of our ways."

"We'll fix that, won't we?"

Eddie wasn't sure if Sebastian meant that for Rachel or for him.

"Let's take our talk to the house," suggested Sebastian.

Eddie was staring at Rachel as the three of them got into the jeep and sped away. He couldn't shake Sebastian's words about Rachel's crying about how she was treating him. Was she telling Eddie the truth about not having any choice in the matter of his confusion? Did it really bother her? These were more pieces of a puzzle Eddie couldn't put together.

The island scenery was beautiful, what he could see of it. The only light in the dark jungle was that of the jeep headlights. The dirt road was smooth, as if it was well used and maintained. Eddie caught glimpses of what looked like footpaths in the jungle undergrowth. He wondered if people made them, or if there was wildlife on the island. The house looked huge and ominous in the lights of the jeep as they approached. The headlights reflected off of the white front. From a distance, dark windows of the house gave the structure a skull sort of a look. From the smile on Rachel's face and the grin on Sebastian's, Eddie realized they had been waiting to see his reaction to the house. Eddie snapped his mouth shut, clinching his jaw tightly.

Sebastian burst into laughter.

The jeep pulled up and stopped. A young man came out of the house. Wordlessly, the man climbed into the driver's seat as Sebastian exited it. Rachel and Eddie got out of the vehicle and the young man drove off.

"Who's coming up behind us?" Rachel asked Sebastian, referring to the second jeep, and the two men in it, at the landing strip.

"Partath called. Said he would be here this weekend and was bringing in some special surprise as well," Sebastian told her.

Rachel spun on Eddie so fast she almost ran into him. "Remember my warning about members with short tempers. Partath has one of the shortest tempers you will meet in the Guide. Stay away from him if I am not with you. He would hurt you and enjoy doing it."

Eddie could do no more than nod at her.

Sebastian led the group inside. The entry hall was large like a grand hotel, with a high ceiling and deeply polished hardwood floors. Eddie looked around the entry hall and his eyes fell on what he wanted.

Rachel saw him staring longingly at the device. "There are phones in the bedrooms. Would you like to make your calls in private or use that phone?"

"I can use the phone?" Eddie asked, not expecting to be allowed to touch the phones at all after what he would call being kidnapped.

"Of course. Sebastian, where are we staying?"

"Come along, I'll walk with you." Sebastian led the group a few feet into the entry hall then turned left and up a staircase there. "So how long are you staying?"

"I'm afraid we're leaving Sunday night," Rachel replied.

"That's hardly two days. Why so quickly?"

"I promised Eddie I would have him back in time for work on Monday."

"Did you not tell me in our last conversation that he was unemployed?"

"Things changed. You know about that. You're always telling us that changes are coming. Well, here's one of those changes."

Sebastian nodded, and then came to a stop at a set of double doors. "Your quarters," said Sebastian. With a gentle push, both doors opened completely. He watched for Eddie's reaction again. Eddie was careful in masking his feelings by not reacting.

Eddie and Rachel entered the suite, and Sebastian followed. Eddie looked around the room and noticed that to his left was one door and straight ahead was a second door. This room, he realized, served as the front room or living room to the occupant's quarters. Of the two doors, one he figured for the bathroom, while the second was the bedroom. The quarters were simple, but nice. He wondered if his room would be as nice. Eddie got the sudden image of stone walls and chains and heavy wooden doors with iron locks.

"I must leave you two now. I'm sure you'll want to rest and I've guests to meet."

"What of my quarters?"

"These are your quarters, my young friend," Sebastian informed him.

Eddie looked to Rachel.

"And hers," Sebastian added, noticing Eddie's look. "Rachel, is there a problem?"

"No, Sebastian. Nothing experience won't fix." Rachel saw Sebastian out, closed the doors, and locked them. She turned to Eddie and pointed to the door across from her. "Bedroom number one, your room." She then pointed to the other door. "Bedroom number two, my bedroom. It is set up like a hotel suite, Eddie, having multiple bedrooms, each with their own private bath."

"Oh," was all Eddie could think of as a reply.

"You'll find a phone in the room. Go call your sister and Frank."

"Yeah, I need to do that." Eddie went over to the door. He opened it, but didn't enter. "Rachel," he called out.

"Yes, Eddie?" Eddie still faced the bedroom, his back to her.

"Is it true what Sebastian said? I mean about you crying to him on the phone about me."

"Yes, Eddie," she replied in a level tone of voice.

Eddie entered the room and closed the door.

CHAPTER 5

After his call to Marsha and Frank, Eddie was sitting on the side of the bed thinking about the last month of his life. How crazy some parts of it had become—a weekend he didn't remember a thing about, talking to people in trees in the dead of night, and the persistent feeling of being watched or followed. Now he was on an island, having no idea where it was located, with people he didn't know. Eddie thought and thought, but couldn't see anything to do about his present situation. He stretched out on the bed and was fast asleep.

Although sleep had come easily, it didn't last long. Eddie yawned his way into the bathroom to freshen and wake up. While there, he looked at the injury he'd reopened. He hadn't torn the scab off, but it looked like it had been punctured again. The day had grown hot, as he'd slept. Upon leaving the bathroom, Eddie headed straight out of the bedroom. He found the living room of the suite empty. He looked to the door of the second bedroom. When he tried it, it was unlocked. He wasn't sure at first if he should enter, if he should knock first, or if he should just go away and wait for her to come out.

What Eddie decided was he didn't know if she was in there or not, and he didn't want to wait if she wasn't or wake her if she slept. He eased the door open and entered.

Rachel was asleep under the bed covers. Eddie stood there a minute and watched her, then moved to a chair and sat down. Not seeing any reason to wake her, he watched the dark haired woman sleep. From his chair, Eddie could also see out the window. The curtains were open, as was the window, allowing a light breeze to enter the room. On the grounds below, the staff was seeing to the lush green grass around the house. Eddie knew a place like this would have staff personnel--maids, cooks, and gardeners. He wondered what else. He wasn't accustomed to running around with, or more accurately being pulled around by, the rich. Not personally, anyway. Pushed around was old hat, a worn old hat, and he was used to it. But this, on a personal level, was different.

Sitting there quietly, Eddie realized something. The scent that had damn near driven him mad in the city was here as well, only not as strong. The cops had almost had him. They thought he was on drugs of some kind. "You're not asleep, are you?" Eddie looked to the still form of Rachel.

"No."

"You've been awake since I came in, huh?"

"Yes, Eddie. I heard you open the door." Rachel opened her eyes and looked over at him.

"The weekend with you I can't remember--this is what you did, isn't it?" Eddie indicated the chair he was sitting in.

"Speculation, Eddie, or have you decided?"

"I've decided."

"Correct. You slept and I watched."

"Why?"

"I'll be happy to explain Monday, but I think by then you won't have to ask."

Eddie listened to Rachel's voice. It was soft and pleasant, he decided. He enjoyed its tone and could remain listening to it for a very long time.

"How about the hole in my side?"

"The puncture?"

Eddie could see her weigh the decision to tell him or not.

"All right, but just the how, not the why. Clear?"

"Not the why?"

"No."

"Agreed," Eddie said, knowing that if he didn't, he would get no answers at all.

Rachel lifted her right hand to him. She waved her right forefinger back and forth with the white color of her nail catching the sun coming in the window.

"Your nail?" he said, making sure he understood her meaning. "But--" He started to ask the why, and then stopped himself. "And why did you reopen the wound?"

Rachel gave him a little smile.

"All right, Eddie. Run along to the living room so I can dress, and then I'll give you the tour of the grounds. Maybe we'll meet some interesting people along the way." Eddie looked at her form under the covers, up and down, quite clearly examining her shape. Rachel waited briefly. "Come along now, Eddie. Lots of things to see and do if you want out of here in time to go to work Monday."

Eddie rose from the chair, his eyes not leaving her until he turned for the door. At the door, Eddie opened it fully and made sure it stayed open, leaving her bedroom in full view from the living room. He took a seat on the couch and watched.

"You're a brat, Mr. Laidlaw," Rachel yelled from the bed.

"I'm learning from the best," Eddie replied with a smile. Rachel smiled back and pushed off her covers. Eddie lost his smile as he found she wore a nightshirt that covered her most completely.

"I don't give peep shows, Eddie," Rachel informed him. She collected her clothes from the end of the bed and headed into the bathroom, closing and locking the door behind her.

A minute later, Eddie heard the shower come on. He sat and waited.

An hour later found Eddie and Rachel outside, deep in he undergrowth of the Island. They hadn't talked much, but Eddie came to understand that Rachel's very presence had a calming effect on him. As they walked, they heard sounds growing louder. Eddie knew from Rachel's expression that she also heard the sounds, but said nothing. Finally, when the noise was very close, Eddie took hold of Rachel's shoulder. He gently turned her to face him.

"Will you tell me about that noise?"

"It's other members of the Guide, Eddie. It can be very unsettling, but if you wish I'll take you to them. I will show you the Sands."

"Lead on."

Rachel nodded and took Eddie to one of the other footpaths in the jungle. The walk wasn't much farther before Eddie could make out some of the sounds. He heard people fighting, and moans and cries of pain, some shouts of anger, and howls of victory.

The two of them walked into a clearing and came to the edge

of a sand-filled area. There was a circle with a dozen people in it. Most were just lying there, unconscious. They were bleeding from injuries, clearly inflicted by one of the two people still standing. One of them wasn't even a man yet. Eddie guessed him to be fifteen or sixteen years old. The second was a powerfully built man. He had dark black hair and tanned, almost black, skin. Eddie judged him not to be a black man, though, based on the fact he had long, straight hair. His long hair was tied back in a ponytail.

The youth approached the man, growling his intentions to attack. The man waited silently, a look of controlled rage on his dark face.

"Do not enter the sand," Rachel whispered to Eddie.

This youth leaped from a crouched position, hoping to drive his opponent backward, perhaps to an off-balance position. The tactic failed. The youth caught a fist in his face. The cracking noise hinted that his nose had broken. The dark man hammered the youth with a second blow to the head. The youth fell backward, blood pouring from his nose and mouth. The dark man kicked his downed opponent, snapping ribs from the sound of the blow. The young man crawled away as fast as he could, trying to protect his injured side from further assault. The dark man laughed while walking around him. He laughed again and lifted his foot to stomp the youth's left arm. Before he could bring his foot down, the dark man was knocked off balance from behind.

The dark man spun to see who was there, who had interrupted his fun.

"You've won. Leave him alone," Eddie growled at the dark man. Rachel had not been quick enough to stop Eddie from attacking the man. She had not expected his intervention. Rachel moved between Eddie and the dark man.

"Partath," she yelled, grabbing the dark man's arms at the shoulders. "He is new. He does not know the rules on the Sands. He does not understand, leave him be."

"He entered the Sands. He issued the challenge," Partath told her, trying to push her aside.

"He doesn't know, let him leave," Rachel demanded.

"Only the victor may walk out of the Sands. You know this. No one may enter who does not wish to give challenge. I have accepted, there is no other way."

"Fine," Eddie growled. "Let him try someone closer to his own size."

Rachel spun on Eddie. "You don't know this place or what you're doing. Leave the Sands."

"No!" Partath yelled. "There is no rule to let him walk out. New to the Guide or not."

"Partath, you are wrong," said a new voice to the argument.

Everyone looked to the side of the sand-filled circle.

Sebastian continued his explanation. "At the time of the beginning of the Guide, the Sands of Combat had a special purpose, and with something of purpose, there are rules. For every rule there is another rule or exception. The Membership of the Guide decided that for this matter, a student wrongly entering the Sands may be allowed to fight, or may be replaced by that student's Mentor." Sebastian's eyes looked to Rachel. "The decision is yours. Do you wish to depart and let them fight, or do you wish to stay?"

Rachel looked from Sebastian to Eddie, then back to Sebastian.

"And do I need to point out that you too have now entered the Sands?" Sebastian added.

"I will remain," Rachel told Sebastian. She turned to Eddie. "Step out of the Sands, Eddie." Rachel had a smooth control to her voice.

Eddie felt himself wanting to listen to her, to obey, just to please her. Something deep in his mind explained to him the switch. Before he had started to move, his mind stopped his body. "No," he told her.

"Eddie--" Rachel started.

"I said no."

She hit him square on the point of the jaw. Eddie staggered. Before he knew it, she had pushed him clear of the Sands.

"Hold him well, Sebastian," Rachel told her friend, as she turned to face Partath.

"I've always wanted to get you in here," Partath said to

Rachel.

"Why? I have no reputation for fighting," she replied.

Eddie's mind cleared to find him restrained by Sebastian.

Sebastian's grip was unaffected by Eddie's attempts at freedom.

Eddie also found the fight had already started.

Rachel's face was bloody. Her abdomen and chest had a dozen deep looking gouges across them.

Eddie looked for a knife but saw none. Her right arm hung limply at her side and Eddie wondered if her shoulder was broken. He struggled harder, to no avail, to get free. He was as helpless where he was as Rachel was against Partath.

Partath would hit or kick her and send Rachel to the Sands. He would look over at Eddie and Sebastian, smile, pick her up, and hit her again.

Eddie looked up at the face of the man holding him.

Sebastian's face was like stone, but it didn't hide the look in the eyes. His eyes spoke volumes of pain and hatred. The beating Rachel was getting was not just for Eddie's benefit, but Sebastian's as well. And he had caused it somehow by breaking one of the Guide rules.

Eddie realized that no matter what, Sebastian would not release him. Partath was continuing his assault on Rachel, in part, because of Eddie's reaction. Eddie forced himself to be still, to calm his rage. The cold hatred of Partath fed his nerves as he watched the brutal treatment.

Minutes passed and even Partath lost interest in Rachel. Eddie sat silently and stared as she hit the ground for what was the last time. Partath gave her injured shoulder a bone jarring kick and walked away from her.

Walking by Sebastian and Eddie, Partath stopped. "Enjoy the show, boy?"

"I'm going to kill you," said Eddie. The threat was cold, emotionless.

Partath looked down at Eddie, looking in his eyes. "I hardly think so." He tried not to show the glimmer of fear that Eddie's eyes instilled in him.

Sebastian saw the fear, too. "That's enough." Sebastian

stopped both of them.

Partath walked away, not looking back. Eddie rose to his feet as Sebastian released him. He turned in Partath's direction.

"No, Eddie," Sebastian commanded him. "Go see to Rachel."

"She needs a doctor." Eddie felt his aid would be useless.

"Take her to her room. Put her into the tub and fill it with cold water. I'll send someone to see to her. Go. Now!"

Slowly, Eddie turned.

Sebastian headed up the path Partath had taken. Seconds later, Eddie heard raised voices. Instead of listening, Eddie made himself collect Rachel from the Sands. He carried her cradled to his chest as he hurried for the house. Eddie took her to her room and straight to the tub. He pulled off her ruined clothing and flipped on the water. As carefully as he could, Eddie started washing the sand from her wounds. He kept looking over his shoulder to the doorway for Sebastian or his help. For him, time seemed to drag on.

"I'll take care of her," a voice said from behind Eddie.

He found a young woman standing there. She was maybe twenty, with green eyes.

"She's unconscious. We need a doctor."

"I'm fully trained. I know what to do. Leave her with me."

Behind the girl stood Sebastian. "Come along, Eddie. Gale will see to Rachel."

Eddie hated leaving her side. He hated more that what was done to her was his fault. Eddie walked past Sebastian wordlessly and collapsed into a chair.

Sebastian closed the door to the bathroom then walked over and sat down on the edge of the bed.

"You're a very sick group to let one of your members hurt others of your group. You could have stopped him, couldn't you?" Eddie wasn't asking Sebastian. Something told him Sebastian could have overruled the rules of the Sands.

"I haven't challenged a right to fight in the Sands in many years, Eddie. I saw no reason to do so now. I think Rachel accepted the fight so you would learn. You see, here, Mentors are responsible for their students until they are blooded members. She is your teacher, here and off of the Island, until you do not require one."

"You could have stopped that fight, that beating she took, and you're trying to hook the blame on me. Like I don't feel bad enough about it as it is."

"That was the point. If you remember, maybe this will be avoided in the future."

"Rachel needs a doctor, Sebastian."

"She has the help she needs. Come along, Eddie, it's time for us to go."

Sebastian got to his feet, put a hand on Eddie's shoulder and waited for Eddie to stand up. Sebastian took Eddie down to the kitchen. When they entered, Sebastian waved the staff out. They put away what they were doing and left the kitchen.

"Hungry?"

"No." Food was the last thing Eddie wanted to think about.

Sebastian nodded, went to one of the refrigerators, and extracted the fixings for a salad.

Eddie watched Sebastian filling a bowl with lettuce, carrots, celery, red radishes, and sweet smelling green bell peppers from the fridge. As he watched, he realized how hungry he was.

Sebastian noticed Eddie's stare and pushed an empty bowl at him. "Eat, I can see you have not been eating properly."

Eddie dove into the bowl of salad like he hadn't eaten in a month. A ravenous hunger filled him as he ate. A hunger the salad didn't settle.

Sebastian watched with the interest of a man trying to learn. He studied Eddie carefully as he pushed more and more types of food in front of him. Sebastian put a large glass of orange juice in front of Eddie.

Eddie sipped the juice. There was a taste to it--different, wrong--but he drained the glass. He surprised himself by asking for more.

Sebastian refilled the glass. "Come along, Eddie. It's time for you to see more of the house."

"Rachel gave me the tour before we went outside," Eddie told him.

"Not what I'm going to show you."

"I want to go check on Rachel."

"She'll need her rest for now. You'll get to see Rachel at dinner. There are a lot of places on this island to see, Eddie. I'll finish Rachel's guided tour." Sebastian took Eddie to a corridor Rachel had not shown him.

Sebastian took Eddie down the corridor to a door. They entered a large spacious room, a warehouse of sorts. Eddie became instantly captivated with the room.

"This is the Meeting Hall. Some of the things in this room, date back to the beginning of the Guide. It will be the last point of the tour. It will be a tour of history, my friend." Sebastian then led Eddie outside, and not to the Sands.

CHAPTER 6

Eddie spent the day with Sebastian. He felt a strange closeness to the older man, even though the man answered questions more evasively than Rachel. Sebastian took Eddie back over the grounds first, and then showed him the sea cliffs not far from the house. For a long time, the two men stood there staring out over the cliff's edge. They didn't talk. They just stood there looking down at the rocks some two hundred feet below, waves crashing over the jagged points.

"This is a strange place."

"The world is a strange place, Eddie. You will find, given time, that we are not as bad as you think."

"I meant the cliffs, Sebastian. There is an eerie feel about them. Almost like I've been here before. Ever since I met Rachel, I've had dreams of places I've never been. Things, that just at waking, feel like they should be familiar but they're not."

"I don't have an answer for you, Eddie. I could tell you about the Guide, not about your dreams."

"Do you have dreams?"

"As a matter of fact, several that has had fresh life blown into them. Those are matters for another time. Come along, Eddie, and I'll show you some history and legend." Sebastian led them back to the house and the meeting hall.

In the hall, Sebastian showed him the past. He started on one wall and walked Eddie completely around the room. There were antiques of all kinds--pieces of furniture, desks, books, and ledgers.

"It's like a vault."

"We use it as such. If a member wishes to store something here, he or she lists it in the computer. Items are stored the same way at any Guide property. This is done strictly for inventory purposes and to keep track of who put what in where. Then the caretaker of the hall will tend to it until the owner wishes to retrieve his belongings. When you are a blooded member, Rachel will show you how to do all of that."

"Why did you let Partath hurt her? You just stood there and restrained me."

"You do not have the background to understand yet, Eddie."

"I understand that my entering the Sands was why she fought. She fought because she thought I could not handle Partath, and now she is all broken up, like that kid. What I really don't understand is why you didn't enter the Sands to help her. It is clear that you two care for each other, but you let that animal hurt her." Confusion touched Eddie's face. He tilted his head sideways to get a better angle to look at Sebastian. Eddie wanted to retract the question after seeing the pain he caused Sebastian. It made his heart go out to the older man.

"Enough, boy," Sebastian hissed. "I was there. There are many things you do not know and there is no way to explain one without the others." Sebastian walked several feet away from Eddie. His movements were stiff, like his legs didn't want to work, and his upper body was held erect only by force of will. It was plain to see he was composing himself. A minute passed and Sebastian turned back to Eddie. The controlled manner was back. "No one has put pointed questions to me in many years, my friend. Your questions of my actions, or lack thereof, are the same questions I ask myself. What I can tell you is that I made a promise a very long time ago. That promise means as much to me now as it did the minute I made it. Rachel's life was not in danger. Had that been the case, I would have intervened."

"Instead she's all busted up. Hell, maybe for life, for a promise." Eddie saw the control almost slip again.

"Let's finish your tour, Eddie." Sebastian ended further discussion of the matter.

Both men were quiet for a time as they walked by portraits of what Sebastian had, early on in the tour, described as members of the Guide. Some he had told Eddie were long dead. Eddie found out that the Guide was at least several centuries old.

One portrait caught Eddie's eye. It was dust covered and sitting on the floor. He walked over to it, blew off some of the dust and stared at the faces there. One man in the portrait Eddie didn't know, but he did recognize the other. The man's black hair was pulled back, and its braid fell over the man's left shoulder. Eddie studied the portrait, and then turned to Sebastian.

"How long have you been in the Guide?"

Sebastian looked down at the portrait. Sadness touched his eyes briefly. "That is Val. He and I were boys together, long before I had any dealings with the Guide. He was my friend, Eddie, when I thought the entire world was against me. He helped turn a mean, hateful young boy into a man. He was a good friend. And, Eddie, then or now, that is hard to find and harder still to keep." Sebastian wiped the rest of the dust from his friend's face. "Let's make our way to the dining hall, Eddie. I don't imagine you've much of an appetite, but it would be impolite not to attend. And you can meet more of the members. There are four others like you here. This is their introduction to the Guide as well. You didn't know about them, I think." Sebastian stopped and turned to Eddie. "There is one matter I must discuss with you before we go. Has Rachel told you of this first dinner for new members? The rules that apply?"

"No." Eddie readied himself at the mention of rules.

"These rules are as serious as the ones for the Sands. Listen and remember."

Eddie did not expect to see Rachel there, and almost bolted to her side when he did. A dozen questions came to mind, but he remembered the rules Sebastian had told him. He saw the empty chair next to her and wished it were for him, but knew it wasn't. Sebastian had explained the seating arrangements as well. Rachel saw Eddie and Sebastian. He nodded and took Eddie to a seat across the table from Rachel. Eddie imitated the nod Sebastian had given Rachel. She smiled, although Eddie knew that it had to hurt the way her jaw was swollen. Rachel's injured arm was in a sling.

The food had not yet been served, but glasses filled with orange juice were on the table. Eddie picked up his glass, sipped, and looked around at the people. No one was talking. Eddie turned his attention to the French style doors that led outside from the dining room. He could see the gardens he and Rachel had walked through that morning. He didn't know what to make of these people, but their place was beautiful.

Before he and Sebastian had come to dinner, Sebastian had instructed Eddie on certain dining rules. One of these rules was that at a new member's first dinner with the Guide, they were forbidden to speak. They ate, were seen, and remained quiet. Sebastian had told him that the Guide did not have many rules, but the ones they did have were strict and strictly enforced, and that breaking them had consequences for the student and their Mentor. At that, a flash of Rachel's fight came to mind and Eddie vowed to himself not to do anything to cause her more pain. He did not like her treatment of him or being kept in the dark, but he didn't wish to see her harmed. He never liked hurting people, but it seemed that he always did. Most of the time the pain he caused was to his family. Marsha, Debra, and Frank had had to deal with his screw-ups more than once. But they also always were there for him. Eddie looked down at his plate, staring at it, wishing they were there on this island with him.

While lost in thought, the rest of the chairs were filled and the serving staff brought in trays of food. The conversations were what returned Eddie's thoughts to the present.

"I hear you fought on the Sands today," someone said to another of the members. "Doesn't it bore you yet? You always win."

"I win because it does not bore me." Partath answered the questioner. Eddie glanced over at him. Partath saw him and smiled. "Something to say?"

Eddie shook his head, and got an approving nod from Rachel.

"You did not fight anyone of skill today, so the battles were of no consequence," Rachel said.

"All battles on the Sands are important. They tell us who is the best," Partath replied.

"Not hardly, but I will not argue the point further." Rachel returned her attention to her meal.

"What are the Sands?" asked a woman not far down the table from Eddie. He judged her to be in her thirties. From the question she asked, he also figured she must be one of the other new members.

On each side of her sat blooded members. The Guide members, as quick as lightening, grabbed the woman's arms and forced her hands out flat on the tabletop. With their elbows and one sharp blow each, they broke the woman's hands. The woman, in shock before the pain hit, just sat there. Then the pain reached some inner part of her brain and she screamed. The members of the Guide pushed her from the table.

"Why?" demanded a man at the far end of the table. He was just getting up from the table to go to the woman when the members of the Guide around him tore into him.

He was an older man, about sixty, Eddie thought.

The man screamed as the members took him to the floor.

Eddie had seen Rachel's fight and that helped him control his desire to scream at these people; to vent his rage at the treatment he and the others were getting from their hosts. He turned his eyes to Rachel. She was watching him as they listened to the older man scream. Eddie was grateful that the man and whatever they did to him was not at a place Eddie could see him. Try as he might, he could not block the screams from his mind, even after they had turned to moans and softer wails. Eddie put his elbows on the table and buried his face in his hands. The most chilling part of this to him was that mixed with the cries of pain was pleasant conversation by the members of the Guide.

Dinner ended and Eddie heard the rustling of chairs as people were getting up. As the members left, they took the injured people with them. He just sat there. After awhile there was a hand on his shoulder. He found Rachel standing there when he looked up. Without a word, he followed her from the dining room.

An hour later the sun was down. Rachel, Sebastian, and Eddie were seated in Rachel and Eddie's suite. Eddie was quiet but not calm. Inside, his emotions were like that of a stranger. He had no one here to talk out his problems with. Rachel and Sebastian had discussed telling him all about the Guide and then they did. There was much information to take in. So many beliefs were destroyed. He was filled with doubt and scared of the truths they had explained to him. Somewhere he heard loud voices shouting, outcries, and screams. Eddie looked to Rachel. She and Sebastian were looking at the door. So, the screams were real, Eddie thought. They hear them too.

"I'll see what the commotion is," Sebastian said, leaving the room.

"Are you all right?" Rachel asked Eddie as gently as possible. She could see his nerves were fraying. She couldn't lose control of him.

"No, I'm not," Eddie screamed at Rachel. "You just told me I'm a monster, in a den of monsters."

"Eddie, please--" she started, and the door to the room burst open. Sebastian was in the doorway.

"Take him and head for my launch!" Sebastian ordered.

"Why? What has happened?" Rachel demanded, getting to her feet. Eddie stood up as well.

"Partath has gone over to the Followers of Delvar and has given Delvar the location of the Island. The Followers are swarming all through the house. We don't have enough members here to face them. Take him and leave."

"I won't leave, Sebastian."

"Do as you are told. The rest of the Guide must be informed."

"Come along, Eddie," Rachel said. Sebastian disappeared back into the hall.

"Monsters killing monsters," Eddie muttered, following after Rachel.

Rachel pulled her injured arm from its sling. If she had to fight, injured or not, she had to be ready. She led Eddie to a dark stairway entrance and down it to the first floor of the house. There were cries from all directions, and several times, Rachel and Eddie skirted fights. They were blood baths far worse than anything Eddie had seen on the Sands. It made his stomach turn and his mind reel to see Guide fighting Followers. And Eddie didn't have time to ask who these Followers were.

Finally, Eddie Laidlaw could take no more. He pushed past Rachel, knocking her down as he ran full speed toward a patio door. The glass door exploded as Eddie went through it. He left bits of clothing, flesh, and blood on the jagged edges of the shattered glass door.

Rachel jumped to her feet and tore out after him. Running full speed with every step, she hardly kept Eddie in sight. Rachel could follow him by the thrashing sounds he made, ripping through the jungle.

Eddie's run through the jungle brought him to his destination. He stopped and stared out over the sea cliff's edge. He could still hear the terrible fighting going on, but only faintly now.

"Eddie!" Someone was screaming. He looked to find a beautiful woman tear through the trees, abruptly stopping when she reached him. Something in the back of his mind told him he knew her. He knew all about her. Try as he might, though, he couldn't put a name with the face.

"Eddie, come away from the edge, the launch is the other way. Come on now, we haven't much time."

"I've all the time in the world."

"Eddie," she said softly, approaching him slowly. She could feel the knot in her stomach building with each step.

"Rachel," he replied finding he did know her name. "I can't." He looked out at the dark night sea. "I can't do what you want, be who you want. Not like that." Tears rolled down his cheeks as he pointed in the direction of the house and the killing.

"I'll take you away, come with me."

"No. No more running, or hurting."

"I love you, Eddie," Rachel said, feeling hot tears in her eyes.

"I can't say that. I don't know how I feel about you." Eddie leaped with the last of his resolve. The last of his strength took him as far out from the cliffs edge as he could get.

Rachel rushed to the edge and watched his silent plunge into the surf below. She knew that at the bottom of the cliff, the waves crashed over jagged rocks.

"Rest in peace, Eddie," Rachel said. His body fell and smashed on the rocks, then the surf crashed over him and Eddie disappeared into his watery grave.

Rachel stood a second longer, then turned and ran for the launch. Her heart's pain gave speed to her feet. She had to warn the Guide, she had to get away from this place. Rachel Anne Westchester ran faster and harder than she ever had.

CHAPTER 7

Sebastian looked haggard. His usually, neatly braided ponytail was a shambles. Dark bruises covered much of his face and upper body. There were deep gouges in his chest and shoulders. Dried blood was caked here and there. Also, fresh blood still oozed from his wounds. Of the remaining members of the Guide left on the Island, all were seated at the dinner table, chained together and to their chairs. The household staff employed by the Guide was dead, killed in the cruelest manner Partath had been able to create. Around the table stood Partath's new brethren, the Followers of Delvar. Partath was not in the dining hall. He was off conferring with Delvar as to what to do with the Guide members. Sebastian looked around at each of the members and the new members that sat at the table. Five new members had come to the Island. Now, there were but three. One of the new members, a boy really, had fought hard and been so ripped apart, literally torn limb from limb that he had expired. Even had the Guide won the fight, there would have been nothing they could have done for him.

And then there was Laidlaw. His mind had snapped at the thoughts of the truth. What had he said, monsters killing monsters? Rachel had told Sebastian of Eddie's choice not to be like them. Maybe they should all be thrown from the cliffs, Guide and Follower alike. Sebastian tried to find it in himself to hate Eddie for his choice, but he couldn't. He did, however, hate him for the pain Rachel would be forced to live with. He could see the lost look in her eyes. There was no spark of life now the pain was too fresh. Their life was a hard one, he knew and sometimes the regrets seemed crushing. That was the reason he couldn't hate Eddie. It was the reason, whether she knew it or not, that Rachel had let Eddie make his choice.

The door from the kitchen opened. Partath strolled in like a great lord. A grin covered his face. He walked around the table, stopping next to Sebastian. "You were right, Sebastian. You spoke often of the change coming. Well, it's here." Partath laughed. "Was it not a good change for you?" Partath rattled the chains wrapped around Sebastian's chest.

"It is a battle, Partath. One of many that has been fought between the Guide and the Followers. It is nothing more."

"A battle?" cried Partath. "You are insane, old man. We will roll from this battle to the next and the next. A war is what will be ended. Delvar has seen changes too, Sebastian. There will be an end to the fight of the Guide and we who follow. One shall rule both of our peoples."

"You learned nothing from us, did you, Partath? We are not two peoples. We are the same. We just have different points of view, different goals to reach." Sebastian's words could have easily not been spoken. Partath wasn't listening.

"We have our goals, Sebastian, that is true. Delvar has his goals, and I have a few myself." Partath's eyes went to Rachel. "Goals, and trophies old man." Partath moved over to her.

Rachel didn't seem to notice.

Partath took hold of her hair and jerked her head backward. There was a howl in the distance.

Rachel looked at Partath as he tore the rest of her ruined clothing from her body.

He saw no reaction in her eyes.

"Leave her alone," Sebastian growled.

"Or what, old man?" Partath laughed. He reached down and ran clawed fingernails up her stomach and chest. His sharp nails cut her skin easily. "What, no threat Sebastian? Come come now. Tell me how the Guide protects their own. Tell me of how I will pay for violating Rachel. Tell me these things or be quiet." Partath backhanded Sebastian across the mouth, then turned his attention back to Rachel. "Sebastian and his rules have protected you far too long, Rachel. When I leave the Island, you are coming with me, bound in chains. I have many plans for you."

"Leave her alone."

"I told you to be quiet!" Partath screamed at Sebastian. As he looked to Sebastian, he saw him staring in disbelief. Partath followed Sebastian's stare.

At the door of the dining room, which led outside of the house, stood Eddie Laidlaw, paler white than a ghost. His naked flesh was wet with seawater, and every muscle was defined in long, smooth perfection. His hair was matted back from the water, and his eyes were cold and dark like the depths of the sea.

"Well, I heard you died," Partath said to Eddie.

Eddie just stood there.

"I have your friends, your Mentor, and their lives at my fingertips. Do as you're told, and maybe I won't kill them all." Partath stroked Rachel's cheek and smiled.

"Followers of Delvar, you are here as guests of the Guide. You will release the members now and bow to our will, or die as Partath has chosen to do." Eddie spoke in a soft, hoarse tone. There was no more feeling in his voice than in his stone-like face.

Partath's smile turned to a grim expression of purest hatred. He slashed Rachel's face with his nails.

The howl that had been heard in the distance, moments earlier, burst from Eddie's lungs. With speed unseen by the Guide for thousands of years, Eddie charged Partath.

Before Partath could react, Eddie locked fingers of steel at the base of his neck and drove Partath's head straight down into the heavy wooden table. There was a sharp cracking sound on impact. Eddie jerked Partath up and slammed his head again into the table. The table cracked with the force of the blow and Eddie felt Partath's neck break as well. Partath's skull was split wide open, and blood and brain were scattered across the table. Eddie discarded Partath like he was tossing away empty peanut shells.

Partath made a heavy thud on the floor where he landed. The Follower nearest him charged Eddie. Eddie spun toward his attacker, lashing out with a solid fist to the man's chest. The man staggered backward but did not get out of Eddie's reach. Eddie drove his fist into the man's chest a second time. Blood spurted out where shattered bones punctured through flesh. The Follower of Delvar, Eddie's would be attacker, crumpled to the floor.

Eddie looked at each of the remaining Followers. The Followers had seen Partath's head crushed, his brain turned to jelly. There was no challenge in their eyes.

"Release the members," Eddie told them. Keys rattled out of pockets as quickly as they could. The Followers released the chains, dropped to their knees, and bowed their heads to the floor in fear of the Guide. Eddie turned his eyes to Sebastian. "You will see to them?" Sebastian stood. "As you wish, My Lord Laidlaw."

Eddie looked at the older man. "Eddie," he corrected Sebastian. Eddie looked to Rachel. "Are you all right?" he asked.

"I'm fine, now." She stared at Eddie. "But are you?"

"I'm starving," Eddie replied.

Rachel pushed her chair out from the cracked table. With a sharpened fingernail Rachel sliced open her left forearm. "Feed, My Lord Laidlaw."

Eddie looked at her and the blood coming from her open vein. He sank to his knees at her feet. Eddie put his mouth to her arm. The blood filled his mouth; he could taste the bittersweet flavor and smell the salt water still damp on his own flesh. He sucked on the blood from her vein. The Young Lord of the Vampires fed.

The first part of the day, the Guide, with the help of the Followers, put the house to rights. The injured were aided, and the dead disposed of. As far as the damages to the house and its contents were concerned, that would take time, and supplies would have to be brought in. All in all, it was restored to a semblance of order. The Followers of Delvar were put to use as the household staff they'd murdered until such time as replacements could be brought in. This was the order of the Young Lord. The memory of Partath was too fresh in their minds to suggest any refusal or disagreement.

Before the sun was down, but with it well on its way, Rachel pulled Sebastian away from the rest of the Guide. "I'm going to take Eddie up to our suite now if you can spare us?"

Sebastian had been running the work crews of Followers and the Guide throughout the day. He had been directing the activities of what needed to be done. "We haven't had a minute to ourselves either, Rachel. Tell your Confessor, how are you holding up?" Concern filled the older man's voice.

"It has been a long day," she told him with a smile. "A long month, Confessor."

"Take him up. The other three new members are already bedded down for the night."

She started to turn away.

"Rachel, should I check on you two tonight, or in the morning?"

Rachel bowed deeply to Sebastian. "We are at your call, Lord Sebastian." She straightened, laughed lightly and returned to the others.

Eddie was talking to a female member of the Guide.

Rachel knew Nancy quite well and could imagine Nancy's side of the conversation. Rachel stopped walking for a minute. A thought crossed her mind. She had been mind touched to come to him as Mentor that was true. And since meeting him, she knew the feelings she had for him. It was also true that she had been the first, and for the moment the only, living blood he had tasted. All of that lead up to a big fat nothing if he had no feelings for her. Rachel, momentarily lost in thought, didn't see Eddie separate from Nancy, but noticed him as he stepped up to her.

"You would not believe the offer that girl just made me," Eddie told Rachel, then noticed the blank look on her face.

Rachel forced her thoughts to the present. "Yes I could, Eddie. She's been making offers for two hundred and fifty years." She looked up at him. "Would you like to go rest for a while, Eddie?"

"I do feel drained. But the others are still working. There's so much to do I doubt they would think too highly of me if I left it all to them."

"First, they are blooded members. Their endurance is higher than yours at this point. They have fed many times--you but once. Second, the other new members are asleep already. You have been through more than your share of events today. They will remember that you saved them this morning before they remember you did not work as long as they to repair the house. Third, if it makes you feel better, I will have Sebastian leave work for you tomorrow." Rachel's expression changed suddenly. "Eddie, I promised to have you home tomorrow. I regret to inform you that will not happen. We can have you there late tomorrow if you wish, or Tuesday at the latest. Do you still wish to go?" The question was there between them. Don't go, Rachel asked with her heart, but was silent.

"I think I'll have to pass on my old job for now."

"Then you need to call Frank. We can use the phone in your room." Rachel took Eddie's hand in hers and led him upstairs.

CHAPTER 8

Eddie looked at the still form next to him. He stroked her bare back with his hand, his fingers following along Rachel's spine. At the small of her back he let his hand come to a stop. On Rachel's back there were fine white scars that the morning before had been open wounds she'd received in the fight with the Followers. She had told Eddie vampires heal quickly, and tomorrow those scars would be only a memory. Rachel had also told Eddie that was why she had healed so quickly after Partath's beating on the Sands.

All of the members of the Guide, new and old were well healed at this point. All, that is, but one new member. Carlo, not yet a blooded member of the Guide, had been so severely torn apart that there wasn't enough left of him to heal. There had been hardly enough to bury. Rachel had explained to Eddie that vampires were hard to kill, but not impossible. That difference in each vampires DNA and personal constitution played a part in the amount of injuries they could take and survive. Like non-vampires, what hurt one person or how quickly they healed did not necessarily affect the next person the same way.

Lying there next to Rachel, Eddie was aware that there was a scent about her that he knew he would always recognize as Rachel, now and forever. They hadn't talked at all after retiring the night before. He had slept like a baby through the night. He looked down at the sleeping form next to him and thought how beautiful she was. All they had done during the night was lay in each other's arms. Even that had tired him to the point of exhaustion. He had fallen asleep and dreamt of nothing.

Eddie stared at his hand lying on her back. His fingernails had changed during the night. They were bone white, extending an eighth of an inch past the tips of his fingers, and he could feel how strong they'd become. His sense of touch was more defined as well. It seemed as though all of his senses were more acute. That was why he now knew Rachel's scent. But it was all of his senses: smell, touch, hearing, even sight. Eddie had always had good eyesight, but it seemed sharper since he walked out of the sea, after his jump from the cliff.

Eddie heard the knock at the main doors to his and Rachel's suite. When no one replied, the visitor opened the door. He could hear their visitor crossing the room.

"Come in," Eddie said softly, knowing that the vampire on the other side of the door would hear him. Eddie pulled the sheet up to Rachel's neck.

Sebastian entered their room. He bowed deeply to Eddie, a solemn look on his face. "Good morning, Great Lord Laidlaw."

"Stop that," snapped Eddie.

"But Great Lord Laidlaw, your servant is nothing but humbled in your presence."

"Sebastian!" Eddie said louder.

"Quietly, Great Lord Laidlaw, or you might wake me, and I can be a real bitch in the morning," Rachel ordered, her face still buried in her pillow.

Sebastian burst out laughing.

Eddie didn't think it quite as funny. He pulled the sheet over Rachel's head.

"So I take it all went well last night?" Sebastian queried innocently.

From under the covers Rachel growled something in a language Eddie didn't understand.

Sebastian laughed. "Hateful this morning are we? Ah well, girl, give the Young Lord a break. I imagine he is very weak."

"What did she say?" Eddie asked his curiosity piqued.

Sebastian laughed. "It is not important, Young Lord."

"Stop that, Sebastian. I'm serious. I don't want to be addressed that way."

"I'm sorry, Eddie. I truly am. I'm afraid you might as well get used to it. What you did yesterday is what legends are made of. The members of the Guide that are here call you Young Lord in their conversations, and they will tell the other members. Word will spread, and fighting it will not help."

"But I don't want a title. Did I do something that you cannot, or Rachel or one of the other members could not?"

Rachel rolled over onto her back and pulled the covers off of her face. "There are two perhaps that could have survived your jump from the cliff. Sebastian here, and our Guide's leader, Orbis Gracen."

"And I, for one, doubt I would survive, certainly not walk away as quickly as you did. Gracen is powerful, but there is one other who comes to mind. Another that might survive." Sebastian looked to Rachel.

"Rachel could have?" Eddie knew she could, he could feel it.

"Delvar," Rachel corrected him.

"Delvar," Sebastian repeated intensely. "He, too, might possibly have survived, but none have ever attempted a suicide as such, except you."

"Will I meet this Delvar?" inquired Eddie. "I know he is not of the Guide but Rachel did tell me last night that there are independent vampires out there. That the Guide still has dealings with them, even if they are not one of us."

"Delvar is not the same as an independent. He was Guide, in the earlier centuries. In our beginnings." Sebastian looked away, and then back at Eddie. "He is evil, Eddie, and God help us, I saved that murderous man from sure death and taught him how to survive and stay unnoticed.

"You did?"

"Like Sebastian rescued me from the French government. He did the same thing for Delvar some two thousand years before that."

"So he is Guide--a blooded member?"

"One of the first," Rachel said. "But not anymore."

"Why isn't he a member anymore? Did you kick him out?"

Sebastian rubbed his chin. "We should have killed him, and one day will likely have to. No, we did not kick him out. Delvar became less and less satisfied with our staff medallion wearers and with non-vampire humans as a whole."

"He left, Eddie. He convinced a small group of our members to follow him. To create a group to counter the Guide's work and goals as much as possible." Rachel patted the bed covers and looked at Eddie. "That is how they became know as the Followers."

"Does this kind of brutal fighting take place often?" Eddie

inquired. "Does he hate the Guide that much?"

"Yes." Sebastian's answer, to Eddie, was simple, direct, and terrifying on many levels. "He was a magnet when he was here, Eddie. Delvar was in many ways the spirit of the Guide."

"When he left, he made this a war," Rachel explained. "For centuries we've fought as quietly as possible. Neither side has the membership numbers to fight each other and non-vampires humans, too."

"One thing, Eddie, to remember. Delvar is special, as you are. He is stronger than perhaps any vampire, save Gracen, and now you. You are going to be a new force in the Guide, once you are a blooded-member. But for now, there are other matters of importance."

"Wait. Special? Please explain more what you mean by special." Eddie questioned how Sebastian meant what he was saying.

"Yes, Eddie. For lack of a better word or way to put it. Your body is somehow stronger, at least in your tissue's ability to heal. I myself, as Rachel told you, may have survived the leap you took. But one thing is for certain, Eddie. I would not have climbed back out of the surf like you did. Not in one night." Sebastian sat there watching Eddie.

"I'm not sure Sebastian or myself can explain this," said Rachel. "Gracen might have more insight into these matters. He is one of the oldest of us. He might know some piece of lore we do not."

Sebastian nodded. "I too am one of the oldest of us vampires. There is little in vampire history about coming back from the dead. The only thing we know for certain is that you did just that. You leaped to your death to escape the thought of what you are and you came back to us. Your body should have been crushed against the rocks, and torn apart in the surf. You are special, and you will very likely have one hell of a reputation to handle from now on."

"Not to mention there will be those that will want you around or at least to be around you to share in the rewards they will think you can get them," Rachel added. "We are vampires, Eddie, but the base stock is still human. Hate, greed, fear, lust for power--they are all there."

"She's right about that. Be wary of Guide members that are too friendly too quickly, unless Rachel or I tell you they can be trusted."

"Did you have to come and depress me first thing in the morning?" Eddie seriously did not like his situation so far.

Sebastian laughed. "That was not my intent, my friend. But I do have other matters to discuss with you, with both of you. It goes along with this subject, sort of." Sebastian pulled a chair over to the side of the bed and got comfortable. "There is the matter of your relationship. I'm presuming you intend to continue it. At least for the present, correct?"

Eddie looked to Rachel. He sat there in the bed, not sure what to say, or if he should say anything. Maybe he'd let Rachel react first. He was lost and looked to Sebastian. The man's gentleness could be seen in his ancient eyes. Eddie looked down at Rachel.

Rachel was already looking at Eddie. "There's nothing to do right now, Eddie. No expectations, nothing to say or worry about. We'll find out more about your strengths and your weaknesses as we train. And I'm here for you," Rachel told him. She did not want to spook him away, so she left the subject of them to him for now.

Eddie couldn't read her expression, and mind reading had not come with his other vampire skills. He decided what was best was to just tell them both straight out and see what Rachel did. "I would like to continue our relationship if Rachel will allow it," Eddie told them.

A small smile touched her lips. His words erased her worries from the night before.

"I'm glad to hear that. I think it's best for the both of you," Sebastian agreed eagerly.

"And for the Guide," Rachel added, trying not to show how little she cared about the Guide as compared to her being with Eddie.

"If we're lucky," Sebastian said with a slight smile.

"But--" Eddie prompted, thinking he was missing some unspoken part of the conversation.

"Yes, Eddie. There are some possible problems. Rachel has been in the Guide a very long time. She has rejected a number of powerful, would-be suitors, some of which are bound to take exception to one so young having her, and also so new to the Guide. That aside, there is Guide rules against mentors and students having relationships. Most of the time, this is not an issue. When it is, the rules are there to protect the mentor, the student and the Guide. This time the rules are against us, and left in the open, there will likely be trouble."

"They have no right to cause trouble. No one has claims on me," Rachel objected.

"Jealousy doesn't have a thing to do with right or claims, and you know that." Sebastian touched her arm. "But before you get angry about things that haven't happened yet, let me assure you I have a plan. You, after all, Eddie, are not even a blooded member yet. Relationships between Mentor and student are not looked well upon in the Guide, not until after the Induction Ceremony anyway. Then you will be their equal and have all the rights of a member. Then no one will stand against you and Rachel's relationship."

"What is this Induction Ceremony you mentioned?" Eddie wanted to know so he could be with Rachel without causing trouble for her.

Rachel smiled. "It is where you become a blooded member of the Guide. There are a lot of things I must teach you before then. But not to worry, we have time. The ceremony is not this weekend. They are never done quickly, and there will be several more weekends here for me to teach you. We will be together a great deal when we leave the Island. A new member does not usually become a blooded member in under a year, sometimes much longer."

"You know what they say about never say never, Rachel," Sebastian said to her. She caught the hint but was not sure of Sebastian's meaning.

"What?" she asked him, feeling dread set in.

"I woke this morning to a phone call. Gracen has thought about all I told him last night--about the attack on the Island and about Eddie. He said to tell you, Eddie's Mentor, to begin at once." Sebastian looked to Eddie. "You have much to learn and no time to learn it. Gracen wants you brought to his house and wants to have the Induction Ceremony for you this next weekend."

"I can't have him ready by then," Rachel told Sebastian. She sat up and leaned forward against Eddie's back. "It would be more work than you can imagine. New members normally have months of training and education about the Guide before they go to Gracen's. Some of them still have to go through the ceremony several times to get through it. And if you don't get through it the blooded members will treat you like meat until you do, and we won't be able to be together except as Mentor and student. I will talk to Gracen and get us more time."

Eddie felt the warmth of her body against him, her scent filling his nose--the thought of being denied her for any amount of time or because he wasn't one of them, made his decision clear. He felt a calm spread over him. Eddie knew right then that if he were special in any way, it was because of Rachel. He drew strength from her.

"Eddie," Rachel called out to him.

"I'll make it. They want a Lord Monster, they'll get one."

Rachel looked to Sebastian. "Buy me some time."

"I'll do what I can, but either way, training needs to start now," Sebastian told her firmly.

Rachel nodded.

"Get dressed Eddie, we have a lot to do," Sebastian commanded the young Lord Vampire.

Eddie looked from Rachel to Sebastian.

"Give us a few minutes?"

"I'll be downstairs, Eddie. Not too long." Sebastian left.

Rachel waited, knowing Eddie needed time. They needed to talk.

He had moved to the edge of the bed and sat there with his back to her. Eddie started to dress and then stopped.

"How do I cope with this? Everything is happening so fast. One day I'm just plain old Eddie Laidlaw, the next I'm a monster."

"Eddie--" Rachel started, but was cut off.

"Lord Monster," Eddie said.

"Look at me," she commanded. "Eddie, you turn around and look at me."

Slowly, he did.

"Do I look like a monster to you?" Rachel sat there facing him. "Do I?"

"Do you drink blood?"

"Yes, to survive. And you will too, but we of the Guide do not kill for it, Eddie. We haven't killed a human for food in centuries." Rachel got up, pulled on her robe and took Eddie out on the balcony. Searching the balcony corners, she quickly found what she was looking for. Rachel pointed to the spider web and the spider on it. She and Eddie stood there a minute, watching the spider suck the life's blood from the moth that had become entangled in the web. "It feeds, Eddie, to survive. It's instinct. Remember Friday night and how you were running the streets. That was hunting on instinct. Your body didn't know what it was hunting for, or that it was even hunting. The Guide, myself in particular, will teach you what you must know. You will feel that hunger, and if the Guide did not exist, you would kill. You would kill, and the humans would find you and kill you. Or worse, they wouldn't kill you."

Eddie saw the shudder pass through Rachel. It came from deep inside of her, and he felt it too. He wondered about the cause, and was about to ask her when she waved him off and continued talking.

"You are entering the Guide from a much different world than I came from. Your life, although not always easy, has never been a fight to live. Sebastian brought me to the Guide and was my Mentor. He taught me well. Let me do that for you. But I need time. You will need time. Please let us try."

Eddie looked down at the spider, then to Rachel. "Jumping off of a cliff didn't kill me, I guess drinking a little blood won't." He tried to sound flippant, but he failed and knew it.

To Rachel, it sounded like Eddie was trying to convince himself. She smiled and took Eddie back inside. Once inside, Eddie finished dressing then Rachel ran him out of the suite, telling him it was time for him to find Sebastian.

CHAPTER 9

Eddie had no trouble finding Sebastian. He stood waiting at the bottom of the stairs. Sebastian did not have an impatient look on his face. Sebastian, Eddie decided, was much harder to read than the face he presented to the world.

"Hope I wasn't too long," Eddie said, walking up beside the older man.

"Alone with a beautiful woman, one can not be too long." Sebastian grinned a soft smile. "But you're with me now, so come along." Sebastian headed down the hall and through a door that led to the basement. The basement had been cold the day before, but it wasn't now.

"Why are we headed down here? There's nothing down here as I remember," Eddie commented.

"That was true enough, the day of your tour, but that's not so now." Sebastian walked Eddie to one of the storage rooms in the basement and led him in.

Eddie suppressed a growl and his fists clinched up, ready to fight.

Sebastian watched his reaction. As Eddie realized his reaction was being observed, he forced himself to relax. Eddie looked from the table, to Sebastian.

"Why did you bring me here?" The growl was still on Eddie's lips.

"Because you have a choice to make." Sebastian laid a hand on the chest of Partath. Partath's chest raised and lowered evenly. "You didn't finish the job. As you can see, he still breathes."

Eddie looked at Partath. The damage to his head from the table was healed, as was his broken neck. Still, he looked slightly different, almost peaceful. "What's wrong with him?"

"As you can see, physically Partath has healed. What isn't seen is the Partath we knew is gone. That which was his mind is gone, destroyed by your fight, drained away with his blood. There isn't a thought in his head."

"So why did you bring me here?" Eddie repeated.

"To finish the job, Eddie. His condition is your doing. I thought it only right that the next step be your decision."

"Won't his mind heal, like his body did?"

"No, Eddie, there is no mind to heal. The tissue is there, but it's a blank slate. You can tear him limb from limb, or would you like an axe? Of course, you could carry him outside and set him on fire." Sebastian offered these suggestions and waited.

"I can't do any of that," Eddie said, feeling almost sick. He looked up at Sebastian; forcing the calm he had been learning from Rachel to replace the spinning in his head. "I'm not a killer. I can't undo what I did to him, and I can't say I would after what he did to Rachel, but I'm not a killer. If he got his mind back and came after me I'd defend myself, but I won't just kill him here. Get someone else." Eddie started to leave.

"Wait, Eddie," Sebastian called out.

Eddie stopped, but didn't turn back to face him.

"I had to see, Eddie. I had to know whom I was dealing with. I don't want you to kill him."

Eddie turned back to Sebastian.

"What I told you about his mind being gone is true. What I didn't tell you, because I had to test you, was that we could re-educate him. He has the mind of a newborn right now. But the decision is still yours. He can be moved somewhere and left in this condition, or he can be re-trained. The responsibility of choice is yours."

"You can re-train him? Will he be as violent and hateful as before?"

"He'll be what his teachers mold him into."

"Who are his teachers to be?" Eddie asked cautiously.

"Myself, for the most part. And we have some very good educators amongst the Membership of the Guide."

"If it's my decision, I say teach him. I say make him a man of peace. I say make him cherish all life. But I would also leave the matter in your wiser and far more capable hands." Eddie turned from Sebastian and exited the basement.

Eddie was digging through the refrigerator as Sebastian came out of the basement and found Eddie in the kitchen. He looked over at Sebastian then back into the fridge.

"That was a good choice back there, my boy. The best of the bunch."

"There were other choices?" Eddie commented.

"There always are, Eddie."

"You hungry? I found stuff in here for making hamburgers. Want one?" Eddie was trying to get away from the subject.

"Sure," Sebastian replied, letting his-self be diverted from the matter of Partath.

"So where do we start?"

"I guess for hamburgers you better start with the grill," Sebastian informed him.

"Like you don't know what I'm talking about, huh?"

"Well, Eddie, the first thing we need to do with you is see what questions you have and try to answer them."

"I've got a bunch of questions."

"Ask them."

"There's so much I don't know. I don't know what's important to ask and what you're just going to laugh at."

"I'll make you one promise and tell you one thing you need to remember. I will not laugh at questions you want answers to. And I operate under the policy that the only dumb question is the one not asked."

Eddie had heard that statement in school so many times, it sounded funny to hear it here now. He chuckled.

Sebastian grinned slightly.

"All right, tell me about the Guide. What do we Guide?"

"Mankind."

Eddie stopped loading the tray. He looked over at Sebastian. "You're serious?" Eddie said after a minute.

"Very." Sebastian collected some of the supplies for the grill and headed outside. "You see, Eddie, the Guide was formed for the protection of our race. The founders of the Guide found the best way to guard our safety was to unite. Vampires have been around as long as man has. For most of that time, though, humans would kill us if we were detected. And in many cases, if the change that you just underwent in the last month happened in a populated area, the vampire was caught the first time he tried to feed. The vampire was either locked away from people in an asylum, or killed."

"So how does the Guide help?"

"Now, as in your case, we have the mind-touch. A sense in us, like our other enhanced senses that help us locate someone beginning the change. We can be there to help them, and to Guide the humans' attention away from them. In the beginning, it was luck if two of us came across one another. Either we saw, or heard of something that told us vampires were in the area. In the old, old days, that meant run for your life as fast as your feet would carry you. If they were looking for one, that made it easier for them to find two."

"How long have you been around, Sebastian?"

"A very long time." Sebastian pushed the electric start on the gas grill as he opened the valve. The grill lit up and soon, Eddie and Sebastian were listening to hot grease pop and crackle.

"So the Guide's mission is to steer humans away from us?" The word human stuck in Eddie's throat. The thought that he didn't count as the standard human being anymore was a bit unsettling.

"Originally, yes, but time made it clear that what we needed to do was to guide them into accepting each other first, and then into accepting different types of humans. The basic fact is still true. We are human, but we also need their blood to live. Whether they know about us or not, we will have the blood. We have to. So the Guide trains vampires how not to kill humans and still get the blood we need."

"It doesn't sound like a fair trade off," Eddie pointed out. "Give me your blood and like it, or else."

"We've done a lot of things to help mankind over the years. And they don't know it because we do it from the shadows."

"Not to change the subject, but that's another question in itself. Aren't we supposed to live in coffins and melt in the sunlight and things like that?"

From behind Eddie, Rachel and the woman Nancy laughed. That was the first time he knew they were there. He wondered if the smell of the meat on the grill had made him miss Rachel's scent.

Rachel sat down next to Sebastian, directly across from Eddie. "I did wonder when we would get to that. Your first lesson, my student--forget what you learned from movies. Most of it is wrong. Are you familiar with the term, disinformation, Eddie?"

Eddie shook his head as he flipped his hamburgers over. They were just about done, he thought, from the smell of them.

"A lot of those movies were produced by the Guide anyway," Nancy added.

"Why?" Eddie asked, startled to hear the Guide produced vampire movies.

Nancy seated herself next to Eddie, closer than Eddie liked with it not being Rachel, but he did nothing. Sebastian's talk upstairs had made it quite clear that he and Rachel were to keep their relationship as anything more than Mentor and student a secret. After the ceremony, all of the Guide could know they had become lovers.

"The movies are a form of protection. If you think that vampires can only come out at night, why look for them on the sunny beach, or in the church, for that matter? Mankind is suspicious of all things they don't understand."

"And they sure don't understand us," Nancy added with a smile. She laid a lazy hand on Eddie's knee. Eddie got up and walked to the grill. He stood there, flipped the burgers, and then turned to the group. He didn't return to his seat.

"We're not hell-spawn, demons, or creatures of evil," Sebastian added. "We are human. There are some of us that are nice people, and some that are not. As members of the Guide, there are rules that we all agree to abide by as long as we are members." Sebastian got to his feet. "I hate to break up this lunch cookout, but Eddie and I have people to meet at the landing strip. Grab your food, Eddie, and let's go."

Eddie took the burgers from the grill, tossed them in buns, and followed after Sebastian.

Sebastian and Eddie stood next to their jeep and watched the jet roll to a stop. It's engines shut down and someone inside opened the passenger door. Sebastian and Eddie walked to the jet as the mechanical stairway unfolded for the people aboard to exit.

Eddie caught a whiff on the breeze--a smell that was familiar and powerful. People started coming off of the jet, and Eddie realized that the smell was their blood--human blood, not vampire blood.

Sebastian stood watching his reaction to the arriving humans. They were the new house and grounds staff Sebastian had sent for to replace the murdered staff.

Eddie looked to Sebastian. Control made his features rigid. What, did he expect me to bite them, Eddie thought but said nothing? He was fast becoming tired of Sebastian's games-- first Partath and now this.

It was like Sebastian read his mind. "I have to know who I'm dealing with, Eddie. I think you're going to be one of our best, my boy, but thinking isn't good enough. I have to know you inside and out." Sebastian waved to the first person off of the plane, a woman.

The woman came down the small stairs and waited by the plane.

"I've parked several trucks at the end of the clearing, they are for running your staff to the house. I have one here for us," Sebastian informed the woman.

Eddie turned his attention to the disembarking passengers, and the woman by the plane. It took Eddie several seconds to realize she was staring straight at him. There was tightness about her stance, and then she smiled and approached with the casualness of a breeze.

"We'll discuss this matter more, Eddie. And yes, meeting this plane and its passengers was a test," Sebastian said.

"I'm getting tired of your tests," Eddie hissed in a low voice.

"I've only just arrived and you're fighting over me already," the woman said to Sebastian and Eddie. She walked over to the two men and stood there smiling up at them. Rita Janel Davis stood all of five feet four inches tall with short blonde hair and green eyes. She came almost up to the bottom of Sebastian's chest.

"Eddie, meet Miss Rita Janel Davis. Rita Janel, Eddie Laidlaw." Sebastian handled the introductions.

"Nice to meet you," Eddie replied.

Rita Janel reached her hand out to Eddie.

He shook it briefly then released it.

"Sebastian, you are getting lax in your old age."

"I know. This disaster is my fault. I've let security down grade much too far, but that will change faster than you can imagine. And I have agreed for Wolf to station some of his people here full time." Sebastian gazed down at her.

"Security," she replied, baffled. "No, no brother. I don't mean this silly island. I mean the boy's manners." Rita Janel held her hand out to Sebastian.

He took hold of it, brought her fingers up to his lips, and kissed them.

"He is young, sister. I will see that he is properly instructed." Sebastian bowed to her as he released her hand.

Rita Janel greeted the bow with a curtsy, and then walked off to the jeep, climbing into the front passenger seat.

"Is she really your sister?"

"Only of spirit, Eddie, only of spirit." Sebastian returned to the jeep and started it up. "Come along, Eddie."

Eddie leaped into the back of the jeep and settled back for the ride to the house.

"I left transportation to pick up the new staff. They'll bring your luggage as well," Sebastian said. I'll admit you surprised me at how quickly you were able to collect supplies and personnel, not to mention transportation here. Good work."

"I do what I must," she answered.

"Your belongings will be delivered soon," Sebastian said.

"As long as it is done quickly. I'd hate to see some monkey swinging through the trees wearing my clothes." Rita Janel turned to face Eddie. "So you're the Young Lord, are you?"

"I'm no Lord," Eddie said quickly, although unintentionally.

"What a shame, we could have had such fun. I guess we'll have to think up something else. After all the time we'll be spending together, my brother." Rita Janel laughed.

"What is she talking about, all the time we'll be together?"

Eddie directed the question to Sebastian.

Rita Janel looked at Sebastian. "You haven't told him yet?" She looked delighted.

"I keep having several things to see to at once," Sebastian answered in his own defense.

"Tell me what?" Eddie asked them.

Rita Janel climbed into the back seat with Eddie. "You have a relationship with Rachel. Sebastian thought you would want to keep it, and Rachel must want to as well. So to keep the rest of the witches off of Rachel's territory, Sebastian called me. We're going to have lots of fun, you and I. What side of the bed do you sleep on? Oh, it doesn't matter, I'm not here to let you sleep anyway." Rita Janel kissed Eddie's cheek and moved back into the front seat.

Eddie sat there speechless the rest of the ride to the house. He would see Sebastian looking at him in the rearview mirror and sometimes Rita Janel would look around at him. Eddie decided it was another of Sebastian's tests, and he would not react or say something stupid.

At the house, Rita Janel latched on to Eddie's arm as soon as they were out of the jeep. The three of them walked inside and through the house, and almost directly out one of the back doors. The members of the Guide were out on the patio. All were looking well after the trouble of the day before. Several members got up at the sight of Rita Janel and came to greet her. Of the members, there were only two groups that did not say hello. The first were the new members of the Guide. The new members knew that their various Mentors would introduce them at some point. And new members did better to stay to the background for the most part.

The other who did not greet Rita Janel, but sat there watching the woman become the center of attention, was Rachel. As the hellos and the when did you arrives got discussed, Rita Janel kept a firm grip on Eddie's arm. Even when he would try politely to disengage from her, he failed. Rita Janel pulled him away from the others briefly.

"My brother, please stop your fidgeting." With that said, Rita Janel dragged Eddie back into the crowd but this time walking over to where Rachel was seated. "Hello, bitch," Rita Janel said to Rachel.

Rachel smiled softly, getting to her feet. "I didn't know the old folks home had an outpatient day," Rachel commented. "You look tired. Need a nap?"

Rita Janel looked to Eddie. "It's really a pity that some of the young of this place forgot what they were taught about respecting their betters. Oh, I mean elders."

Eddie stood there, not knowing what to expect or do with these two women.

The two women solved that problem before he had long to think about it. They fell into each other's arms, clasping each other tightly in a hug. Their reaction to one another only caught the new members of the Guide by surprise. Rita Janel had released Eddie's arm to hug Rachel, but his arm wasn't free long. From behind him, Nancy came up and wrapped her arms around his.

She smiled at Eddie and greeted Rita Janel with a wicked smile when Rita Janel turned back to Eddie after the hug.

"What's that on your dress?" Rita Janel asked Nancy. "It looks like blood."

"Where?" Nancy asked, looking down at her dress.

"There." Rita Janel pointed and stabbed four hard fingernails into Nancy's belly. All four nails punched holes easily, and blood stained the dress as Nancy gasped in shock and surprise. Rita Janel took hold of Eddie's arm the instant Nancy released it to grab her injuries. "Come along, Eddie, we don't want people dripping their bodily fluids on us." Rita Janel licked her fingers clean as she left the group, with Eddie in tow.

She took Eddie to the den in the house and closed the doors behind them. She sat down on one of the sofas and watched Eddie pace the room nervously. "Sit down or Sebastian will need to replace the carpet."

Eddie stopped pacing but made no move toward a seat.

Rita Janel patted the sofa seat next to her.

"I'm fine, I'll stand," Eddie informed her.

"I don't bite," Rita Janel told him.

"A vampire that doesn't bite?"

"Well, maybe sometimes."

"Let's go back out with the others. I'm sure Sebastian and the others are wondering what we're doing in here."

"Don't be naive, Eddie. They don't wonder in the least. They know, and some of them are even right. In case you missed it, I just laid claim to you for the whole Guide to hear about. None of the female members will oppose it, and maybe some of the men will think you lucky, but regardless of what they think, they know you're taken." Rita Janel leaned back in the sofa. "So, now that that is seen to, want to play a game? I'll chase you around the room then you can chase me."

"No thanks," Eddie told her.

"Eddie, come here and sit by me for a minute. I won't do anything, promise."

Eddie stood there staring at her.

"Promise, Eddie."

He moved to the sofa and sat down.

"I know you have a relationship with Rachel. I won't be doing anything to jeopardize that. She is my dearest friend. Sebastian knows this, and that is why I'm here. I'll keep the other skirts off of you until you and Rachel can be together. I've set the wheel in motion with that incident with Nancy, but we'll need your help in this too. Don't fight me out there. As far as the others must know, you are with me by choice."

Eddie thought about the brief conversation in the jeep coming to the house and everything up to this point. His thoughts were all about Rachel.

"Besides, Eddie, I'm the show off. I'll do all the work. All you have to do is make like you're enjoying the hell out of me. You might even like it."

Before Eddie could think of anything to say Rita Janel looked around at the double doors to the den.

"Someone's coming." Rita Janel pulled her shirt open, and grabbed Eddie by the back of the head. She pulled him in against her bare chest a half a second before the door to the den opened. "Oh Eddie, Eddie," she laughed. "That tickles." Rita Janel jerked her head around as if startled by the door opening. Rachel was standing there. "Oh, it's you." Rita Janel pushed

Eddie away from her chest and closed her shirt again.

"Hate to break up the party," Rachel said to Rita Janel. "But you get out. Eddie has to get started on his training."

Rita Janel got to her feet. She headed for the door, stopping beside Rachel. "Just warming him up for you." Rita Janel exited the room.

Eddie was sitting on the sofa, watching the two of them until Rita Janel was gone then Rachel came and sat by him.

"I didn't--" he started. "We haven't done anything," he told Rachel.

She laughed. "I know, Eddie. Rita Janel is a lot of things, one of which is loyal to her friends. I trust her. And I know I trust you. The reason I came in here is just what I said though. We must get started with your training so you can pass the Induction Ceremony." Rachel became very serious.

"Tell me something. I can't be with you, the way I understand it, because of your position in the Guide--my being a new member and not a blooded member, correct?"

"Yes, Eddie, that is correct."

"So why would I be allowed to be with Rita Janel? Doesn't she have a position of power or honor or whatever it is your system is based on?"

"Rita Janel has a very powerful position. Powerful enough that even Gracen won't disagree with her actions. But beyond that, Rita Janel also has a reputation of eating new members for lunch and going on to the next one." Rachel touched Eddie's hand. "In this instance, Eddie, Rita Janel is using her reputation as a flake to our advantage. One thing to remember about her is that Rita Janel is not what she shows to the public or the membership."

CHAPTER 10

"All right, from the top. The music will play while the blooded members are being seated. When the music ends, the speaker will step up to the podium and announce Gracen's entrance into the leader's balcony box. What happens after that?" Eddie was seated on the sofa, Rachel in a chair directly across from him. He sat there with his head forward, resting in his hands, and his elbows were on his knees. They had been at this all day without a break. The sun was down now and Eddie felt exhausted. Rachel had covered every detail of the Induction Ceremony backwards and forwards a hundred times each. She told him many of the different tests they might require of him. She had made him repeat them back to her, starting over from the beginning on any mistake or slip of the tongue. His head was spinning with facts that he thought to be useless information.

"Eddie, answer me," Rachel called out to him in a slightly raised voice. Her words reached through the mental distance between them. His thoughts had been drifting back to the city, to Marsh, to Frank and Debra, and how his changes would affect them.

"What?" Eddie said, looking up at her. "I'm sorry, Rachel. I didn't hear the question."

Rachel could see the weariness in his eyes. "I asked if you'd like to stop for the night," she told him, changing her question.

"Please," he replied, his voice weak from exhaustion.

"Come along, Eddie." Rachel led them from the den. They walked slowly through the house. Rachel thought this might give Eddie a chance to relax his body as well as his mind. As they walked, they came across one of the other members. It was a woman Rachel had introduced Eddie to the day before, but he didn't recall the member's name. The woman looked up from feeding as they approached. Bright red blood was on her lips as she nodded to them.

"Evening," the woman said.

"Hello," Rachel replied.

Eddie nodded to her. He looked to the man lying on the table before the woman. "Is he--" Eddie couldn't bring himself to ask the question.

"Dead," Rachel finished for him. "No, Eddie, I told you we do not kill humans anymore." Rachel took Eddie's hand and placed it on the chest of the man.

Even before he made contact with the man Eddie could see his chest raise and fall in even breaths. The heartbeat Eddie could feel was strong and steady.

"Michael is asleep," the woman told Eddie. "He will sleep here tonight for the members to feed. Tomorrow he will return to his room and rest. You are new. Consider this one of your lessons, Young Lord. Do you wish to feed?"

Deep in Eddie's soul he heard a voice screaming yes, yes, feed. Eddie started to move forward even as his mind fought the idea of sucking blood.

Rachel blocked him. "You are not ready for this. Feeding from one vampire to another is one thing, but from a human is different. You could kill him accidentally, but kill him. And no one wants that. Rita Janel will feed you later, or I will." What Rachel did next, Eddie found, both turned his stomach and fascinated him at the same time. She turned to Michael's sleeping body, seated herself at the table, and lifted his bare arm. She punctured a small hole in Michael's forearm with her forefinger and fed as vampires do.

Eddie watched intently as his Mentor showed him what it was to be a vampire.

Rachel fed quickly, then stood up, licking her lips. She looked to Eddie to see how revolted he was by her actions.

He met her gaze easily with a warm, half-smile. Eddie knew what she was thinking and how it worried her. "You'll teach me to do that properly, I take it?" Eddie wanted to wrap her up in his arms but knew he couldn't, yet.

Rachel nodded. "Come along, Eddie. If I don't get you upstairs before long, Rita Janel will be looking to suck my blood--all of it." Rachel looked back to the woman. "See you in the morning, Teri."

"Yes, I imagine you will." Teri brushed her short blonde

hair back with her hand and returned to feeding.

Rachel and Eddie left her to herself.

"How does the Guide select who becomes a vampire, Rachel? What made you pick me?" They continued their slow walk to their suite.

"I thought I explained that, Eddie. Let me go over it again so you have a better understanding. I explained to you how a member is mind-touched by someone entering the change, as I was with you. You see, Eddie, I didn't select you. Your mind, on a level we of the Guide are just now learning about, reached out for help. It touched me, my mind. After the touch, the Mentor usually has a rough idea of where the person undergoing the change is located. The mind-touch grows stronger as the Mentor nears the person undergoing the change. That Mentor will find this new vampire as quickly as possible. The first days are the hardest. The Mentor must drain almost all of the blood from the body of the student. That is what I did to you. That is the puncture wound you woke up with when we first met. You see the change comes at different times in us all. It has something to do with our DNA code--some little signal in the cellular make-up that causes us to become vampires. Think of it like entering puberty as a young adult. Your body changes as its genetic code demands. With vampires, no one can tell you how it works exactly, but everyone has a theory. So will you, someday."

They reached the door to their suite and entered. Inside, they found Rita Janel sitting there, a wine glass in one hand, a book in the other.

"Done for the night are you?" Rita Janel asked them.

"Hardly," Rachel replied with a grin. "But we are finished working."

"What are you reading?" Eddie tried to change the subject before it got going.

"It's probably her 'See Spot' reader," Rachel answered before Rita Janel could.

"At least I can read."

Rachel seated herself in a chair. The only other available

seat was next to Rita Janel, on the sofa.

Eddie took it and Rita Janel gave him a little smile. "How does it work?" Eddie asked Rachel. "I mean the man downstairs didn't even flinch at your or Teri's bites. And what about the bleeding after you feed?"

"Watched you feed, did he?" Rita Janel asked. "As far as the bleeding, it is controlled by a chemical in the glands of a vampires mouth. A blood-clotting agent is produced by these glands and is left in the wounds after feeding. The agent also speeds up the healing and repairs tissue damage so no scars are left. As far as a staff member flinching is concerned, you will find out that your saliva has a numbing effect on non-vampire flesh. You will also be taught how to make an incision or puncture without the person feeling it. You will need that skill when you are not around Guide properties and have no staff to feed from." Rita Janel ended her explanation there.

"Here, or at any Guide property, the humans that we employ as staff also serve as our blood supply. They are trusted with the information that we exist after we are sure we can trust them. We employ two types of humans. Those that have been in our service and have proven their loyalty are the ones that know about us. They wear a silver medallion on a silver chain around their neck. That is so every vampire will know they are talking to, or are around someone that knows of us. Then, there is a group that has the same medallion, only it is gold on gold. The wearers of the gold medallions are a step above the silver, only in that they know of us and let us feed on them, like Michael downstairs. They have accepted what we are and know we will not kill or harm them in drinking their blood. It does not take much to keep us healthy, so a dozen of us can feed on one human without harm to them."

Rita Janel nodded. "There are ways to do it, Eddie, that you will learn. And rules. One of which is that Michael will not be touched again for a month, perhaps longer. We have a large supply, for lack of a better word, of humans as food."

"How often do we need to feed?"

"Well, Eddie, that depends a lot on the person. But a new member, like you, will normally feed off their Mentor once a day, everyday, for the first few weeks. That way you learn how to feed from someone that can control you and stop you from feeding too hard. It doesn't take a lot to sustain us, but feeding tastes good, Eddie. I know how that sounds, but it is the truth. After I've taught you how to judge your need against your desire, you will be safe to feed on a human and taste the difference. As for us old timers, we can go weeks between feedings if we choose to or have to, barring that we are not injured in some manner. Injuries cost us blood to repair the damaged areas, and it is best to feed as soon as possible after an injury."

"Those that wear the medallions are the first type we employ. The second group is the one that does not know about vampires. Remember this. If they wear a medallion, silver or gold, they know about us. All others don't," Rachel explained to him. "You're new to this, and if you're not sure about a human ask a vampire around you."

"How can I tell the difference between a vampire and a human that doesn't know? I haven't seen any vampires wearing any medallions."

"Part of the training is scents. I know you know mine, and I know you can detect human blood. I'll just have to refine your skills a little." Rachel looked to her bedroom door. "That is enough talk for tonight. Sit here and relax a couple of minutes, Eddie. I need a few moments alone, then I'll come back out and feed you." Rachel got to her feet.

"I can see to his dinner, Rachel," Rita Janel offered. "Go see to your needs."

Rachel looked to her friend, smiled and nodded. She headed into her room.

"She looked tired. Is Rachel all right?" Eddie asked Rita Janel.

"She'll be fine before you know it."

"What's wrong?"

"I know your understanding of vampire bodily functions are limited right now, but how is your knowledge of female anatomy?"

"What?"

"Let's just say this is the wrong time of the month for all this activity," Rita Janel told him.

Eddie understood then. "Great. I turn into a blood sucking vampire and my Mentor has P.M.S." Eddie shook his head as thoughts of his sister's black moods, came to mind. Then Eddie looked to Rita Janel. "It's been a real good month." He laughed.

Rita Janel laughed with him. Sebastian had told her earlier in the day how hard the change was affecting Eddie. To her, he seemed to be adapting. He could laugh at himself, and that was a good sign.

"Should I be feeding off of her then, Rita Janel?"

"Eddie, she's fine, believe me. For female vampires, it's not exactly the same as it is for humans. That's something else to store in your memory. We consider ourselves human as well. We are human, so a lot, but not all of us, refer to the non-vampire humans as N.V.'s. So if you hear the term, that's what it means. Second thing, as far as female vampires and P.M.S. goes, it doesn't occur in us the same as N.V.'s. It doesn't happen on a regular basis. You can't chart it and go, 'Oh, I'll be a bitch from this date to this date.' For Rachel, this hasn't happened to her for a year. That's about how often she has to deal with this. And it only lasts a couple of days, so relax." Rita Janel started rolling up her sleeve.

"Now what?" Eddie asked.

"Time to feed you," she answered. Eddie shook his head. "Eddie, Rachel said it was all right. Now the first thing you should be taught is the areas in which to feed. Some are easier to drink from. Fleshy areas are good, easy to get suction on. Arms, legs, bellies." Rita Janel noticed Eddie shake his head again. "Eddie, it's fine with her that I feed you," she repeated.

"It's not the feeding I'm saying no to," Eddie told her.

"What then?"

Eddie reached to Rita Janel's shirt and tore it open.

She didn't react.

Eddie reached to her bare breast, stroked it, and then pushed two fingernails into her. He had his mouth over the bleeding holes before the first drips started to run down her breast.

Rita Janel sat there stroking Eddie's hair. Her thoughts were a million miles away, thinking of the day she'd met Rachel Anne

Westchester. They had met when Rachel was Sebastian's student. She was hardly more than a child then, afraid of the world. Not now, though. Sebastian had left Rachel with him when a matter of Guide business had come up. They had shown up on Rita Janel's door step in the wee hours of the morning, with Sebastian explaining in a hurry that there was trouble he had to see to and couldn't take his new student.

Rita Janel and Sebastian had been close and trusting friends for centuries. Rita Janel welcomed Rachel with open arms the night Sebastian had brought them together. Sebastian had taken on Rachel as a student to teach her how to survive as a vampire and to introduce her to the Guide. Rita Janel accepted his charge into her home with nothing more than a simple request from him.

Rita Janel remembered taking Rachel upstairs to a room similar to the very one she and Eddie sat in now. It was still several hours before sunrise, and Rita Janel remembered how tired she was. Her new student/guest had arrived when it was not the best time of the month for Rita Janel. The scared kid, then twenty-eight, only had Sebastian at the time. No one was close to her except him. He had taught her all there was to know about the Guide. And back then, the important things to know were much different than today. "Sit down, relax," she told Rachel.

Rachel sat as if she were ready to bolt and run down the path after Sebastian, but that didn't happen. They spent the next five years together. Sebastian had taught Rachel about the Guide, and Rita Janel had taught her all about life.

Rita Janel's thoughts returned to the present when she realized Rachel was standing over the two of them.

"He seems to be doing just fine," Rachel commented.

"He's asleep, like you used to do." Rita Janel stroked Eddie's hair.

"I remember. You know, I used to imagine I was feeding from my mother when I fed from you."

"If I had a daughter, I would want you to be that daughter, Rachel."

"Have you been thinking about that again?"

"Almost never, but sometimes."

"So have a child, Rita Janel."

"I don't know. I'm over 10,000 years old."

"So? Your body doesn't know that, and outside of Sebastian and me and a couple of others, neither does anyone else."

"I don't know if I could watch my child grow up, grow old, and die before I have one gray hair. I don't know how I could do that, how Sebastian does it."

"Ask him how he deals with it."

Rita Janel pushed Eddie from her breast. "Take your man to bed, my sister, my daughter."

Rachel guided the half sleepy Eddie to her room, stopping at the doorway. "Pleasant dreams, my mother."

Eddie woke to find himself in the dark with a body next to him. The scent told him it was Rachel. Eddie ran his hand along her skin. "Are you awake?"

"Yes."

Eddie stopped his hand from moving.

"You can continue if you wish." Rachel lay there as Eddie caressed her body. Before long, teacher and student became lovers until the light of the next day.

Eddie heard voices in the living room of their suite. Rachel was still asleep, so he dressed and slipped from the room. Sebastian and Rita Janel were sitting, talking softly. To a vampire's ears it was still loud enough to hear.

"Good morning," Sebastian said on seeing Eddie.

"Good morning." Eddie sat down on the sofa next to Rita Janel. He looked at her.

"If you wish to feed, Young Lord, please give me a minute to remove my shirt first. You're proving to be very hard on my wardrobe."

Eddie reached over to Rita Janel's shirt, wrapped the material in his fingers and dragged her to him. "I am a Vampire Lord. You will not talk to me so. Do I make myself clear?" Eddie's eyes were the dark color of a deep ocean.

"Eddie," Sebastian said cautiously to him.

Eddie looked to him, but did not release Rita Janel. He flashed Sebastian a wink and a smile, and then turned his cold expression back to Rita Janel. "If I choose to feed from you, I will let you know."

Rita Janel surprised him. He expected to have his head torn off verbally if not literally. Rita Janel bowed her head. "Yes, my Lord Laidlaw."

Eddie would have thought it all in fun, that Rita Janel was having a little fun with him, as he was having with her. He would have, except for the shudder he felt coming from Rita Janel. Eddie knew then, even more than from his confrontation with Partath, that he possessed awful and fearsome power. He couldn't release Rita Janel quickly enough. "Rita Janel, I'm sorry. I didn't mean to scare you. I would no more harm you and Sebastian than I would Rachel."

Rita Janel looked up at him. Shades of the power she had seen in his eyes shone in hers.

Eddie could say nothing to take back his actions.

"Might I suggest, Lord Laidlaw, in the future you be more careful with your humor." Rita Janel rose from the sofa, walked into his bedroom, and closed the door.

Eddie looked at Sebastian. "I was joking, Sebastian. I don't want her fearing me. I don't want any of you fearing me."

"Eddie, some of the Guide already does. They think that you are the beginning of the end of the Guide, as we know it. For a long time, I myself have told the members that change was due, was coming like a storm. Now you're here and they wonder if you are the change I spoke of."

"Am I?" Eddie asked, still worried about Rita Janel.

"I couldn't tell you, not yet. It's to soon."

"Can you talk to her?" Eddie asked.

Sebastian looked at the door Rita Janel had gone through. "I will talk to her if you wish, Eddie, but I would think it would be better if you did."

Rachel's scent was more strongly in the air. He glanced around as she had just entered the room. "Problem?" she asked, seeing the expressions on the faces of the two men.

"Not if you can talk it away," Eddie told her, deciding to have her go see Rita Janel. Woman to woman might help. Eddie told her what he needed and sent her off. Sebastian then took Eddie down to the Sands.

"This is part of your training also, Eddie," Sebastian told him. "As a vampire, you will find that you are stronger and faster than anything you have ever imagined. You have a lot of normal ability and you are well tempered. You are a bit immature, even for an N.V., but that will come with time and responsibility. Today's lessons are for the body not the mind." Sebastian kept Eddie on the Sands, throwing him this way and that, punching him, it seemed to Eddie, at will. Eddie tried to fight back. He tried to bring the fight to Sebastian, but by the end of the day, it was all Eddie could do to defend himself. As the sun dipped, Sebastian called it a day. The two men walked back toward the house.

"As a vampire, I thought I wasn't supposed to hurt." Eddie was rubbing his left shoulder. He was sure the skin, and some of the muscles only attached it.

Sebastian laughed. "I'm afraid, Great Lord Laidlaw, that you are under the wrong assumption. We hurt, we bleed, and we suffer the ravages of being beaten, but we heal and bloody fast."

Eddie stopped walking. "Do you think Rita Janel has gotten over this morning?"

"Truthfully, Eddie, I have known her a very long time and I have never seen this reaction from her. I've seen the woman stand toe-to-toe with powerful people, bend them around her finger, and make them beg for more. Her reaction was unexpected."

"I hope I didn't ruin a possible friendship. From what you've told me about the Membership of the Guide, I'll need as many friends as I can get."

"I might be giving you the wrong idea of the Guide, Eddie, and after this matter with Partath, I can understand your confusion. The Guide has never been betrayed before like it was here. Never has Guide fought Guide like this. Yes, we have internal troubles--no group of people together can avoid that--but our membership is better at working them out than any I know of."

"I still have a lot to learn for this Induction Ceremony, huh?"

"Yes, Eddie, a great deal."

"Then Rachel will begin round two, tonight. After dinner

she and I will be in the den. I would like you and Rita Janel there as well. Is that possible? Is it against the rules to throw a staff of Mentors at an immature student?"

Sebastian laughed and promised to get Rita Janel there, but made no promise as to how much help she would be after the morning.

As planned, after dinner Rachel and Eddie went to the den. The first hour they were alone. Studying Guide ways and conducts went slowly during that hour. Rachel stressed conduct and behavior of one Guide member to another. She told Eddie that it might help him in avoiding such problems as the one from the morning. By the time the second hour was starting, Rita Janel entered and asked Rachel for a minute alone with Eddie.

Eddie sat there nervous, scared of what she wanted to say to him.

In seconds, Rita Janel composed her thoughts. She had all day to think about this. She went to stand in front of Eddie. "I have two things to tell you. You scared me today, and that hasn't been done in nearly 10,000 years, Eddie. I don't like the feeling. Now I understand that you didn't mean to, you were joking, and you apologized. I want you to know that you were wrong, Eddie. Not for what you did to me, but for apologizing. Like it or not, you are a Vampire Lord. You do not apologize to anyone but a Greater Lord. That is the first thing I must tell you. I've known nearly all of these people since before there was a Guide. Take what we offer in knowledge and experience, and make these people of the Guide and the Followers of Delvar accept you as a Vampire Lord. If it sounds like a lot, it is, but you will do fine. The only other thing I must tell you is that I am your most faithful servant." Rita Janel sank to her knees at his feet, bowing forward until her head was lower than his knees.

Eddie was speechless. What does someone say to a person that promises to serve you? Was he man enough to deal with such responsibility? Then Eddie knew what to say. "Rita Janel, my servant. As my servant, I then command you, above all others, to keep me honest to myself. As long as I have the right to command you, you are so commanded."

"I will follow your orders, my Lord Laidlaw."

"Bring in the others, Rita Janel. I have a lot to learn."

Rita Janel rose and summoned the others.

Eddie sat there as the others entered. Not just Rachel and Sebastian, but all of the available members of the Guide. Every member that did not have a task to see to that night went into the den to assist in the education of a Vampire Lord.

CHAPTER 11

Eddie kept at his instructors until just before dawn. He was trying to learn what he could from them, but he knew his mind was turning to mush after all of the hours he had put in studying.

"Eddie, I think we could all use a break," Rachel said to him, her voice revealing her own weariness.

He looked too her, then to the other faces around him. Rita Janel had told him, "Make them accept you as a Vampire Lord." In doing that, Eddie had been trying to run the training session, or at least control the people teaching him.

One of the members thought Rachel's statement meant they were done, so he got up and started for the door. Eddie got to the door before him. Patrick was caught by surprise. He started to say something to Eddie but stopped himself. Eddie, and every person in the den, knew what Patrick was thinking. How dare a new member think to block his way or decide when a training session was to start or end? Patrick said nothing. Instead, he looked to Rachel.

Rachel made no move to intercede.

Patrick looked to the other members, saw no support, and turned back to Eddie.

Eddie's gaze was cold and unyielding.

Patrick returned to his seat.

"I think your counsel, Mentor, is well advised. We will break until a later time. Thank you all for your assistance." Eddie opened the door and returned to his seat. After a second of thought, the members of the Guide started filing out of the den.

Rachel made no move to leave as Eddie was still sitting down.

"Rita Janel, please stay," Eddie asked her as she reached the door.

"Of course." Rita Janel walked back to stand next to him.

"I'll talk to you later, Rachel," Eddie told her.

As much as Rachel didn't like it, it was clear to her that she had just been dismissed.

"Yes, Young Lord Laidlaw." Rachel got to her feet and curtsied. There was coldness to her voice and stiffness to her movements as she left and closed the door behind her.

"Did you see the look on Patrick's face?" Rita Janel commented to Eddie. "I think he wanted to tear your head off." Rita Janel laughed.

"Who cares what he wants? Did you see the look on Rachel's face?" Eddie looked to Rita Janel, took her hand in his, and pulled her down to the sofa. "I don't know how long I can hold this lofty attitude with these people, or with Rachel."

"You can discuss the matter with Rachel. Tell her, or I can, but you're doing fine with the rest of them. They will learn to expect it and then you can relax."

"I'll talk to Rachel when we go upstairs."

Rita Janel could hear the weariness in Eddie's voice. She could see the tired, drained look in his face and posture. Eddie was still new to this and although he carried himself well, very much like he was used to the demands being put on him, he wasn't. "I think we have time for one more lesson."

Eddie looked at her, too tired to fight.

Rita Janel picked up the end of the coffee table and dumped everything on it.

Eddie jumped at the clatter the fallen items made. He hadn't expected her to just pour the stuff on the floor. Eddie looked to Rita Janel.

"I needed the table," she explained innocently. "Now, I want you to stretch out on it, facing up."

He looked at her, puzzled. "What do you have in mind?"

Rita Janel smiled and tapped the table.

Eddie lay down as she had requested and waited, watching her.

Rita Janel moved next to his body. "This is Vampire Magic, Eddie. As old as vampires, perhaps older." She clasped her palms together and began rubbing them vigorously over his abdomen.

For an instant, Eddie thought he saw a glimpse of green light between her fingers. As she opened her hands, there was no green light or anything out of the ordinary that he could see.

"Are you ready?"

He nodded.

Rita Janel extended her right hand over Eddie's lower abdomen. She lay her palm on him and felt every muscle in him tense up, then strain, and then Eddie screamed.

Eddie thought he was hit by electricity. His fingers clamped down on the edges of the coffee table to the point of his nails digging into the wood. The sound of cracking could be heard. Every muscle in him twitched. Eddie's head smashed back into the hardwood table with a thud. He jerked once, then his body relaxed. Eddie opened his eyes as he realized that the flash of pain was gone. He started to raise his head to look at Rita Janel.

"No, no, child," Rita Janel said to him in a voice that was not her own. "You just lie still." She brought her left hand down on the center of Eddie's chest. He felt warmth spread from that point, out over his entire body. Eddie could feel the fatigue and weariness in his-elf fade away. Rita Janel then moved her hands to the temples of his head.

There was a knock at the door to the den, with concerned voices talking through it.

"Go away, we're fine in here," Rita Janel ordered.

Even through the door, Eddie smelled Rachel's scent, but she had not said a word.

"This is called the Touch of Life. It is a power beyond description." Rita Janel's voice was her own soft tone again. "It is a matter of great concentration, to start with. I will teach you, but the benefits are what you are feeling. There are two things you must know at this point. First, this is Vampire Magic, not Guide teachings. Second, no living vampire, save me, knows of this magic. It is my gift to you, Eddie. You and I alone will share this secret. Promise me this or I will teach you not of it."

Eddie felt the energy moving through his limbs.

There was no way he could not make this promise she wanted. There was also no way, if he knew this Touch of Life, he would not share it with Rachel. The feeling was too good, too strong not to. "I would tell Rachel. I won't deceive you on that. Teach me, please, but know I will tell her."

"I will consider it. Rest now, though. I'm not finished."

Eddie could feel the blood moving through him, from his heart to the smallest blood vessels and back. It was one of the greatest feelings he'd ever felt. He drew in a deep breath, his lungs expanding more than he remembered them doing before.

"Now, Eddie, open your mind to everything around you. Can you feel life in the very air? That is a sense you will develop from my technique. It is a sense beyond this world."

"Rachel and Sebastian are your best friends, but you haven't shared this with them. Why me?"

"They are great vampires, powerful people, and the only love I have known in years but they are not a Vampire Lord. You are the first in five thousand years, Eddie. Knowledge can be a powerful tool or a powerful weapon. One must be careful about who knows what." Rita Janel moved back from Eddie.

He felt wonderful, rested, and strong. Eddie looked to her.

Rita Janel was holding her head.

"Are you all right?" Eddie moved beside her, wrapping an arm around her.

"I'm fine, Eddie. It has been a lot of years since I've used the Touch of Life. I just have to catch my breath."

"Should I get help?"

"No, Eddie. Give me a minute." Rita Janel closed her eyes and Eddie could feel the energies of the Touch swirl through the room again. When Rita Janel reopened her eyes, the familiar mischief was back and blazing.

"You can do that to yourself as well?"

"You felt the flow again?" A look of surprise was on her face.

"Yes."

Rita Janel smiled broadly. "You will be easy to teach, my brother." With this she got to her feet, Eddie right after her, and they left the den.

Rachel was in bed when Eddie walked into their room. He could tell she wasn't asleep, although her eyes were closed. Eddie undressed and joined her. He reached for her nightgown and started undoing it, to remove it.

"I'm asleep."

"Not for long."

Rachel suppressed a laugh in her pillow then wheeled around on him with a stern look on her face. She said nothing. Rachel noticed the lack of weariness in his face. She saw the energies in his eyes. "It would seem Rita Janel lifted your spirits more than I could have." There was a bit of jealousy in her voice.

"No, my love. She talked only of you, and that aroused my heart."

Rachel looked sideways at him, waiting for the comment to let her know what he was after. She watched Eddie's eyes, looking for the joke, the humor, and the lie. She found nothing but truth and love there. His soul was hers, she realized.

Eddie pulled Rachel to his chest and held her. She had brought disorder and confusion to his life, at first, but now that was over. He still had much to learn, and not just about vampires, but he had her love and nothing could change that. Eddie Laidlaw kissed her head and then moved down her body.

Rachel held Eddie tightly against her. His nails shredded her nightgown with ease, not touching her flesh at all. She grabbed him by the shoulders and tossed him to his back. She was instantly on top of him. With her mouth down on his, their lips pressed firmly together.

Behind them, morning's light slowly crept up the sky, its fingers reaching through the curtains to make shadows paint ever-changing pictures in their room.

Unknown to the two lovers, a discussion was at the same moment taking place in the kitchen. It was the talk of worried and confused people.

"I can't believe how calmly you people are taking this.

Laidlaw isn't even through the Induction Ceremony, and he thinks he can order blooded members around like he was Gracen himself." Patrick spoke to the others at the kitchen table.

"Please note, at this time, that it was Patrick that backed down, not Rachel's student," Teri said, getting a laugh from all but Patrick.

"This isn't funny. What about what he did to Partath, huh?" The laughter stopped.

"Partath, that pig, deserved what he got after betraying us to the Followers of Delvar. A quick death was too good for him." Little Stevie looked serious. The day before Partath's betrayal, Little Stevie had fought Partath on the Sands, and Partath had not let up even after he was in no condition to defend his-self. He could not shake the image of Partath's raised foot about to stomp down on him. The image he could see, just beyond that, he couldn't shake either. Eddie Laidlaw pulled Partath off of him as blooded members stood there and watched. Little Stevie knew that Eddie had thought he was just a kid, and that had probably weighed in his decision to intervene. Still, the fact of the matter was, he did stop Partath from hurting him anymore. Little Stevie had undergone the change at sixteen, and had looked sixteen for over 400 years. It was a real problem with bars and women. One thing he had learned though, was that you backed your friends where you found them. "As far as I'm concerned, Eddie can do anything he'd like. He kept Partath off of me once, and he stopped him from hurting Rachel."

"Not to mention hurting and killing the rest of us," Teri added.

"Still, though," said Nancy. "He can not be allowed to just do as he pleases. He should not order us all about like he did in the training session that Sebastian asked us to help with."

"Sebastian will keep him in line. As will Rachel," Teri commented.

"We don't know that. Rachel has never served as a Mentor of a new member before, and Rita Janel was once with Partath, also," Patrick pointed out. "What if we've just exchanged one Partath for another? His powerful reputation is what brought Rita Janel here so quickly. We all have heard or seen the way she laid claim to him almost before she landed."

Teri agreed. "I'll admit I wasn't pleased about that, or about her moving right in with him. There are rules about that, aren't there? That is the way I remember it being taught. No new member would have a relationship with any of us until after induction ceremonies."

"No. All the rules only apply to us. When is the last time a Guide rule applied to Rita Janel?" Nancy asked.

"Perhaps we should call Gracen. He could talk to her, or to

Sebastian. And Sebastian could talk to him," Patrick suggested. "Or maybe--" Before he could continue, Sebastian walked into the kitchen. The room got silent.

Sebastian got a glass of juice from the refrigerator, and then sat down at the table. No one said a word.

"We're all friends here, aren't we?" Sebastian asked.

"Yes, of course," Nancy agreed nervously.

"I heard rumors that there are some concerns about Eddie and his--" Sebastian stopped talking, looking for the right wording. "Arrogance. I think everyone here has heard comments. I need your help, all of you. You see Eddie, is in a very difficult position. One that none of us has had to deal with. He has shown great potential as a Guide member, and he came back from the dead, as it were, to do that. Not an easy task, is it?" Sebastian let his words sink in.

"What help are you asking for, Sebastian? You know we are discussing that same matter right now," Patrick demanded.

"Always the impatient one, Patrick. That is why it took me years to mentor you to the point of the Induction Ceremony. But that is where I need help. I pulled all of you for the training session last night for a reason. You see, what no one's told any of you is that Eddie doesn't have that kind of time. Gracen wants Eddie at his house in a week. A week, and ready to enter the Induction Ceremony then."

They all gasped, as he knew they would, as Sebastian told them of this.

"A week?" Teri cried out, stunned with disbelief.

Sebastian nodded. "You can all see how it was important to give this new member extra leeway around here. The pressure is quite intense for him and on Rachel trying to get him ready."

"Her first student, and this kind of push," Little Stevie commented. He was grateful Eddie wasn't his student.

"Yes," Sebastian added.

"We didn't know," Nancy told him. Regret laced her tone.

"That's still not much of a reason to let him act the way he does," Patrick argued. The rest of the group was watching Sebastian.

"True, but it is a matter to be addressed later. There is much work to be done. I wasn't going to tell you this and add to the pressure, but I decided pressure was better than tension amongst us. With this knowledge, maybe you could be a bit more understanding when he acts up or seems a bit bossy."

"How else can we help?" Little Stevie spoke up to offer what aid he could.

"I'll call on each of you as I need you." Sebastian stood and left the kitchen. The minute the door closed behind him, he heard Patrick start in again. Patrick was a solid member, and all but Sebastian knew, and had known for years, that Patrick was still the peasant beggar that he had been when the change came to him.

Sebastian headed down to the basement. It was time to check on Partath. Sebastian stopped dead in his tracks. Partath was dead and his name would go with him. Since Sebastian had to re-educate him anyway, he would give him a new name--a new name for a new man.

In one room, lovers slept, quiet and content. In another slept the empty vessel of a name that was no more. A third room had discussions of the Young Lord Vampire. In a room not far away from that sleeping Vampire Lord and lover sat a woman alone. She was ten thousand years plus, but she knew that once you passed the five thousand year mark, there wasn't much point in counting.

Rita Janel Davis sat back in her foam filled tub and thought about the past. It was a warm summer day when she had changed. She had a good man and was a simple farmer's wife. The thought made her laugh. She had seen a show on television that had explored the era that was the time of her birth. The professor on T.V. had told the world that man did not yet have civilizations. He told the world that although there were a few signs of nomads, there was definitely not civilizations. Rita Janel laughed again and thought back to the day of the change, letting tears run down her cheeks that disappeared into the hot bath water.

"Rita Janel!" Cleve had yelled for her from the fields.

Cleve, her husband, was a big man, all muscle and heart. He was twenty-five years older than she when he'd taken the wisp of a girl that she was as his wife. Her father, Cleve's best friend from before she and her brothers and sisters were born, had promised Cleve one of the girls as a new wife when Cleve's wife of twenty years had died. Rita Janel remembered standing there, her five sisters and she, as Cleve walked back and forth looking them over. Finally, Cleve reached into his pocket, took out a coin and tossed it across the yard.

"First one to the coin gets to keep it." Rita Janel watched her sisters tear after the coin.

Cleve watched her just standing there. "You didn't even try for the coin, girl. Would it be so bad to be the wife of Cleve? Isn't it worth the effort?" he asked her.

"It is not that. All of my sisters are older and stronger than I am. Chasing the coin would only get me hurt. I would not be able to keep it. Surely one of them would take it, and I am not old enough to be a proper wife to you. I would lose there, too."

Cleve reached out to her shoulder and pulled her thirteen-year-old body to his side. He informed her father of his choice and left, with Rita Janel.

Rita Janel remembered how scared leaving made her feel. She knew she was a child and not ready for marriage. She could cook and clean, but there was much more to a husband and wife relationship than that. That part of the marriage was what scared her. Rita Janel got a second surprise that day she was selected by Cleve. He sat her down at their kitchen table and told her he would build a room for her until she was comfortable enough to come to his room, as his wife. True to his word, he did just that.

Rita Janel wept bitter tears for that man from her youth. There were no tears of joy, only those of loss and sorrow, and sadness at the way it ended.

For more than twenty years, Rita Janel was Cleve's wife. She had made her decision to enter his room two years after she'd moved into his home. They did not have children unless you counted Rita Janel herself. Life was hard, working the farm with Cleve and seeing to the house, but he helped her with the house as she did him with the farm. They were happy and she almost never regretted being with him.

Several months before the end, Rita Janel started getting

strange feelings and pounding headaches. She fought them off alone, not telling Cleve. His first wife had died of a head illness that no one knew any treatment for at that time, so they could do nothing to help her. She didn't want to scare him if it was nothing. The headaches always passed, so she suffered in silent pain when they did come. This went on until one summer day when she collapsed in the fields.

Cleve carried her to the house and tended to her. He couldn't go for help for fear of leaving her alone. She did not remember much of the next several days, but she did remember telling him of the headaches and strange feelings, and that she loved him. She remembered him telling her that her body was hot to the touch. She knew now that it had been the fever of the change.

Rita Janel slipped from thought, for how long she did not know. When she awoke from awful dreams, she found herself sitting in the middle of the floor with blood covering her naked flesh. Pieces of Cleve were scattered around their bedroom as though a wild animal had torn him apart.

She sat there, scared, confused, awake, and unharmed. A choking noise caught her attention. She jerked her head around to find Cleve lying not far away--what was left of him. She jumped away at the sight of him. Rita Janel threw up an enormous amount of blood. Crawling through the blood, she forced herself to go to Cleve.

It took him several minutes to focus on her with anything close to a conscious thought. One of his arms had been torn off, as had half of the side of his head and neck. His belly and chest were ripped to shreds, and many of his organs were hanging out or missing altogether.

With total disbelief, at first, Rita Janel realized the horrible dreams she had remembered weren't dreams at all, but reality. She had done this horror to Cleve. The worst part, as she sat there holding his dying body, was Cleve looking into her eyes. Barely louder than a whisper, Cleve told her, "I forgive you my wife."

Rita Janel ran from their house, her home, into the night. She remembered running for what seemed like a lifetime before she finally did stop. Rita Janel sickened herself, as she stopped only to feed, then ran again. She did that for years before she controlled herself, mastered her body's new needs, and learned to cope. Then, as more and more years rolled by and she was counting in centuries, Rita Janel started a search for a cure to her condition, as she thought of it. Her search led her to find out about vampires and eventually to the discovery of Vampire Magic, as she called it. Rita Janel knew now, after decades of research, and trial and error, that it wasn't magic anymore than they were hell spawn or cursed. But the ability wasn't in all vampires, and Rita Janel had taught no one of what she had dubbed as Vampire Magic.

Telling Eddie of it earlier had brought up all of these memories. Rita Janel had asked herself a thousand times why she had to be different. She had stopped asking God. He knew the question, and as of yet, had not had the time or the desire to answer her.

Rita Janel soaked in her bath of foam and wondered if the reason for her difference had just arrived at the Guide. She had cried many tears for her long dead husband, and only once in all of the years since then had she found a man of kindred spirit. Now perhaps there was a second.

Rita Janel let herself slip into a restful sleep.

CHAPTER 12

With the new household staff on the island, Sebastian shipped the Followers off. He sent them away with a message for Delvar. They were to inform him that this incident would be overlooked, and not to attempt such actions again. They would not be dealt with kindly again.

For Eddie, the next few days raced by, and for all of the members, really. The other new members and Eddie almost never saw one another because they were not getting the intense training sessions he was. He was either in the den with someone, mostly Rachel, or on the Sands with Sebastian.

Eddie was learning more about fighting than he ever thought about knowing. In his fighting experience, it was toe-to-toe slugfest until there was a winner. Sebastian told him how, as a vampire, he would have more strength, speed, and agility than most N.V.'s. What Eddie found out was just how lucky he'd gotten with Partath. His instincts and desire to protect Rachel had overcome his lack of knowledge about fighting. The element of surprise cost Partath. Sebastian explained it was akin to animal instincts with speed and power Partath couldn't match.

Now, on the Sands, Eddie was fighting with logic. He was thinking, planning his attacks, and worrying about injury to himself and about injuring Sebastian. His instructor with the long ponytail had told him that was a common enough reaction to new members learning the Sands.

"In ages past, Eddie, training to defend yourself or to subdue another was more of a necessity. Today, in our world, you don't have the need to fight for your life every day. We train so that if the need arises, we can defend ourselves and the Guide."

"If I were confronted then, in a life or death struggle, do you think that the instinct you've talked of would come out naturally, putting your training and the animal savagery together?"

"I think it would depend on the situation," Sebastian told Eddie. They were resting, taking a break from the rigors of the Sands. They had worked harder each day. "You've made a great deal of progress, Eddie. More than any other student I've had, new member or not."

Eddie wasn't sure how to reply to Sebastian's comment, or if he should. He had grown fond of the older man. Eddie found he was very much at ease with all of the members. It was like a home he had never had. He had Marsha--she was family--but the ten years between their ages might as well have been a lifetime. Eddie laughed at the thought.

"What is funny, my brother?" asked a voice behind Eddie and Sebastian.

Eddie looked around at Rita Janel and Rachel standing there. He had smelled their scents and knew of their approach. "I was just thinking of the differences between Marsha and myself, like an entire lifetime. And now I'm running with people that have lived several lifetimes."

"Some of us more than that, Eddie," Rachel told him.

Eddie noticed she and Rita Janel were dressed in workout clothes.

"You two fighting?" Eddie asked.

"Yep," Rita Janel replied, and then smiled.

"I asked them to come out today and fight you," Sebastian informed him.

"I can't fight them. They're girls," Eddie argued.

"What a sweet boy," Rita Janel said unconvincingly.

"Yes, a dear." Amused sarcasm laced Rachel's reply.

Rachel stepped in front of Eddie and grabbed his shirt with both hands. She dropped backward, kicking a foot into Eddie's stomach as she pulled him over forward. She neatly rolled along the curve of her spine and tossed him like a rag doll into the circle of Sand.

He laid there, more stunned than hurt.

Rachel, Rita Janel, and Sebastian walked over to look down at him. "I suggest you defend yourself," Sebastian said to Eddie, then left the Sand.

Eddie looked up at the two women. "This isn't fair," he complained. "You two aren't a match for me. I'm not going to hit either of you."

Rita Janel looked to Rachel. "He's right." Rita Janel offered him a hand to get to his feet.

Eddie ignored it, rolled to one side and got up.

"Are you all right after my flip?" Rachel asked.

"I'm fine. Sebastian hits harder than that," Eddie answered.

Rita Janel landed a punch to the point of his chin as Eddie glanced her way. He staggered backwards.

Rachel spun, slamming her tennis shoe against his head. Eddie went down face-first into the sand. Rita Janel stomped on his right forearm, and then kicked him in the ribs.

Eddie cried out in pain and tried to get away from their attack. After almost two minutes of a constant assault, Rachel and Rita Janel stopped, stepping away from him.

Eddie tucked his head under his arms and pulled his knees up to his chest. In his little ball, he took the pounding dished out by the women. He stayed there, not moving.

They stood there watching him.

"We appreciate your sentiments about not hitting women and all, but this is training, Eddie," Rachel said. "Now get on your feet and face us."

Eddie felt every pain in his body from their blows. His arms hurt the worst, and he was sure his right forearm was broken. There was blood in his mouth and some dripping from it. His right eye hurt, as did his ribs, back, and legs.

"Eddie, we are vampires. Any damage you do will heal, remember that. This is a testing ground, of sorts."

Rachel nodded. "Look at it this way, Eddie. What if you were out in the world somewhere and you had to hit a woman, N.V. or not? Maybe for her own good. Could you control the force you would need to subdue her? Could you hit her without injuring her?"

"Rachel, Rita Janel, give me a minute with him," Sebastian said, walking past them to kneel in front of Eddie.

"I can't do it, Sebastian."

"Is it because it is them, or because they are women, my boy?" Sebastian took Eddie's right forearm in his hands and set the bones. Moving them into place made Eddie clinch his teeth against the new wave of pain.

"I can't hit Rachel. Or Rita Janel, for that matter."

"All right, Eddie. We'll call it a day. Later, sometime, we'll get a couple of other women out here for practice. But when I arrange that, I want more fight out of you. Understand?" Sebastian grinned. He took hold of Eddie's shoulder and helped him to his feet.

"Do we fight?" Rachel asked, concerned about situations Eddie could find himself in.

"No, ladies. Thank you for your assistance, but that will be all for today."

"Not much of a workout," Rita Janel said, sounding disappointed.

"Fight each other. I'm going to see Eddie back to the house."

"I can make it. You can stay and referee for them." Eddie moved off. Moving away, he could hear the sounds of Rachel and Rita Janel starting to fight. From the sound of it, he decided they didn't have a problem hitting each other. A short distance up the path, Eddie stopped. There was an old fallen tree on the side of the path and Eddie sat down. He closed his left fist tightly--his thoughts on the energies Rita Janel had exposed him to. Eddie saw the flash of green light between his fingers, and then opened his hand to apply the radiant heat to his broken arm. He could feel the bones knit, the damaged tissue heal, and his soreness drain away.

Rita Janel had been shocked when he picked up her magic so quickly. She was even more stunned when she realized he could use it on her, or anyone for that matter, better than she could. He still hadn't shown it to Rachel. Rita Janel had agreed to teach him all the Vampire Magic she knew and told him that the decision to tell Rachel would be left to him. However, to tell no one else had still been part of her terms. So far, this was all she had taught him, even though she had told him it was only the tip of the iceberg.

He opened his eyes and drew in a deep breath, then continued on his way to the house.

On the Sands, Rachel landed hard from Rita Janel's flip. Rita Janel smiled down at her.

"It really is a good thing Eddie won't fight you, sister. Even as a beginner, he would kick your butt." Rita Janel laughed.

"You know I am not good at this. Never have been. Not against members anyway." Rachel rolled to one side to get up.

Rita Janel let her get halfway to her feet and then put her knee in the center of Rachel's back. This drove her face down in the sand. She seized one arm, and pulled it behind Rachel in a joint lock and grabbed a handful of hair to pull her face up from the sand. "You're lucky we're friends or I could really hurt you."

Rachel spit sand from her mouth. "Well, Rita Janel, you know what people say. With friends like you, who needs enemies?"

Rita Janel laughed, got up and offered Rachel a hand. She accepted the offer and got to her feet. They walked to the edge of the Sands where Sebastian stood watching them.

"Sebastian, you need to work with her more. She is getting very sloppy."

"I noticed a little slop in your performance, as well. Should I work with you?"

"Slop from me?" Rita Janel looked shocked--thinking her side of the workout had gone quite well. She stepped back, swinging her arm in an offer for him to join her on the Sands.

Sebastian smiled and stepped forward. As his foot touched the sand, he landed a staggering punch to Rita Janel's jaw. She had expected him to move to the middle where she would meet him. That wasn't the case. Sebastian followed the punch with a kick to the abdomen that doubled her over. He swept her legs from under her, putting her on her back. Rita Janel, still stunned from the punch, tried rolling over to get away from the assault. When she got to her hands and knees, Sebastian laid a kick into her ribs that tossed her almost to the center of the Sands and onto her back. Sebastian walked over to her. "Oh, by the way, just in case you forgot, I don't have a problem hitting you like Eddie does. As one of the head instructors on the Sands, it's my job."

Rita Janel lay there coughing up blood from the broken ribs that had punctured her lungs. She wanted to reply. She wanted to jump up and fight back, but she knew the fight was over. So did Sebastian.

Sebastian bent down, picking up Rita Janel as carefully as he could. He cradled her to his chest and carried her from the Sands. Instantly, Rachel was at his side.

"You really did a number on her," Rachel commented angrily.

"She didn't pull any punches on you. You two didn't pull any punches on Eddie. Was I supposed to?" Sebastian snapped back at Rachel. "I'm sorry," he said at once. His anger was not her fault, but his own for the injuries he'd just caused.

"No, I wasn't suggesting that. Just commenting." Rachel looked embarrassed at the stupid disagreement when Rita Janel was hurt so badly.

Sebastian and Rachel headed back to the house, with Rita Janel lying in Sebastian's arms.

Rita Janel touched Rachel's arm. "You'll need a new sparring partner, my daughter." Her voice seemed weak, and almost distant.

"She'll have Eddie to work with now. That'll help. I'll show him things to teach her." Sebastian offered words he thought might comfort his injured charge.

"Teach me?" Rachel reacted to that statement.

"Fighting techniques," Sebastian clarified. "He's a quick study. I don't think he realizes how quick."

Rachel nodded. "What he can do already and what he's picked up, is incredible. A lot of what he retains he doesn't even realize. I heard him correct Teri yesterday when he heard her teaching her new member. He pulled her aside, she told me later, and informed her she was incorrect and moved on. After thinking about the matter, she said he was right. I asked him about correcting her. Eddie told me it was just that her error was so blatant that anyone would have caught it. Frankly, he was surprised she hadn't caught it herself. Sometimes, Sebastian, how quickly he's taken to this scares me."

Rita Janel had been lying in Sebastian's arms, listening to them discuss Eddie. She reached out again to Rachel. "Don't let it, don't let him. You have his heart, girl. Embrace him and all he is. Good and bad."

"I'm trying," she told Rita Janel.

"Do it. Promise me," Rita Janel demanded, a desperate tone

to her voice.

"I promise, Rita Janel. But for now, you rest until we get you to the house and a healer."

Rita Janel laid her head back against Sebastian's chest.

Rachel looked to Sebastian, wondering if his thoughts echoed her own. The Guide had only lost two members to age, and neither of them had been as old as Rita Janel. Aging was rare with Members, or Followers for that matter, but it happened. Not many knew Rita Janel's age, so if her age started to get the better of her, it would be a shock to the membership. Rita Janel had always been there, and no one had expected otherwise.

Sebastian pulled her a little tighter to his chest, silently cursing himself for the degree of his attack on her.

Eddie had just finished showering. He toweled off and was pulling on his robe when he heard the door to the suite open. He stepped out of the bedroom as Sebastian carried Rita Janel through the suite to the bedroom, Rachel a step behind Sebastian. Eddie ran to join them. "What happened?" he asked.

"Me." Sebastian replied with displeasure filling his voice.

"What?" That was all of a question Eddie could manage.

"Sebastian met her on the Sands," Rachel told him. "Normally, that is not a problem, but Rita Janel is old, even if she doesn't look it. She's old even for one of us."

Sebastian had placed Rita Janel on the bed. "I'll get a healer. You'll be fine," he told her.

"Liar," Rita Janel told him. "But it's all right. I have my promise." Rita Janel looked to Rachel.

Rachel nodded, forcing back tears.

"Get out," Eddie told both Rachel and Sebastian. "Get out and leave her to me. I can fix this."

They looked to Eddie.

"There's nothing to be done, Eddie," Rachel snapped.

Eddie turned to Rita Janel. "Tell them to leave."

"They won't. They don't understand. And you can't cure death, Eddie," Rita Janel told him.

He started for her side, but Sebastian blocked him.

"Let her rest," Rachel told him.

"Let her sleep, Eddie," added Sebastian.

"You mean let her die." Eddie pushed the man aside.

Sebastian moved with the push, latched onto Eddie, and pulled him bodily away from the bed. "Stop it, Eddie! Just stop it!"

Eddie gripped Sebastian, picked him up and tossed him against a wall ten feet across the room. Rachel grabbed Eddie from behind. He twisted around faster than she realized he could. Eddie pulled her free of himself, with Rachel's nails cutting gouges in his flesh. Eddie pushed Rachel to her knees beside the bed.

"Don't move, don't even think about it," Eddie instructed her. He turned to Rita Janel. "I'm sorry to break my promise, but I can't leave you like this."

Rita Janel nodded.

Eddie clasped his hands together as Rita Janel had taught him. The green light didn't flash this time. It came into existence gradually, growing stronger as Eddie's total concentration locked on to one thought, purifying Rita Janel's health. He lowered his green glowing hand to her body.

Rita Janel jerked up as voltage coursed through her. Her lungs let forth a scream not unlike the scream Eddie had made when first exposed to her touch.

Sebastian was just reaching the bed as the scream ended. There was pounding on the door to the suite, and lots of voices. Sebastian started to reach for Eddie.

Rita Janel looked to him. "No, my brother, please," she begged him.

Sebastian watched from then on.

Rita Janel turned her face to Eddie. His expression was unreadable, his concentration complete. Rita Janel could feel every cell of her body rejuvenate. She hadn't felt this great in many, many centuries.

Eddie smiled at her. He then reached out his hand to Sebastian.

Sebastian's reaction was a sharp intake of air. Then he relaxed as the energies flowed through his body. The power he felt in his body returned to levels he thought long gone. Shock filled him and he laughed. Eddie smiled at him.

Slowly, Eddie turned to Rachel. Tears ran down her face. He reached to her shoulders and she cried. Eddie pulled her to his chest and held her. "I love you," he whispered. Rachel sobbed and held on to him as the last of the green light caressed her and faded.

"Sebastian, get the door before they break it down," Rita Janel told him.

Sebastian couldn't get his voice to work. He nodded, left the bedroom, and headed for the door of the suite.

"How did you do that?" Rachel asked between tearful chokes. "What was it?"

"Later, Rachel. He needs rest. Believe me, he needs rest, we all do," Rita Janel told her firmly. "Take him to your room."

CHAPTER 13

Hours after Eddie had revealed the Touch of Life to Sebastian and Rachel in order to save Rita Janel's life, he stood at the balcony window, watching the sun sink into the ocean. Rita Janel had dropped into a deep, restful sleep. Sebastian was watching over her.

Rachel lay in the bed behind Eddie. He could feel her eyes on him. He couldn't blame her for that. "What I have become seems to be my question of the month."

"You've become far more than anything I could have expected."

"I'm sorry," Eddie said, turning to her. "I never meant to hurt you."

"Hurt me? You stunned me, yes, but you didn't hurt me, my love. Come, sit here."

Eddie walked to their bed and sat down beside her.

"That Touch of Life saved the life of one more dear to me than words can explain. And to know it came from another so dear to me makes it even more special. You promised Rita Janel secrecy, but broke it to save her. I give you that same promise. I'm sure Sebastian will agree. We fought you because we thought it best to let her die in peace. We both should ask your forgiveness and hers."

"You've given me more than I've dreamt possible. There is no need to ever ask forgiveness from me." Eddie pulled the blanket down to gaze upon Rachel's body. He ran his hand along her flesh.

Rachel felt the gentle touch and her thoughts all said one thing--don't stop, don't ever stop.

"I won't," Eddie told her, and Rachel realized she had spoken her thoughts aloud. Eddie brought his face down to her body. Rachel seized his head with both hands, pulled Eddie's lips up to hers, and kissed him.

They had made love a dozen times in the span of just a few hours, both letting their lover roam over them. They felt that the world beyond their door did not exist. Sleep came and went and returned again. Eddie slept wrapped in a dream of Rachel. As he dreamt on, Rachel decided to check on her friend.

Sebastian was sleeping when Rachel entered Rita Janel's room. Rita Janel looked over to her. "I knew you'd come to see me."

"Can you talk? Are you all right?"

"I'm fine, now."

"I can come back later."

"Come sit with me." Rita Janel patted the bed.

Rachel walked over, sat down and took Rita Janel's hand in both of hers.

"You scared us so badly."

"It wasn't my intention. As I told Sebastian when he and I talked, I didn't realize my body was getting tired. I just didn't. He still feels so badly about hurting me, and I can't do anything about it. It just isn't his fault."

"I'm sure you two will work that out." Rachel just sat there. She had nothing to say to Rita Janel, but she had so much she wanted to discuss with her. The fact that Rita Janel was alive and well was good enough for now.

Rita Janel reached out to Rachel and pulled her to her chest, stroking her hair the way she had hundreds of times. Rachel was lying there, listening to the strong, steady beat of Rita Janel's heart.

Sebastian stirred after an hour. He looked at the two women whom he'd known so long. He thought of them both as his children, even if Rita Janel had a number of years on him. When Sebastian met Rita Janel, she was a roamer, never in one place too long. That was before Orbis Gracen and the beginnings of the Guide. There had been lots of changes in the world and the Guide since those days, but Rita Janel hadn't changed. Sebastian wondered if he, Gracen, and Rita Janel, and Delvar for that matter, were the old guard getting ready to retire as the young hearts stepped into the center light. He looked to Rachel, thinking of young hearts.

Sebastian remembered back to after her rescue, how scared and fragile she was. Rachel had spent the next year living with him. Although he had not been mind-touched by her, he took on the job of her Mentor. He had to first teach her that she wasn't a beast or a monster as her village had labeled her. It had been much the same thing she had just had to teach Eddie. When Rachel accepted that, he then taught her what she needed to know to become a blooded member of the Guide. She was a fast study and was a blooded member within four months. Over their year together, Sebastian taught Rachel to read, write and also taught her basic mathematics. She had a doctorate in mathematics now, but back then it had been so hard to learn. She improved his French and he taught her his German. That was years ago, and a great many languages had been learned by each since. They, like most of the membership, had worked very hard to lose any sign or hint of accents. Looking at Rachel, now, Sebastian could see shades of the girl he had left with Rita Janel hidden beneath the elegant woman he had returned to find.

"Sebastian," Rita Janel called out to him. "Would you be a dear and call for the jet? I think it's time Rachel took Eddie to meet Gracen."

Rachel sat up and looked at her. "He isn't ready," she protested.

"Yes he is, Rachel." Rita Janel's reply was simply a statement of fact.

"But--"

"No, Rachel, he is ready, and you must take him." Rita Janel rubbed Rachel's left arm.

"Yes, Rachel, I agree with her."

"So do I," Rachel reluctantly agreed. They all three looked to the door as it swung open.

Eddie was standing there. "So this is where you slipped off to," Eddie said with a scowl to Rachel. He looked to Sebastian and then to Rita Janel. "How are you feeling?"

"Alive, Eddie. Very much alive."

"You're a little pale," Eddie mentioned.

"I'm still weak. I'll need to stay in bed a few days. Nearly dying takes a lot out of you."

"So does dying itself," Eddie commented, thinking about his leap from the cliff.

"Are you all right?" all three of the others asked Eddie.

"I'm starving."

"Come along then. We'll find you some food." Rachel got off of the bed. "What sounds good?"

Eddie took hold of Rachel's arm as she reached him. "Something red," he told her, only half joking.

"That can be arranged, but I'd better go downstairs and feed first. You have quite some appetite."

"Wait," Rita Janel called to them. "I think we could all do with a feeding."

"Do you think that's wise?" Rachel inquired cautiously.

Rita Janel threw Sebastian a glance.

"I'm inclined to agree with her."

Rita Janel tossed the covers aside and started for the edge of the bed.

Sebastian was out of his chair in a flash. He gently stopped her, putting her back under the covers.

"You stay right there. I'll bring someone up when I call for the jet." His tone of voice said not to argue with him. Rita Janel smiled innocently and reclined back.

"Rachel, go with him. Leave Eddie with me."

Rachel eyed Rita Janel carefully, then nodded and left with Sebastian.

Eddie took Sebastian's chair. "So, Mom, what am I getting lectured on?" Eddie asked with a wide grin. He didn't care if she did complain about his fighting Sebastian and Rachel to treat her. He'd let her chew him out about breaking his promise to her. Eddie would take any anger on her part and smile happily that she was there to correct him.

"I wanted to thank you, Eddie," Rita Janel informed him.

That caught him a little off guard. "You're most welcome," he told her.

"I won't go on and on about what you did but there is one thing. What you did was incredible to say the least--the power you called up. I'm surprised you're up so soon. You pulled my body back from the brink of death--not an easy feat."

"You didn't tell me that the Touch of Life could fix the dead," Eddie said to Rita Janel.

"It can't. Had I died, your powers would have been useless. But I would say as long as there's a spark of life in the member you touch, you could likely save them."

"Member, you said. Will it not work on the Followers?"

"They are vampires like us. It would work on them as well."

"Why haven't you ever told anyone else?"

"A healing power can do a lot of good. It can also be a curse. I've sworn Sebastian to silence. I suggest you do the same with Rachel."

"I have," Eddie told her. "She agreed to be silent before I brought it up."

"After I teach you what more I do know, what to do with the Vampire Magic is up to you."

"What will it do to N.V. humans?"

"In truth, Eddie, although I call it magic, it is a chemical reaction in our bodies, on the cellular structure level. Their bodies are different. It would destroy that tissue. The energies produced in vampires' bodies are very powerful. That is the reason we heal from things that would kill an N.V. human."

Eddie sat looking at Rita Janel and listening to her words. She made it clear to him that the differences between N.V. humans and vampires were so very vast. Since she had introduced him to Vampire Magic, Eddie had wondered how it could benefit humans, especially Marsha, Debra, and Frank. Could he come to their aid as needed? Maybe he could help them live longer, better lives before the natural aging process had its way with them. Before he could question Rita Janel further about the idea of use on humans, there was a knock at the door.

"Come in," Rita Janel answered. The door opened and in came a young female of the house staff.

"Miss Westchester said I was needed up here. She said Sebastian and she would be along shortly."

"Yes, Janet, but we'll wait for the others. Just have a seat," Rita Janel told the woman.

Janet sat down and waited.

Eddie stared at the woman's gold medallion. "What's it like?"

"Sir?" she replied in confusion.

"I mean to live amongst the Guide."

"To be a Non Vampire amongst vampires?" she asked with a smile.

"Yes, I guess that's what I'm asking. I mean, you not only know about us, you actually feed us."

"I'm a blood donor." Janet thought a minute about how to explain her feelings on this matter. "You see, sir--"

Eddie put up his hand. "Eddie," he told her.

"All right. You see, Eddie, it isn't that big of a step from silver to gold." She touched her medallion. "Not for me it wasn't. Not for a lot of the other blood donors, either. People donate blood to hospitals, and services like the Red Cross all the time. Once you've been entrusted with the information that the Guide are vampires, nothing more seems quite beyond acceptability."

"But those services have trained personnel taking the blood. The needle is much smaller than a nail. Doesn't it hurt?"

"As far as trained personnel, that is what your Mentor is. Miss Westchester has never injured me, or anyone that I know of, during her feedings. She'll teach you how much pressure to use and what areas are best. Once you are practiced in the techniques, I'm sure your donors will feel nothing more than a little pressure and a pin prick."

"How long have you been doing this?"

"I've been employed by the Guide for just over five years. I've worn a medallion for a year and a half. I've been a blood donor for a year."

At this time, Rachel walked into the room with Sebastian just behind her.

"The jet will be here in the morning for you."

"Us, you mean," Eddie corrected.

"No, Eddie. Rita Janel is better, but weak. She'll be up in a day or two and I have other duties here that require my attention. The jet is just picking up you and Rachel, and a few of the others that need to return to the States."

"Where are we headed, anyway?" Eddie asked.

"Orbis Gracen's home--the headquarters, if you will, of the

Guide. Colorado."

"It's a mountain fortress of sorts. You'll see all of that when we get there. For now, though, let's get down to business, Janet." Rachel indicated the bed.

Janet rose from the chair, unzipped her one-piece dress and stepped out of it. Under the dress was a one-piece body suit. The body suit left her arms and legs bare for the Guide members. She lay down on the bed next to Rita Janel.

Rita Janel took Janet's right arm and brought it up to her mouth. With her fingernail, Rita Janel made a small opening in the fleshy underside of the forearm.

Eddie watched carefully.

Janet didn't even flinch at the puncture.

Rita Janel fed slowly, not drawing hard on the opening. She knew how much she needed as opposed to what she wanted. Within minutes, Rita Janel stopped. Rachel went next. She made use of the same puncture Rita Janel had made.

When it came to Sebastian, he made a fresh puncture in the left thigh. Janet laid still for all three members.

"Now remember, Eddie, this is not the same, exactly, as feeding from Rita Janel or myself. You could kill her if you're not very careful, but relax, we three will not let that happen. The first thing you will do is select an area. You will find that arms and legs are good. Abdomens work well, and on women, breasts, of course.

"Fleshy areas. Yes, I remember you told me that," Eddie said.

"Fleshy areas nearest a strong vein, but not to near the heart," Rachel reminded him.

Eddie knelt next to Janet. He put a hand to her left side. "Would this be all right with you?" he asked Janet.

"That's fine," she replied.

"Eddie, why don't you pick or start with a thigh or calf?" Rachel suggested.

"No." He was determined to learn this most important lesson.

"I could order it, Eddie," Rachel told him, letting him know his boundaries.

"And if you do so I will obey, but I'm asking you not to. You three are here to stop me if I go too far. Janet has faith in that, or I think she would not be here. You three have trust in her, or she would not be here. Let me earn your trust and hers."

Rachel sighed and nodded.

Janet sat up, slipping the body suit down to her hips, then laid back down.

Eddie reached to her side. Before he applied any pressure, Rachel took a hold of his hand.

"You're shaking, Eddie, let me help," she told him. Rachel brought his forefinger fingernail to Janet's side, just below the rib cage. "This is where you would puncture a vampire as I did you. It is too high, however, for a human." Rachel then repositioned his fingernail. "Very gently, Eddie. Your puncture does not have to go deeply into the body." Rachel let Eddie apply the pressure, keeping her hand ready to stop him if he went too deep. "You can feel the skin and tissue separate under your nail." A sharp intake of air from Janet got everyone's attention. "Too far, Eddie, ease your hand back." Rachel looked to Janet. "Are you all right, shall we stop?"

"I'll be fine. Go on." Pain filled her eyes.

"I'm sorry," Eddie told Janet.

She nodded, but her concentration was obviously on her pain.

"All right, Eddie, take your finger out of the hole and put your mouth over it. Suck gently like you were sipping a cup of tea, not downing a milk shake."

Eddie drank from the opening. Blood filled his mouth and ran down his throat. He had tasted his own blood from too many fists in the mouth in fights, and he had tasted Rita Janel's blood and fed several times from Rachel. Never had he tasted any blood like this. It was like his taste buds had only just started working. The blood was almost sweet, and there was richness to it. Eddie realized how easy it would be to drain every drop of this taste. He thought of the expression on Janet's face as his nail had gone too far. He thought of the trust she and his friends were placing in him. Eddie leaned back from Janet's side. Every fiber of his being was screaming, "feed." The smell was thick in the air, and on his own breath. Eddie pushed himself to his feet, stepping back and turning away from the group.

"Eddie," Rachel said softly. She touched his shoulder.

"I could have killed her. The taste, so good, so strong."

"Seductive," Sebastian added. "Yes, Eddie, you could have, but you didn't."

Eddie turned to Janet. "Are you all right?"

"Yes, Lord Laidlaw," Janet said. She had heard he was the Vampire Lord. Everyone on the island had. A lot of the Guide Membership around the world had, also."

"I'm going for a walk," Eddie announced. "Alone, please," he added, knowing Rachel was sure to follow.

Janet pulled her body suit back up over her bikini top and started to get up.

Rita Janel restrained her with a pat on the shoulder. "Lay still, child. Let your strength return."

Eddie left the house and headed out through the surrounding jungle. The sun had already gone down.

CHAPTER 14

Rachel had stayed up late waiting for Eddie, and got up early to pack for the flight. One of the staff took her and Eddie's luggage out to the airstrip. Teri was also going to fly out with them. She told Rachel she wanted to see Eddie's Induction Ceremony. A lot of members had expressed the same desire, and would be attending. From the sound of it, the Grand Hall would be filled, assuming they had a Young Lord to present. Rachel had waited long enough. It was time to go find him. She left the house and took the first path she came to. She hoped he had stayed on one of the paths. That would make finding him easier.

After an hour and ten different paths, Rachel met with success. She saw him in the distance, standing on the cliff's edge.

"Eddie," she called out. Worry touched her expression. Thoughts of that horrible night she'd watched him jump came to her mind.

He looked around at her and smiled.

"What are you doing out here?"

"Good morning to you, too," he answered.

She laughed lightly, shaking her head. "Good morning."

"Want to see something?"

"What?"

"A trick, of sorts."

"Is it quick? We have a plane to catch."

"Very." Eddie turned his back to the cliff's edge, bent his knees and leaped up, arcing backwards.

"Eddie!" Rachel screamed. Breaking into a dead run for the cliff's edge, he sailed out over the rocks and surf below. She got to the edge and looked over in time to see his body twisting toward the cliff face. To Rachel's stunned disbelief, as Eddie was falling, he righted himself, and then reached out a hand to the cliff's face. His nails made sparks as they contacted the rock. His descent stopped as his left hand found a hold. Then his right hand and his feet hit, and his toenails found cracks to grip.

Eddie smiled up at her and started up the cliff. He was moving at a running pace when he reached the top and leaped up beside her. Eddie tossed his arms open wide, a smile beaming from ear-to-ear. "How's that? Impressive, huh?"

Rachel slapped him so hard across the face that Eddie thought his jaw broke. "You ever scare me again like that, I'll toss you off this cliff myself."

"But--" Eddie started to explain.

Rachel slapped him again. "I don't want to hear it. We have a plane to catch. Get back to the house."

Eddie dropped his head forward like a punished dog and started walking back to the house.

At the house, he showered, put on fresh clothes, and then Sebastian drove Rachel and him to the airstrip. The jet was there, ready, loaded and waiting for them.

On the jet, Rachel sat next to Eddie, making no comments or small talk for the first hour of the flight. The jet wasn't empty this time like the flight to the Island. Even with other people on the jet, Rachel and Eddie were as good as alone, as far away as the rest of the members sat.

"Rachel," Eddie said softly, looking at the other members. "Do I have the plague or something?"

"Why do you ask?"

"The others. Nobody comes near."

"I am your Mentor and we are going to prepare for your Induction Ceremony. They're letting us have space to study, talk, whatever we need to do to get you ready."

"Rachel."

"Yes."

"I'm sorry I scared you. I guess I should have warned you." Eddie sat back in his seat. He didn't expect a reply to his apology and he didn't get one.

"How's the jaw?" Rachel asked.

"I think it'll mend," Eddie said teasingly.

"What ever possessed you to jump off there a second time?"

"I didn't. When I was walking around last night, it was dark and I just wasn't watching where I was going. I walked too close to the edge of the cliff and lost my footing. I fell."

Rachel gave Eddie a stern look. "Eddie, it is that kind of carelessness that could get you killed. You could get caught by the world of man as a living, breathing vampire."

"I'll be more careful," he promised.

"Yes, you will. That's what we'll work on from now on."

"Do you really think it would cause that much trouble getting caught as a vampire?" Eddie saw the shadow cover Rachel's eyes like a curtain.

"Let me tell you about their world and ours. When I was fifteen, life was easy and all planned out for me. I married. That wasn't an uncommon age for a woman to marry then. By the time I was twenty I had three children. Yes, Eddie, I have had children--two sons and a daughter, at the time. All went well and as expected until my twenty-fifth birthday. I was pregnant again, almost due when I got sick. I started getting headaches, cramps, and I was fatigued easily. My family didn't know what was wrong or what to do, but then the sickness quit. It went away. About the same time when I got better, grisly murders started happening--brutal, bloody murders. The men of the village started a patrol. One afternoon, a member of the patrol came across two people. One was hunched over the other, tearing the flesh from the body and sucking the fresh blood. This patrol member raised his club to bash that murderous devil's brains in. When that murderous devil looked up at him, the patrol member could hardly believe it. It was his wife. The mother of his children and the mother of his still unborn child."

Eddie couldn't picture Rachel in such a situation. "What did you do?"

"I begged him, Eddie, to walk away. To run, for the children, our children, to look the other way."

"Did he?"

"He brought the club down as hard as he could. As he beat me unconscious, he screamed for the rest of the patrol." Rachel thought about the events of that day so many years earlier. "Before the sun set that day, I was chained and loaded on a wagon, taken to a much bigger town near what is now Paris, and given to a group of men that were the center of religious and scientific knowledge in the area, at the time. The religious sect declared me a daughter of Satan and started in with the rituals to purify my soul. The scientists all said it was a disease, or that I was a freak of nature. With their scalpels in hand, they were determined to find out. I was their prisoner, their guinea pig, and the center of their attention for several months." Rachel closed her eyes against the memory of the horrible things that had then been done to her. "My screams, Eddie, only made them think they were getting somewhere. I spent most of my time chained to a cold stone rock they used as a table."

"How did you get away?"

"This was the start of my change. That's what the headaches and sickness were--my body rejecting my blood. You would have had the same sickness had I not drained your blood. I told you it would drive you mad, remember?"

Eddie nodded.

"Every time they cut me open, Eddie, more blood drained away. The loss of blood drained the madness away with it. I wasn't feeding, and the body had to work hard to keep me alive. I grew weaker all the time. This made this group of men overjoyed. They were winning their battle with Satan and learning more about the human anatomy than they thought possible."

"How did you escape?"

"I didn't. I was rescued. One night, late, the door to the lab exploded off its hinges. Before my keepers could think to move, this other devil was amongst them. He killed them all and burnt the place to the ground. As he lit the last torch and put it to the building he unchained me and carried me away. He nursed me to health and told me of an organization called the Guide. He was a member and he knew well what I was going through. This gentle man became my Mentor and taught me so much."

"Sebastian saved you?"

Rachel nodded. "So, Eddie, you can see I know about what I speak of as far as care and caution are concerned."

"You amaze me, Rachel. You are a member of an organization to help them, the very people that caused you so much pain."

"The reason I'm with the Guide, Eddie, is because of those people. We have to close the rift between knowledge, understanding and acceptance. Those people's actions were because of fright. I killed almost a dozen people before I got caught. If you got caught today, it would be the same. It might not be from the religious standpoint, but the doctors would cut you apart to watch you heal. They'd do it twenty times in the name of research. One day the Guide will get caught. Or the Followers of Delvar will, or even some of the free roaming rogues of our kind. When it happens, we have to bring them to an area of understanding.

"How long ago did that happen to you?" Eddie wasn't too sure he should ask.

"My birthday is in two months. I'll turn 1146 years old." Rachel smiled and leaned back in the chair, giving Eddie full view of her shape. "How am I holding up?"

"I want to make love to you. How is that for an answer?"

"I'd love to, but remember, to the rest of the Guide, at least until after you're a blooded member, you're sleeping with Rita Janel. I'm only your Mentor."

"So teach me, Mentor," Eddie teased her.

"I've taught you enough for now. Rest, Eddie, there will be much to do when we reach Gracen's house."

"I have something for you--a promise."

"I've asked no promises of you, Eddie."

"If you have to ask, then I think the promise wouldn't be worth much. I promise you that no one will ever harm you again--not like those people you've told me of. Not in any way at all."

"Eddie, you made me that promise when you came through that dining room door to face Partath for me. I knew then I would be safe as long as I had you." She took his hand, brought it to her lips and kissed it. "You killed for me, Young Lord."

"Only half killed," Eddie said before catching himself.

Rachel looked around at Eddie. "What do you mean, half killed?"

"Nothing, its just that he was dead when he betrayed the Guide. That's all."

"Nice try," Rachel commented. "Try again." Her eyes sparkled with the intensity of a predator targeting its prey. This answer was refused without exception.

"Nothing, really," Eddie tried again. The look on Rachel's face told him he would have to answer. "All right, but you can't tell Sebastian I told you. You can't breathe a word of it."

Rachel said nothing, making no promise or agreement of silence.

Eddie waited, but it was clear she was going to remain silent until he told her more. "All right, Partath isn't exactly dead."

Rachel remained quiet, waiting for more details.

"You know he's a vampire. The tissue healed."

"Where is he?" she hissed.

"Sebastian has him in the basement. But it's not as bad as you're thinking. Only his body healed. The mind is gone, a clean slate. Sebastian is even going to rename him when he reeducates him."

Rachel reached for the phone near her seat and began dialing. After a minute, Rachel was connected to the island. "Get me Sebastian, this is Rachel," she said to whomever answered the phone.

Eddie heard Sebastian come on the line.

After a friendly hello, Rachel replied. "Give my regards to your patient, Partath." She hung up the phone. Rachel then looked to Eddie. "Why did he tell you?"

"He said it was my choice whether he lived as a new man or died for what he had been. I've never killed in cold blood, I've never killed at all."

"That's one thing, Eddie, half the membership will have on you. Some of us were born at a time when we had to kill to survive."

Not two minutes after Rachel hung up, the phone rang. Eddie and Rachel exchanged a glance and after several rings Rachel picked up the receiver.

"What?"

"I didn't think it was a good idea to tell you right now. I was concerned about your reaction. I'm so pleased I was wrong." Sebastian's voice was crisp but pleasant.

"You should have told me," Rachel replied. Anger was present, but not much.

"You know now, and I'm asking you to remain quiet about it. Please, Rachel."

"Why didn't you trust me? I just want to know."

"It wasn't, and isn't, a matter of trust, Rachel. There was no reason for you to be concerned or get worried over nothing. There was a lot of bad blood between you and he, but he is gone. His body lives, but Partath has the mind of an infant right now. He is not the man you knew."

"It hurts, Sebastian," Rachel told him.

"I know, I'm sorry. My decision could have been wrong, but I did what I thought was best."

Rachel closed her eyes, gripping the receiver in both hands. "All right, I'll tell no one. Do what you think is right and please keep me informed."

"I will. But do something for me. Keep our Young Lord's mouth shut for me."

"I'll keep him occupied." Rachel hung up.

As she hung up, the pilot came over the intercom. "Buckle up, please, we'll be landing very soon."

CHAPTER 15

The jet landed, and everyone disembarked just long enough to board a helicopter. Then they were airborne again. Eddie watched out the window as cities turned to towns, and then to forest covered lands. The helicopter headed into the mountains.

After an hour, they could see what looked like a fortress cut out of the mountain. "Dracula's Castle?" Eddie jokingly asked Rachel. She and the other members in the helicopter laughed.

"I guess you could call it that," Teri replied. "Or Vampires Village."

Everyone laughed again.

"It's the home of Orbis Gracen, leader of the Guide," Rachel told him in a tone that was to let Eddie understand not to joke around too much about it. "What you see is very little compared to what lies inside and below. There are multiple levels in the mountain--meeting chambers, guest accommodations, labs, and libraries. You name it, we probably have it here."

"Including the Induction Ceremony Hall," Teri told Eddie.

"You were telling me earlier that this wasn't a scheduled Induction Ceremony, that it's especially for me. Does that mean it will be quicker with it being just me?"

"I would love to tell you yes, but not likely. These things drag out. And I must have been unclear when telling you about the ceremony. You won't be alone, Eddie. True, this Induction Ceremony was not scheduled to take place at this time, but there were others drawing close to completing their training. Gracen moved them forward and added you."

"When will I meet Gracen?"

A member, one that had met the group at the helicopter, open-handedly slapped Eddie across the face. "Lord Gracen, to you new member. Lord Gracen, until after the Ceremony."

"Montgomery!" Rachel said, intervening. "He is my student and I will thank you to let me see to correcting him."

"I haven't seen you correct him yet. He speaks to blooded members like he is one. I will not stand for it. Do I make myself clear?"

"You're an ass, Montgomery. You always have been," Teri told the man. "This new member is the one that saved our island and rescued all of us."

"I've heard the stories--the tales of him leaping to his death, and then returning as if by magic. As I see it, his Mentor could have been mistaken, or just lied about his jump--a little something to make her student special."

"Your ignorance is showing again," Rachel told Montgomery. He drew back his hand to hit her as he had hit Eddie. Before he could strike, Eddie jerked open the passenger door of the helicopter, shoved Montgomery out on the landing skid, slammed the door shut and locked it into place. Some of the Guide members on the helicopter laughed, thinking it funny to watch Montgomery trying the door and banging on it when it wouldn't open.

Rachel was not one of the amused members. "Open the door. Now!" she ordered sternly.

Eddie sat there, arms folded, staring at her. "He was going to hit you," Eddie said flatly.

"He was going to try. I'm much faster than he is. I could have handled him. Now, let him back in here."

Eddie kicked the door open so fast Montgomery tumbled in, falling flat on his face. He bounced up and started to turn on Eddie.

Rachel grabbed Montgomery and slammed him back into his seat. "I will deal with my student. You will not interfere, or so help me I'll feed you to the dogs."

Eddie had heard this tone of voice from Rachel in their learning sessions when he wasn't doing something well enough, or not concentrating when he should have been.

Rachel spun on Eddie next. He hadn't expected that. "As for you, I've put up with all I'm going to. You are on notice. As of now, you obey the rules I've taught you. Don't press me on this, Eddie. You won't like the results." Rachel returned to her seat, arms folded across her chest, staring down one man and then the other. She was almost daring them to oppose her. They didn't.

When the helicopter landed, all of the members of the Guide, except for Rachel, headed off in different directions. Eddie waited for her, and they left the landing pad together.

"I will see you to your room, Eddie. I'm afraid I won't see you again today, but I'll have Teri or someone come check on you. It would be best for both of us if you stayed in your room today, but I know you, so at least restrict yourself to the wing of the building your room is in."

"I take it we won't be sharing a room here," Eddie said disappointedly to Rachel.

"Unlike the island, where it is customary for students and Mentors to have an adjoining suite, here it is thought that a new member coming to this place has been with their Mentor long enough to handle themselves around blooded members. New members are on the second floor. Blooded members are on the third floor. Staff personnel are on the ground floor." Rachel stopped walking and turned to Eddie. "Eddie, behave yourself. I know I told you that on the island and things got out of control there. The blooded members there were very lenient with your behavior because they owe you their lives. You will not have that going for you here. What I suggest Eddie, is that you try to remember everything anyone has ever told you about manners since the day you were born. Don't let them piss you off or egg you on. Be better than that. You can do it, Eddie. You can do anything, I think."

"I'll be so nice it'll make you sick," Eddie told her.

"Good. I need something to make me sick of you." Rachel laughed and walked on. She saw Eddie to his room. To his surprise, there was a refrigerator in the room, stocked with fresh fruits and vegetables. There was no place in the room to cook, but he had some food, so he wouldn't starve before morning. With the fridge there, Eddie again promised Rachel he'd stay put until she returned for him. She left Eddie to his own devices and headed upstairs.

As was expected when visiting any house of Guide property, Rachel stopped in and paid her respects to the House Master. In this case, it was Orbis Gracen. Then she found her assigned suite and went there. A place to hide for a time, Rachel thought, entering the suite.

Rachel pulled off her clothes and entered her shower. She stood there a long time, letting the hot steam fog up her mind, as it did the bathroom. She stood there and forced all thoughts from her head. She needed to go home, get in her own shower, be around her own things, and give up fronts for a time. She knew more than anything else, all she wanted to do was curl up in Eddie's arms and be held. By vampire standards, he was a kid. By Guide thinking, he was below her just because he wasn't a blooded member yet. Rachel laughed, thinking how he had been more of a man to her than any, except Sebastian. She and Sebastian had never had a relationship except as Mentor, student, and friend. Even so, many of the Guide, thought differently.

Rachel stood there feeling like she should be crying, but she knew that wasn't about to happen. She didn't cry anymore--not for herself, not for anyone--until Eddie. Something about him ignited a part of her soul she'd thought long dead. Rachel turned off the water, found a towel, and began drying off. She wrapped her hair in one towel, and wrapped a second one around her body. Entering her bedroom, Rachel received a surprise.

"I heard you were back."

"Jim," Rachel said with disdain.

"Figured you'd contact me as soon as you got in. But as you didn't, I decided to come see you."

"Jim, I told you and your friends I want nothing to do with you. Please leave." Rachel raised her hand in the direction of the door.

James Albert looked over his shoulder at the two men with him, and smiled. "I don't think just yet."

Rachel then lost all sense of politeness. "Get the hell out of here. Now!"

Jim snatched the towel away from her body. He and the other two men laughed for a heartbeat. They stopped laughing when an unearthly howl filled the air. It seemed to be coming from everywhere at once. All three men looked at one another and around the room.

Rachel stood there glaring at them as their gazes returned to her. "I would advise you to leave before my friend arrives." Rachel was almost hoping they did remain.

"I advise it anyway, Mr. Albert," said a new voice to the conversation. Rachel and the three men looked to the bedroom doorway. "Now."

Jim Albert and his companions threw Rachel one last look, then exited.

"Thank you, Colonel," Rachel said, retrieving her towel and wrapping herself up again.

"You and I don't like each other very much, Ms. Westchester, but I like Mr. Albert and his friends even less," the Colonel told her. He started to turn and leave, then stopped. "It's your own fault, in a way."

"Oh, it is?"

"You're a beautiful woman, Ms. Westchester. You've had numerous offers here, and I would imagine as many away from the Guide as well. If you had taken one of them, there would be someone here now. Albert and his kind would stay away." He looked her square in the eyes.

Rachel thought she saw a sadness cross them.

"Or am I wrong?" he continued. "Is there someone here already?"

"I don't know what you're talking about," Rachel replied. The answer sounded like a lie to her.

"That was he wasn't it? That cry was your student?" Although he worded it as a question, Rachel knew it wasn't. "Coming to your defense, I would say. Coming to his mate's, I mean Mentor's, defense."

Rachel had no reply. Any statement would seem hollow.

The Colonel nodded goodbye to her, and left.

Rachel went to the door of the suite and locked it. She then went back into the bedroom. Next, she closed and locked that door. Rachel pulled off the towel, climbed into bed and went to sleep, wondering how Eddie had known she was in trouble.

That night, Rachel dreamt of pleasant days on the island, of relaxed moods and moonlit nights. She felt safe and content in Eddie's arms. In her dream, there was just the two of them. They were in a world of their making, a world amongst the heavens.

In the waking world, in the morning, Rachel felt revitalized, energetic even, but she knew it would be a long day. Rachel dressed and headed down to Eddie's room. She wanted to talk about the events of the night before. She knocked at his door, received no answer, and knocked again. Rachel tried the door, it opened and she entered. Before Rachel could react, she was pulled into the room, and the door was closed and locked behind her. She didn't move. Eddie was off to her left. He held her by the throat at the full extent of his arm. Rachel stood there not moving, not looking to her left at him. She just waited. Eddie moved behind her, not releasing his grip on her throat.

"Eddie," she said softly.

Eddie applied more pressure to her throat.

She understood the added pressure meant to be quiet.

"Beyond the door I am your humble servant and obedient student, but here, now, at least for the minute, you are mine. "

Rachel nodded her agreement and waited for him to continue.

Eddie moved his free hand to her shirt, undoing one button after another and slipping his hand inside onto the warm flesh of her belly.

She could feel his warm breath on her neck, just behind her right ear. Rachel's heart raced at his touch--she smiled, she couldn't help it. It was silly to get so nervous inside, over a man so much her junior. But she couldn't resist his touch. Anything he wanted she'd do. The thought of having to wait for him to be a blooded member before she declared herself his tore at her heart. All thoughts of troubles and problems that could arise disappeared from her mind as Eddie pulled her firmly against his body.

An hour later, Rachel was fully dressed again, her hair slicked back flat to her head. She stood at the mirror in Eddie's room. He was in the bathroom. They had made love that morning, but beyond that, they had pledged themselves to each other no matter what.

Eddie came out of the bathroom dressed in sweats as she'd instructed him to. "I guess I'm ready for the first test," he told her.

Rachel turned his way. "How did you know I was in trouble

last night?"

"You're my heart. I just knew."

"How did you know when Colonel Wolf appeared?"

"It's hard to explain. I can feel you. I can smell your scent. You could walk out that door, go hide and I could follow you an hour from now to where you were hiding." Eddie looked at her. "Can't most vampires track their Mentors?"

"True, there is a bond between student and Mentor. As best that has been determined, it is from the mind-touch. But I have never heard of a bond as strong as ours, not even in vampires that have been together for centuries. It might be because of how vigorously your vampire skills are expressing themselves, being a vampire lord and all of that."

"I can feel Rita Janel almost as strongly as I can you," Eddie told her.

"Really," she commented. "That's unusual. What about Sebastian or any of the others?"

Eddie shook his head.

A chime echoed through the hall outside of Eddie's room. Rachel looked to the door. "We'll discuss this later in more detail." Looking over at Eddie, she asked, "Are you ready?"

He nodded and they left for the arena, and for Eddie's first test of Induction.

The arena area was a high ceiling room built like a small gym. On two sides of the room were bench seats for the membership of the Guide. At the far end was a section for the Guide leader and the Mentors of new members entering the arena that day. On the fourth and last side of the room was the point where the new members entered the sand filled arena.

"Now remember what I told you. This is a test that will be given only once. It is not like most tests, none of the testing here is. You are not judged on a pass or fail basis. You are merely observed by Gracen, his council, and the blooded members that are here. That is the best explanation I can offer. After today you will never enter the Sands as a new member again. You will not enter again until after the Induction Ceremony. Failure to complete the Induction Ceremony correctly and you will be barred from the Sands until your training is repeated. Then you will be tested again."

"If I don't pass this week, how long before I can try again?" Eddie inquired, not remembering the matter of failure that was discussed before.

"If you cannot complete the Induction Ceremony, Eddie, you will live here as servant to the members for fifty years before you are allowed to try again," Rachel explained. "Do not worry about failing. And remember one thing Eddie--it is not a question of passing each test. It is a matter of how you do overall on all of the tests."

They joined a group of people. Mentors and students lined up from the edge of the Sands of the arena, back to their position about a quarter of the distance from the entry point. More people were coming and joining the line. One at a time, the two people Mentor and student, walked to the edge of the arena. The Mentor would bow to the man standing in the center of the arena, and ask that his or her student be allowed to enter the arena. The man would wave them in. The student would enter as his or her Mentor moved around to the seating reserved for Mentors.

Eddie stood watching, as the man turned no one away. They attacked him, and he defeated all comers. Eddie and Rachel moved up in line, his turn getting closer with each minute. "Has he ever lost?"

"Never in the history of the Guide. But you will only face him once."

"Not to insult the man, but I haven't seen anything impressive. He's slow," Eddie told her.

"He is much faster than you think. He is the Sand King, a most honored man, an ancient warrior and an honorable member of the Guide."

Eddie mulled over Rachel's comments. He also listened to the comments of the other Mentors around them as they gave their students instructions. He heard statements like--he's ruthless attack him quickly. He's an animal--fight him as hard as you can.

Eddie watched student after student enter the arena and fall to the man out there, the Sand King. What gave Eddie a cold feeling, he realized, was that these students were poorly trained in the Sands of Combat, by Sebastian's standards. With cool detachment, Eddie knew he could take the Sand King down, and probably all of these students as well. A minute later, he was next.

Rachel bowed to the Sand King. "Honored Sir, my student wishes to enter the arena. What is your word?"

This man, the Sand King, waved Eddie into the arena. With a quick look at Rachel, Eddie walked to the man. Eddie had watched students charge him head on, trying to be clever, with moves their Mentors had taught them. Students lay all around Eddie and the Sand King. Some were unconscious, and some were moaning in pain from the injuries they'd received. Eddie looked them over, the Sand King watching him carefully.

After a minute, the Sand King moved closer to Eddie. "Well, did you come here to fight or to just sightsee?"

Eddie looked over at the old man, the Sand King. "To learn."

The Sand King screamed his attack cry, charging Eddie.

Eddie let the Sand King land a punch to his jaw. He fell back, rolling with the force of the blow, so the strike was lessened. The Sand King followed him swinging and kicking as Eddie wrapped himself into a ball to minimize what the Sand King could hit.

Eddie could hear a dull droning sound coming from the audience. The dull sound grew louder, to the point where he could make out what they were saying.

"The boy's a coward!"

"Coward!"

"He's scared!"

"Murder the wimp!"

Rachel sat in her assigned seat watching in confusion, as Eddie made no attempt to defend himself. She watched until she could stand it no more, and then dropped her head.

The Sand King stopped and stepped back from Eddie. "You do not fight me, why?"

Eddie uncurled from his ball. "I am not your enemy," Eddie's reply was direct.

"You are a coward then?" the Sand King asked him.

"No."

The Sand King lashed out with a kick, catching Eddie in the shoulder, knocking him backward. "Then sit and watch as others enter the arena of the Sand King." The Sand King returned to the arena center, not waiting for the Mentor to ask for his student to enter. He just waved him in.

Eddie sat in the sand and watched student after student enter the arena. He watched as the Sand King defeated each one until none were left.

The Sand King returned to Eddie. "So, non-fighter, have you learned anything?"

"No," Eddie replied. "You have shown me no move or technique I do not already know. You are slow and these students are poorly trained."

A collective gasp came from the audience of members. A scowl twisted the features of the Sand King. He attacked again. Swinging as hard as he could, he attacked.

Eddie rolled away from the Sand King, and then bounced to his feet.

The Sand King threw punches and kicks as fast as he could.

Eddie blocked each intended strike with ease. His speed made it simple. The Sand King attacked steadily for five minutes.

Eddie, although blocking every strike easily, threw no punches or kicks of his own. He made it quite clear that the Sand King could not hit him unless Eddie allowed it.

The Sand King stopped his attack. "So you think you are the King of the Arena Sands now, don't you, boy?"

Eddie shook his head. "No, sir. You are the Sand King. I am the Vampire Lord."

The Sand King looked at Eddie. Then, so did the students on the ground around them. He extended a hand to Eddie. "I'm Mitchell, Sand King here."

"Eddie Laidlaw," Eddie told him, shaking hands.

"Come along, Lord Laidlaw, we have much to talk about."

Rachel left her seat racing around to the entrance of the arena. She met them as they left the arena. "Sand King, Eddie, where are you going?"

"He is with me for a time, Rachel. I wish to talk with him."

"He has a lot to see to today before the ball tonight. Do not be long, please," she told Mitchell.

"I will see you get him back directly."

Mitchell and Eddie walked off together.

CHAPTER 16

Traditionally, after the new members met the Sand King in the arena, they were treated to a ball. Passing or failing the arena didn't matter where attending the ball was concerned. They all received this little reward before the next phase of the Induction Ceremony began.

Early the next morning, the new members, one-by-one, would be taken before a panel of blooded members to be questioned about many aspects of their lives since before the change and after. But that was tomorrow. Tonight, the new members, their Mentors, and all the membership of the Guide at Gracen's house, were readying themselves for the ball.

"Eddie leave the tie alone, it's perfect," Rachel told him disgustedly for the hundredth time.

"It's too tight. I can hardly breath."

"You're a vampire, you can do without air a very long time." Rachel folded his handkerchief and put it in the breast pocket of his jacket. She stepped back to look at her handiwork. "You're very handsome tonight, Lord Laidlaw."

Eddie bowed to her. "I wish I could say the same about you. You can't be seen with someone of my caliber the way you look. No, I'm afraid we'll have to fix you up or leave you." Eddie stepped over to her and tore open her shirt, ripped it from her body leaving her standing there, with just her bra and skirt on. Eddie stepped back to have a look. "Much better," he commented, grinning.

"I can be seen in your presence now?" Rachel asked, enjoying his amusement.

"No, but you're more fun to look at now."

She hit him in the chest. "You're ready. When you hear the chime three times, the ballroom is open and the Guide will start showing up. I have to go change into something a little more ballroom style. I'll meet you there." Rachel took a shirt out of Eddie's closet and slipped it on to replace her torn one. She stopped next to Eddie and gave him a kiss on the cheek, then left him to ready herself.

Eddie watched her go, thinking how beautiful she was, and wondering what she saw in him. He looked at himself in the mirror. He wasn't fat, but he wouldn't disappear from sight if he turned sideways either. Rachel had his brown hair all neatly combed and set in place with some kind of a gel. He didn't know what it was. Rachel said the gel would keep his hair styled the entire night. He could wash it out in the morning. He noticed, as she fixed his hair, that it was longer than it had been only two weeks ago. When he asked her about it, Rachel explained it was because of the change. His body's metabolism was working on a much different level, much higher than before. That was part of why they healed and were harder to kill, but one of the side effects was that the hair and nails grew faster and stronger. Eddie was still looking in the mirror and noticing other changes in his-self when the chimes rang out. He listened to the three consecutive rings and headed out of his room and upstairs. He had been told that the ballroom was five levels up and couldn't miss it. Walking there, Eddie came across blooded members and new members alike, all headed where he was. He scanned the growing crowd for Rachel but didn't see her.

"Who are you looking for?" a soft voice asked from behind him. Eddie twisted around to find Teri.

"Three guesses." He turned back in the direction he was walking.

Teri snagged his arm and fell in step beside him. "Play escort, huh, at least until you find Rachel."

Eddie laid his left hand on top of Teri's hand that was wrapped around his right arm. For a time, they walked on without a comment between them. Gradually, he stopped looking for Rachel, figuring to see her at the ball. With his mind off of Rachel, Eddie took notice of the beautiful woman at his side. Teri was wearing a dark pink dress that covered one shoulder, leaving the other bare to show off the tan from her time spent on the island. It was a ballroom gown, extending to the floor, with ruffles and fine lace. To Eddie, it looked expensive, and sexy as well.

"You look great tonight," Eddie told her, returning his eyes to where they were walking.

"Thank you. My first compliment for the night."

"I'm sure you'll get plenty. You do look great."

"Good enough to eat?" she teasingly asked.

Eddie looked at her sharply.

"Sorry, old vampire joke. Speaking of Rita Janel, how is she?"

"I haven't had any time today to call and find out."

"When you do, wish her my best."

Eddie nodded.

They walked on in silence the rest of the way to the party. As they neared the double doors to the ballroom, Teri threw out her chest and stepped even closer to Eddie.

"Make all these bitches jealous," Teri whispered to Eddie.

"Is that what you want to do?"

"You got that right."

"And walking in with me is going to do that?"

"They may not all act like it, Eddie, but every man here would love to have the reputation they think you have, and every woman here would love to replace Rita Janel with themselves."

"Everyone, you say. Does that include you?"

"You got that right," Teri didn't back away from his possible interest. "If for no other reason than having the status of being the woman of the young Vampire Lord. When you are made a blooded member, you'll have your pick of the lot of us."

"I'm still unclear on this matter of my being a blooded member, as opposed to not. What difference does it make?"

"Well, Eddie, you see we have a couple of reasons. Most of the Guide is out of old Europe and Asia, regions historically dominated by station and class. So that's part of it. You also should have been told, but maybe not, because of the rush to get you here, but we had a young student and a Mentor mate once, before the student was a blooded member. Everything the Mentor did, after getting together with this student, was what the student wanted. The Guide suffered heavy losses straightening out the messes they put in motion, both financial loses and in losing several very good members who went after them. So it is not looked well upon for a Mentor or any blooded member to become involved with a new member before completing the Induction Ceremony."

"Are you telling me that Rita Janel will get in some kind of trouble because of me?" Eddie asked, as they entered the ballroom.

Teri couldn't suppress laughing at his comment, but she thought his concern was touching. "Rita Janel couldn't get in trouble with the Guide if she walked in here with Delvar on her arm."

"Then why will walking in here with me make anyone other than her jealous?"

"Because, my dear boy, we'll all be jockeying for position, Lord Laidlaw."

Eddie nodded. He reached to her neck, taking her firmly in grip, and twisting her face up to his, Eddie leaned down and kissed her strongly on the mouth as if he'd kissed her a hundred times. Everyone in the room noticed and tried to pretend they didn't. As Eddie broke off the kiss, he whispered to her, "Thanks for the information, and the kiss will give them something to talk about." He winked, straightened, and led her to the buffet tables set up for the ball.

It was an hour before Rachel appeared at the party. Eddie was across the room with Teri and a small harem of other females, but he saw her enter. Rachel saw him, smiled, and shook her head. Before she was five feet into the ballroom, half a dozen people approached her. None stayed with her long, and all threw quick glances Eddie's way. As Rachel spoke to them, she nodded as if in total agreement with them and continued on her way toward Eddie.

Eddie watched her approach. She wore a slim, floor length black dress, with no ruffles or lace to distract from her shape. It was low cut in the front, and Eddie was dying to see the back. From one of the women around him, Eddie heard the word bitch escape just louder than a breath. He had to laugh because he knew she had the eye of every man in the room, and the women knew it, too.

"Are you enjoying yourself?" Rachel asked, as she

approached Eddie.

"It's not exactly a normal ball dress, is it?" commented one of the women, before Eddie could speak.

"It seems to be doing just fine," Rachel replied, not looking away from Eddie.

"Yes," Eddie said. He forced himself to stop staring at her. "Yes, I'm enjoying myself immensely."

"I'm surprised you're not on the dance floor."

"I don't know any of these dances," he explained.

"And these little ladies let you use such a poor excuse." Rachel took hold of his arm and pulled him away from his harem.

"But--" Eddie started.

"I'm your Mentor. It's my job to see you learn what you don't know. Don't argue with your Mentor." Rachel took him off to a far corner of the dance floor and started telling him how to stand and hold his partner. After a few stumbling starts, and a toe or two getting stepped on, Rachel and Eddie were moving around their area of the dance floor easily enough.

"I received a variety of reports on you as I came in." Rachel smirked at Eddie as she told him.

"I know. I saw them. It looked like they couldn't get to you quickly enough."

"You're the talk of the ball tonight."

"I was until you entered. You look wonderful."

"Thank you. I hear you thought Teri was looking pretty tasty, too."

Eddie smiled. Now he understood. "So the green monster rears its ugly head."

"You think I'm jealous?"

"Aren't you?"

"Do I have reason to be?" She turned the question back to Eddie.

"Rachel Anne Westchester, you are the most beautiful woman I have ever laid eyes on. You don't have to worry about Teri or any other woman, ever."

"Thank you." Nothing more needed to be said. "I've showed you the basic steps, so why don't you go step on someone else's toes for a time. I have to visit a lot of this crowd before the night's over." Rachel released him and started to walk off.

Eddie held her arm another second or two, pulling her back his way. "Leave your bedroom window unlocked tonight," he told her, and then let her go.

As soon as Eddie and Rachel separated, Eddie again found himself lost in a sea of smiling females. He grinned wildly, grabbed the closest one and headed off for the dance floor. Eddie spent the rest of the night changing partners and raiding the buffet table. Once in a while, he'd catch a glimpse of Rachel on the dance floor. She didn't seem to notice him, but he knew all too well that it was part of the game.

The rest of the evening did not go as he thought it would. When people starting retiring for the night, Eddie noticed that the sun was coming up. He located and approached Rachel.

"I was just going to come looking for you," she said. I think we can call it a night."

"Not the night I was thinking about."

"I know, but we have time," Rachel assured him. "As for the day, it's yours to do with as you choose. But whatever you choose, be in your room at eight p.m. sharp. I'll see you then." Rachel turned away from him, walked over to a man in a military uniform and took his arm. They left the ballroom together.

Eddie watched her go, and then realized he was just standing there. Eddie felt an ache in the pit of his stomach at her leaving without him. He knew the reason was to keep their affair private for now, but he didn't have to like it. Deception was a game that he wasn't very fond of. Eddie found himself wondering if he would have to get used to a lot of deceptions, being in the Guide. It was time to leave, though, and he started for the doors of the ballroom. He had been up all night and knew he should be tired, but he wasn't, not in the least. Eddie headed down to his room, changed clothes, and decided to have a look around this fortress. No one had bothered to give him the tour. He really didn't feel like being inside, so when his self-guided tour took him to the ground floor, Eddie made a beeline for the first door he saw leading outside. There was a stone driveway that led up to the front of this mansion. Where the island house looked like a southern plantation house, this one was every bit the opposite. It looked like something King Arthur would have lived in. It sat on top of Mount Olympus, Home of the Gods. At first, Eddie just started walking along the driveway. He veered off and was walking over rougher ground, heading he didn't know where. Eddie came out of a small stand of trees that were part of the path he was following, surprised when he realized he wasn't the only one on the path. Ahead of him, sitting on an outcropping of rocks, was a man. Eddie approached the man and stood just a short distance away, staring at him. The man noticed Eddie after a minute, looked over at him, and then returned to watching the mountainside below.

"Are you looking for me?" the man asked, sounding impatient and irritable.

"'Fraid not," Eddie replied deciding he'd rather move on than talk to a grouch first thing in the morning. "I'll be moving on if I'm bothering you," Eddie offered.

"Did you know that if you sit here long enough and watch the clouds roll by, you'll see a dragon every day." All manner of distaste was gone from the man's voice now.

Eddie smiled, walked over and sat down next to the man. "Have you seen any dragons today?" Eddie asked.

"At dawn, that's when they like to come out." The man was old from the looks of him. He had white hair and deep wrinkles. His voice was soft and pleasant, his movements smooth like unseen strength filled him, and his green eyes could have been crystals. "No one comes up here. What made you?" the man asked. His eyes flashed with curiosity.

"I needed to get out of the house for a time."

"Aren't you one of the new members, here for the Induction Ceremony?" the old man asked.

"Yeah."

"You don't sound that enthused."

"Well, it's not like it doesn't come with its draw backs. I get to watch the people I know and the family that I do have grow old and die. And there seems to be a lot of fighting amongst the members, from what I can tell."

"It didn't used to be that way. In more recent years, the newer members have lost respect for the older members."

"Doesn't Lord Gracen have some way to change that? Can't the Mentors teach them better?"

"That old fool," the man growled. "That is where the trouble lies. Nowadays, every member wants to replace him." The man looked over at Eddie. "From what I hear, they think you might be the perfect replacement, Mr. Laidlaw. You are Eddie Laidlaw, aren't you?"

"Please, call me Eddie. I'm afraid I don't know anything about replacing Lord Gracen. I do know he has the trust and support of Sebastian, Rita Janel, and Rachel." Eddie paused. "I'm new, but I trust them. If they support him, so do I."

"It is nice to hear that some youths do use their Mentors as examples, like they are supposed to. I've heard that you died the night that the Followers attacked."

"I jumped from a cliff just like this one." Eddie and the old man leaned forward to see over the rocky terrain below. "But there was an ocean, there."

Eddie decided he wouldn't want to try the same thing here.

"Why?"

Eddie knew what the man was asking.

"Why did I jump? I couldn't handle what was happening. I was scared, confused, and thought it would end my problems," Eddie explained.

"If that was the way you felt, what made you climb back out of the surf?"

"I didn't think about it at the time. Later, though, I realized it was a calling, of sorts. I heard Rachel crying, and--" Eddie stopped as he realized he'd just blown their secret to a man he didn't even know. The man knew it, too. Eddie could tell by the change of expression on his face.

"She cried for the man she loved and lost, and you came back," the old man finished.

Eddie said nothing.

"I understand, Eddie. Your secret is safe with me," the old man assured him. "Rachel is a good girl. She deserves a good fellow."

"I know it's against the rules, but we're in love."

"You'll find there are two truths in this life, Eddie. The first is love. When you find it, fight with every last breath in you to keep it. And the second is that rules are only for those that don't have the strength to find the first rule."

Both men sat in silence for several minutes. Then the old man turned to Eddie.

"Did I ever tell you about the time I was planning a trip to China?"

"No, I don't think you did," Eddie replied, suppressing a grin.

"Well, somehow the Chinese were under the impression that I was a deviant of some kind, so they put up this wall all around the country to keep me out. Can you imagine the surprise I felt at finding out someone disliked me that much?"

"So tell me, did this unfriendly attitude make you reconsider, and cancel your trip?"

"Of course not. I went to their country, pushed down a section of their silly wall, and visited anyway."

Eddie laughed as the man started recounting stories of his adventures and the places he'd seen.

Rachel walked up to the door of Eddie's room, raised her hand to knock, but didn't get the chance to.

"I'm not there," Eddie yelled to her from down the hallway.

Rachel turned to find him walking toward her.

"You said I had to be here by eight. I'm here." The look on his face was relaxed, even happy. "It's open." Eddie twisted the knob, pushed the door open, and escorted her inside. Once inside, after closing the door, Eddie grabbed Rachel in his arms and kissed her. He pulled her tightly to his chest, and kissed her again.

Rachel was stunned as he released her and stepped back. "I'd ask what you've been up to today, but I don't give a damn." Rachel grabbed Eddie by the collar and kissed him with what Eddie decided was the most sensuous kiss of his life. She saw the flame she put in his eyes. A smile touched her lips as she broke off the kiss.

Eddie was ready to continue, and reached for her, but Rachel evaded his touch.

"I'm sorry to do this to you, but we have to be somewhere in fifteen minutes. You jump in the shower and I'll lay clothes out for you."

"A shower?" Eddie repeated.

Rachel nodded.

"A cold shower."

Rachel nodded and smiled innocently.

Eddie didn't smile and walked off.

A short time later, the two of them were walking down a hall two floors above his room.

"So how did you spend your day?"

"I went for a walk outside."

"You've been walking all day?"

"Well, no, not really. When I was out walking, I met up with a man. We got to talking and he kept me laughing all morning. Then he and I went to the kitchen and had lunch."

"Who was he?"

"You know, I never really thought to ask him. I did ask once, when we were eating lunch, but until you just now asked me who he was, I didn't think about him not answering me. He changed the subject on me. I could describe him to you. Maybe you'd know him."

"Not likely. There are too many of the members with similar features. And there are a lot of members here right now to see the Young Lord. Unless, of course, there was something distinct about him, something that made him stand-out."

Eddie thought about it a minute. "No, not really, except that he was fun. Very entertaining company."

They walked on a little further.

"Where are we going?" Eddie asked.

"This is part of the induction process. I'm taking you to a panel of members who will ask you questions, all kinds of questions. Don't let them fluster you, Eddie. They want to see how hard it is to rattle you, get you nervous. They're only questions, so just take your time. Keep in mind that every new member goes through this."

The two of them walked along several hallways and up two flights of stairs. Rachel explained more of what Eddie might expect and again emphasized not to let any of it worry him. She led him to a door and stopped. "It's really simple, Eddie, just don't get rattled."

Eddie shook his head. "Yep, all the rocks are loose. I should rattle fine."

Rachel smiled. "This is where I leave you. Mind your manners, please. They'll call me when they're done." Rachel opened the door she had stopped in front of. Eddie looked into the room. He looked to Rachel then walked in. Rachel closed the door and left.

"Come in, Mr. Laidlaw, and please be seated. I'm Colonel Wolf, and we of the membership panel will be with you in a minute."

Eddie took the indicated seat. It was the only seat in the room on his side of the wide table. Five members sat across from him. They talked in low whispers to each other. Eddie sat there listening to them, not sure if they didn't realize how sharp his vampire hearing had become, or if they were testing him. He listened as they discussed things they'd heard from members that were on the island when he was there. He heard Partath's name come up and the Colonel remarked, "Good riddance for the loss of that member." Eddie suppressed a snicker as he thought how Sebastian was going to surprise this bunch. His snicker jerked the Colonel's attention his way. He and the Colonel's eyes locked for a brief second.

"You can hear our conversation, Mr. Laidlaw?" Colonel Wolf put it as a question, but he and Eddie both knew it wasn't.

"I assumed it was part of this interview, a test of sorts." Looking at the faces of members other than the Colonel's, Eddie knew it wasn't. They truly had not thought he could hear them.

"That's very good. Most times, a recently changed new member isn't able to hear that well, this soon. You're developing at a very fast rate." This statement was from a female seated to the left of the Colonel, who had the center chair of the table.

"Mr. Laidlaw, what is the first and main goal of the Guide?" asked a man seated at the far right of the table.

Now Eddie understood this little interview. Rachel had taught him all of what she called the important stuff as far as the Guide, its purpose, and its anticipated future goals. Now they'd see how much he remembered.

"The first and main objective of the Guide is to bring man to a better understanding of himself, help him accept differences between peoples, and to ensure the safety of our people, as well as theirs."

"What is Rachel Westchester like as a lover?" asked the woman sitting next to the Colonel.

"I'm sure I don't know, but I'll ask her for you. Who should I tell her wants to know?" Eddie acted innocent, knowing now they would try to trick information out of him.

"We'll ask the questions, Mr. Laidlaw," replied the woman. Then the next question came, and one after that, and another, and the night grew very long. Eddie sat there and answered the questions about the Guide. He answered them all quickly and directly, as long as they were not questions like the one the woman asked. Through the hours that passed, Eddie asked questions of his own, like the names of the panel members, but received no replies. Eddie kept asking his questions, and asked even more, until one of the panel members jumped to his feet and started screaming at him. Colonel Wolf grabbed the yelling member by the shirt and forced him back down into his chair. The panel members turned on one another, arguing, about Eddie's attitude.

After the Colonel restored order to his panel, he turned to Eddie. "We'll continue this at a later time, Mr. Laidlaw." As for now, thank you."

"I'm at your call, Colonel Wolf. Members." Eddie acknowledged the blooded members of the Guide. He left the room and heard the arguing start again as the door closed behind him. Eddie grinned and walked away. Rachel had not told him where she was going to be, and Eddie did not feel like tracking her through Gracen's house. He decided to return to his room. She'd find him when she was ready. In his room, Eddie stretched out on the bed. Sleep came easily and he slipped into a world of dreams.

CHAPTER 17

"Knock, knock," Eddie said, sticking his head in the room. Rita Janel pulled him into the room as he held the note she'd sent out to him. "I got your note, but I'd have dressed up if I'd have known it was to be a party." He looked to Rachel as Rita Janel wrapped herself around his side. Rachel smiled that secret smirk of hers that told him to enjoy it while it lasted. Eddie looked to the big man. He held his hand out toward the man. "How you doing this morning, big guy?"

"Just fine Eddie, yourself?" Gracen asked.

"Much better now," Eddie told him pulling Rita Janel tightly to himself.

"Eddie," Rachel said. "You two know each other?"

"Yeah, this is the guy I told you about. I met him on my walk."

"Let me do the introduction then," Rachel said to Eddie, knowing he had told her that he had not gotten the name of the person he had met. "Eddie Laidlaw, this is Orbis Gracen, Leader of the Guide."

Eddie looked to the big man. "You didn't tell me that," Eddie said to Gracen.

"You didn't ask. Why, does it make a difference?"

Eddie thought about the afternoon he'd spent with this man. They had kept each other laughing, and they seemed to get along well enough. Eddie couldn't see any reason they should change the way they treated each other. "You should have told me, but I guess we'll overlook it."

"Gracen doesn't have to explain himself to you Eddie, or to any of us," Rachel said. It was her duty as Mentor and her loyalty to Gracen that made her reprimand him.

"Don't harass my young friend, please. He has to worry about people spying on him enough that I understand his discomfort." Gracen headed toward the door.

"You're leaving so soon?" Rita Janel asked him.

"I only came down for a minute. I have Guide business to

see to, and I have to stop in on another new arrival as well."

"Thank you for coming."

"Rachel, we'll have dinner tonight. You and I must talk. Eight o'clock, my quarters."

"Yes, Lord Gracen." Rachel replied with a curtsy.

When Gracen left and Rita Janel closed and locked the door, she and Rachel both turned on Eddie. They lectured him on his, "we'll overlook it this time" remark, and gave him a quick talk about respect. Gracen was the leader of the Guide, after all.

When they finished, Eddie told them about Gracen's concerns about a lot of members wanting to replace him. He informed them that Gracen also knew the truth about the three of them, and how Gracen had promised to keep their secret safe. They were not happy, but there was nothing to do about it.

"So. Why are you here?" Eddie finally got around to asking Rita Janel.

Rita Janel looked at him. "You didn't think I would miss tonight, did you? Miss your investiture into the Guide? Neither Sebastian nor I would do that."

Eddie looked confused.

"I didn't tell him yet," Rachel told Rita Janel.

"The ceremony is tonight?"

Rachel nodded. "You've done very well on all of the testing so far. I thought it would be best to take you into this without knowing it was the last step until we were there. You do extremely well on the spur of the moment notice, Eddie."

"We'll get you through it, Eddie," Rita Janel assured him.

"There is something we need to see to before tonight. I was just going to come get you, Rachel, but I got the note and knew you'd both be here."

"What needs to be seen to?" Rachel asked.

"You'll see, Rachel. And as it is, your timing couldn't have been better, Rita Janel." Eddie led the two women up one level in the house and to a large dining room. The three of them entered to find the room full.

"What's going on?" Rita Janel asked, as they walked into the room.

"I was approached by a committee representing this group of

people," Eddie told Rachel and Rita Janel.

"Go on." Rachel was not willing to risk more of a comment than that.

"They have expressed a desire to pledge themselves to me. Their loyalty to the Guide is not a question, but they wish to make it clear that they know I am a Lord Vampire, not just a member of the Guide. I told them before I could accept any such promise I had to talk to you. Now you know. What should I do?"

Rachel looked over the faces of people she'd known for years. They all were solid members of the Guide. Some were even members longer than Rachel. "All you people wish to bind yourselves to Lord Laidlaw?"

"Yes," was the answer from the thirty or so men and women in the room.

"You will be loyal to him no matter what, as loyal as you are to the Guide?"

Again, the answer was yes.

Rachel looked to Rita Janel.

Rita Janel stared back at her. "If it is to be done, then it must be done correctly. Wait here." Rita Janel left the room. No one talked or seemed willing to talk the entire time she was gone. Rita Janel returned with Sebastian in tow. She had explained to him as she brought Sebastian to the room.

Sebastian's usually happy expression was now like stone. After a quick glance at Eddie, then he turned to the crowd. "You all understand that once commenced and completed, only Lord Laidlaw can break the bond, and your life is his to use as he wishes, second only to the Guide." The group's reply was the same as it was to Rachel's questions. Sebastian turned to Eddie. "They wish to be your subjects, my Lord. The decision is yours." Sebastian could see the conflict on Eddie's face. The decision was his. "Might I suggest that you take some time to think about it, my Lord? It would be best."

Eddie thought about it. Delaying sounded good to him. He wondered, though, if it would give these people who wanted to swear loyalty to him a bad impression of him.

"It would be best, Lord Laidlaw," Rachel urged.

He trusted her feelings more than his own on the matter, and had Sebastian dismiss the group. Sebastian, Rita Janel, Rachel, and Eddie were the only ones left in the room.

"I knew I needed to talk to someone about this matter before it went too far. How can I accept responsibility for another when I have enough trouble seeing to myself?"

"It is not a matter of taking responsibility for them, or taking care of them. They might come to you for help now and again. It would be a responsibility, but mostly it would be a pool of people that you could rely on when you need them. They pledge to serve you and you pledge to do what is best for all concerned, like the way monarchies are supposed to work."

"Do you think it would be wise to accept their pledges then?"

Rachel exhaled, then nodded. She stepped in front of Eddie directly. "You and I have a relationship stronger than any bond can make. Would you take my pledge, Lord Laidlaw?"

"You don't have to pledge to me. You're my woman, Rachel."

"I'm not. You have my pledge, my life as you need it." Rita Janel sank to her knees. "How do you answer, Lord Laidlaw?"

Eddie had no idea what to tell her.

Sebastian reached for Eddie's arm. He pulled the sleeve back and put the thumbnail of Eddie's other hand to the exposed forearm. "This is the first step in how you bind people, members to you." Sebastian cut Eddie's arm open with the thumbnail and let the blood run. He turned Eddie to Rita Janel, extending Eddie's arm to her. Rita Janel put her mouth over the cut, sucking the blood. She stopped, leaned back from him, and swallowed the blood.

Rachel took Eddie's arm next and drank his blood. She had drunk a great deal of blood in her life, and never had she tasted blood like this. The taste wasn't even the same as it had been when she had all but drained his blood to prevent the madness at the time of the change. There was something different about it, something she just couldn't put her finger on.

Sebastian brought Eddie's arm to his own lips as Rachel stepped back. He too drank Eddie's blood. "Now, Lord Laidlaw, you must strike each of us. I suggest snapping the neck. The blow would be fatal to a non-vampire human, but we will heal. When our bodies do heal, we will have your blood in us, and the bond will be complete. From that time on, no matter about the Guide or its existence, we are with you."

Eddie looked from one person to the next. "I can't kill you." Eddie started to step away but was stopped by Rachel.

"Yes, my love, you can. We are Vampires. Use the skills Sebastian has taught you by striking quickly and hard." Rachel went to her knees, sitting as Rita Janel already was. Sebastian copied their posture. Rachel stroked Eddie's calf, smiled at him and waited. She did not shake or tremble as Eddie reached for her. Remembering how he could not strike her or Rita Janel on the sands, Eddie wondered how he could do so now. But as he contacted her smooth, cool skin, he followed the ritual Sebastian had explained. Eddie twisted her neck sharply to the side. Rachel slumped in his arms and he placed her on the floor. Sickened by his actions, Eddie knew he must finish with Rita Janel and Sebastian before his nerve failed him. He seized Rita Janel next, breaking her neck more quickly than he had Rachel's. Sebastian's neck broke with a bit more effort, and then he lowered him to the floor next to the two women. Eddie quietly sat beside their bodies. Stone would have looked softer than his grim expression.

Sebastian was the first to recover. He jerked as though hit by lightning, then sat upright. Confusion raked at his expression. A glassy hollowed look of death consumed his eyes.

Eddie's cold stare scrutinized him. "I will try my best to be worthy of your trust," Eddie told the older man.

Rachel cried out as her body breathed life anew.

Eddie grabbed her up and held her as the disorientation past. Then Rita Janel awoke from the dead. Her gaze searched out Eddie and she bowed forward toward him. There was nothing to say to them. He could feel the steel hardening around his nerves that he would need to be a vampire lord. Lord Laidlaw rose to his feet, and together the four of them left the dining room.

Sebastian and Rita Janel returned to their rooms, and Rachel took Eddie to hers to get him prepared for the Induction

Ceremony that night.

The Induction Ceremony was in a cavernous hall deep in the mountain that was Orbis Gracen's house. It was set up with seating for the blooded members of the Guide on two of the four walls. Coming from the third wall was a rock platform twenty feet above the open floor--the platform was where the Mentors would bring their students for the Ceremony. There were two stairways to the platform. The first faced the third cavern wall. It was the stairway students and Mentors would ascend to stand before Orbis Gracen and his advisors. The second stairway was the exit for blooded members, and blooded members only. If a student for whatever reason did not leave the platform a blooded member, they exited by the first stairway. Their Mentor would meet them after the ceremony, if that were the case. The fourth wall held the booth of the Leader of the Guide. His advisors also had a booth on that wall. Their booth was lower on the wall than his. Both the advisors and the Leader of the Guide could look down on the platform of the students.

Eddie watched all of the other students and Mentors approach the stairway up onto the platform as he and Rachel walked toward it.

"Now Eddie, the ceremony goes like this. We will file up there in groups of ten students and Mentors. The speaker will already be on the platform. He will announce Orbis, then the council, then each student and Mentor on the platform." Rachel had gone through all of this with him twenty times today, but Eddie liked to listen to her talk. He loved the sound of her voice. The line they stood in came to another stop in the procession. As it did, a man approached them from one side.

"Miss Westchester," he said, coming up to them.

"Yes," Rachel replied, not wanting to lose time with Eddie right now. She knew the man was one of Gracen's personal staff.

"Mr. Gracen would like to see you and Mr. Laidlaw for a few minutes. If you'll follow me."

Rachel knew this was unusual but nodded. She and Eddie were led to a private chamber that Gracen and his council used for Guide business.

"Come in, Rachel, please be seated," Gracen said. There was one open chair at the table. It was clear that Eddie was to remain standing. Rachel didn't like the smell of this already, but she took her seat.

"What can I do for you, sir?" she asked politely.

"It seems, Rachel, that some members of the council believe that Eddie needs more testing before he is allowed to enter the platform. They simply do not believe he has earned the right to stand with the others yet."

"This is a very poor attempt to unhinge my student," Rachel remarked. "Waiting until he is in line to file such complaints is improper."

"The timing is always questionable on such matters. I assure you that we just wanted to wait as long as possible to let our council view him as much as possible without added or undue pressure on him. Or you, for that matter," Gracen explained. "But the extra time did not ease the issues that have arisen, and I am forced to remove him from tonight's Induction Ceremony."

Rachel was on her feet the instant he finished. "Remove him?" she snapped. "This is unthinkable. In all of the time I have been with the Guide, this has never been done, and I have been with the Guide longer than over half of this council. Lord Gracen, I respectfully request you rethink your decision. I will take it as a personal favor if you do and an insult if you do not." Rachel felt a hand on her shoulder applying pressure to put her back in her chair. As she turned to rip the hand away she found it was Eddie's hand. A look from him steadied her composure. Rachel turned back to the council. "What issues?" she demanded, every drop of venom she could muster in the question.

"As you know, students are given pieces of Guide business to see to as part of their training, to see how they handle themselves. This is standard training which takes place over months as new members learn about who and what they are." Gracen looked to Eddie. "This is part of the training you have not received because of the speed in which you were brought here."

"You wish Eddie to be a courier for a time?" Rachel said,

knowing that was the first standard job given to a new member as they trained with their Mentors.

"No, we were thinking of a more difficult assignment. He has, after all, been brought to this point of the Guide Induction Ceremony in rather a hurry. We decided to send him on a retrieval job."

"When do we leave and what are we retrieving?" Rachel asked, resigned to the situation.

"I am afraid that isn't the case. This is his test. If you go, how are we going to know his qualifications, his resourcefulness?"

Rachel looked at each member of the council, some she had counted among her list of friends for years. She found no friends at the table. She saw it as a painful betrayal. Four of these advisors to Gracen received their positions on her recommendations to him. And then there was Gracen himself. He had said nothing to her at dinner only two hours ago. He had asked her to dinner and spoke of nothing in particular. Her own words to Eddie from that morning rang back to her. "Orbis Gracen didn't have to explain himself to you or any one of us," she'd told Eddie. Rachel smiled and forced herself to calmness. "I have complete confidence in my student," Rachel informed them. And she did.

"Then it's settled. Eddie will find it an interesting assignment, I think." Gracen stood up and left the room through a door behind his chair. The other members of the council asked Rachel and Eddie to leave them.

Rachel agreed with a nod and took Eddie back to his room. "From this time on, Eddie, do not trust one living soul in this place except Rita Janel, Sebastian, and me. They are playing some kind of a game. They'll contact you or me about this trip they're planning. I'll be with you in spirit if I can't arrange to go with you. Just don't trust them."

"I never did trust anyone but you," Eddie told her.

Rachel turned to him. "The Induction Ceremony for the others will take the rest of the night. We have until then before they come calling." Rachel reached to her shirt, unbuttoned it, and dropped it on the floor. Eddie took her in his arms.

CHAPTER 18

In the morning, Rachel and Eddie were sitting in the kitchen eating breakfast when Sebastian entered the room.

"I can hardly believe what they did, canceling you out last night." Sebastian dropped heavily into the chair beside Rachel.

"Believe it my old friend," Rachel commented, as she chewed on a carrot.

"Why, is what I want to know?" Sebastian asked them. "Have they given you a reason?"

Eddie and Rachel exchanged a look, and then nodded.

"They have a little job they want me to see to first. I don't have any details though."

"I'll see what I can dig up."

"That won't be necessary. I have a meeting with Gracen in a little while. He said he'd tell me everything then." Rachel bit into her carrot like she meant to hurt it. "The advisors will be there as well."

"You feel up to a two-out-of-three-falls wrestling match?" Eddie asked Sebastian with a leer, daring him.

"I'm feeling very good, of late, Eddie. I'd be happy to make you sore for a while."

Getting up from the table, Eddie headed for the door. "I'll meet you in the arena in say, twenty minutes?"

"Twenty minutes," Sebastian agreed. After Eddie left, Sebastian turned to Rachel. "So tell me. Do you know more than you are divulging?"

"Someone is running a game I think. I smell it more than anything I can lay a finger on. They wish to send him off without me, his Mentor. That is uncommon in itself for such a new member, even a new member with Eddie's abilities. He has skills which most of the Guide know nothing about."

"You're worried about the game being directed at you?"

"I don't know, Sebastian. I can't protect him if I'm not with him."

"He has grown much from the boy you brought to the island.

He may surprise them and you."

"He surprises me everyday," Rachel confessed.

"So what's to worry about?"

Rachel looked to him. "This place, the Guide I mean, and the people of it have been a home to me for more than a thousand years. Last night was the first time I ever felt betrayed by them. Last night, if not for Eddie's strength, I would have been coming to see my Confessor to cry on his strong shoulders."

"I don't think it is Eddie's strength you face them with. Eddie has only given you the reason, not the will. They do not know how strong you can be, Rachel. You've never had any reason to draw on your inner core, but that can be good. It takes a very long time to make a diamond." Sebastian got up from the table. "You remember what I've told you. Keep it in mind as I go beat the stuffing out of your student."

Rachel nodded, accepting Sebastian's words. She was going to show Gracen and his advisors a side of herself they were not expecting. Rachel hurried to Rita Janel's room. She would need her old friend's help.

"So, where is she?" demanded Colonel Wolf. He had been called in to advise them all on the situation Eddie was to be sent to face. "She should have been here half an hour ago."

"Maybe she isn't coming. She was pretty mad about last night."

"Mad or not, she swore oaths to the Guide and the leader of the Guide. She'll be here or I'll tear the hide from her body myself," Gracen told the group. He had to sound like he would show no favoritism, even if he knew he would.

"When she does, I'm going to give her a piece of my mind about her actions concerning this matter," Montgomery told them.

"You can't spare it," Colonel Wolf said sarcastically, disgusted with the situation at hand. The door to the advisor's chamber opened. The group fell silent. Rachel walked in and looked at each member. It appeared as if every one of them had a comment they wished to express on the tip of their tongues, but every member remained silent. She entered, found a seat, and took her place at the table.

"You were saying, fellow members?" Rachel inquired innocently. No one spoke up at first. They all stared at the new look she presented to them. Her hair was slicked back on each side, but the top was loose and combed to the left. Her halter-top couldn't have been any tighter, but it was doing its job. Rachel hoped that between the top and her short skirt, she would have the advisors and Gracen unbalanced just enough to get them to slip and give her some piece of information she might find useful. She was sure not much of the information she'd get otherwise would help her or Eddie. The men were distracted from the business at hand, and for that matter, so were the women. The men were trying to see what wasn't shown, and the women were furious at her coming to the meeting dressed this way. Rachel kept the smile off her face as she enjoyed their discomfort. Even so, their discomfort wasn't the point of the revealing clothes.

"You're late," Gracen finally said. It was clear his attention wasn't on her attendance.

"My apologies for the delay." Rachel opened the notebook she'd brought with her. "Now what is it Eddie is going after?" she asked.

"What?" Montgomery mumbled with his eyes locked on her chest.

"I said, what is Eddie supposed to retrieve?"

"It isn't a what, but a who."

"Explain," Rachel replied to Becky's statement.

"The Colonel could explain better," Becky told her.

Rachel looked to him.

"There is a vampire loose in New York City. He's not one of us, and we don't think it's one of Delvar's Followers." Colonel Wolf passed papers to Rachel. They were newspaper clippings on a string of ghastly killings and copies of police photos of the crime scenes and the victims. There was no doubt that it was a vampire, possibly a rogue.

"One hell of a first assignment. He comes back a hero or in a box," Rachel commented, not letting the anger she was feeling show.

"We don't want to hear any whining about the job. We've all taken risks since we've been with the Guide," Donna said to her.

"And you'll hear none. I am simply expressing an opinion. Now stay out of this conversation unless you have something pertinent to add."

Donna's eyes looked like they were going to pop out of her head. She started to get up from the table but was close to Gracen, who barred her way.

"Be quiet and sit down," Gracen told Donna harshly.

Rachel dismissed the woman from that point on.

"What do you have for him to go on?"

"Very little, Miss Westchester," Colonel Wolf replied somberly. "The attacks are frequent, but sporadic. This has only just started, three weeks ago tonight. The police have nothing. They have run it through all of their computer links and haven't a clue." Colonel Wolf handed Rachel a map and a folder. The map had the times and locations of the killings. Rachel looked into the folder to find a wallet, plane tickets, and cash. She had her share of these folders, tickets to the problem area, cash, credit cards and identification. Rachel removed the wallet and looked at the I.D. "EDDIE LAIDLAW," was printed on the driver's license, and the credit cards. That was not standard on a job like this.

"You will please note, Rachel, that it is all in his name. The reason for that is we don't what him pretending to be someone else without training in that kind of operation. If he gets in a jam, we don't want him to get caught in lies about whom he is. In the wallet is a number to one of our operators. He can call there for a pickup if he thinks he's in over his head, or if he should find out something. The information will get sent directly to me and then I'll inform you," Gracen told her. "Will that be satisfactory?"

"Yes sir, fine." Rachel knew any other answer would be useless or met with argument. "What time frame are we looking at to get Eddie on his way?"

"The helicopter will be here to pick him up in a little over two hours. You'll have until then to have him ready."

"A question, please. Is Eddie to bring the rogue back or take him down by any means necessary?"

"Exterminate, if need be. It would probably be the best solution. Tell him to count on that scenario," Wolf told her.

"Are there any more details I should know?" Rachel asked, admitting to herself that so far, she hadn't received the sort of information she was hoping for.

"Colonel, this is your line of work. If you'll brief Rachel, there are several other matters that my advisors and I need to see to." Gracen and the others got up from their chairs.

"There is one other matter that concerns me. I have taught Eddie most of the basics to get him through the Induction Ceremony, and how to survive easily at Guide properties, such as how to feed here at home and how to know who to feed from. I have not taught him anything about feeding away from our medallion staff people."

"You're saying he can't feed away from here?" Montgomery asked, getting to his feet. "I knew this was a bad idea. We should have sent in an insertion team like we discussed before there was a suspicion that Rachel and her student were having a relationship. I--"

"Montgomery, shut up!" Becky said. "Just shut up and sit down."

Rachel and Gracen's eyes were locked on one another. Neither spoke, they just stared. The betrayal, as far as she was concerned, was complete. She didn't show a reaction to the reason Eddie had been denied his membership at this time. Finally, Gracen got to his feet and walked over to Rachel.

"No one has made an accusation, Rachel," he told her unconvincingly.

"No?" she questioned him, tilting her head slightly.

"No," he replied more firmly. "But there has been talk. Talk I have suppressed on all levels except for this one. For the safety of the Guide and for us, we have to know he is worthy of us. We have to know that he won't turn into another Dane."

"And I into another Carolyn?" Rachel replied bitterly.

"I didn't say that. I didn't even consider the possibility," Gracen assured her. He lied.

"I will not interfere in this assignment, Lord Gracen. I will send him off to face this rogue, but understand this. Upon his return, he is to be accepted as a blooded member. I will hear no more talk about his worthiness to stand with the Guide." Rachel turned on her heel and left the room.

Colonel Wolf was only a second behind her. He caught her by the arm.

Rachel turned, ready to remove the arm of the person grabbing her, but Wolf released her first.

"There is more for him. Do you wish to hear about it?"

Rachel wanted to tell him where to go, but she wanted the information more.

"Can you brief me as we walk?"

"Of course." Colonel Wolf fell in step with Rachel as she headed for her quarters. "Before we get started, Miss Westchester, I want you to know two things. For this operation, Mr. Laidlaw is one of my staff. I do not send my staff out with anything less than the absolute certainty of getting them back safely. Secondly, I have heard the rumors of you two, and you know I know the true of the matter. My point is that I did not say anything to anyone. I thought if we're to work together that you should know these things."

"Colonel, you're sure that Eddie and I are lovers because he was coming to my defense the other night, but that is very little to go on," Rachel replied, her voice not having the conviction she was striving for.

"True. You tell me straight out that you aren't. The answer goes no farther than here," the Colonel told Rachel.

She stopped walking and turned to face him. Rachel looked deep into the eyes of the man before her. She didn't care for him, and he didn't much care for her, but she did know Wolf to be an honorable man. His word was good when he gave it. "Promise me this mission is not just someone's scheme to get rid of Eddie."

"My word on the matter. I will do all I can to see to his safe return."

"Yes, we are lovers. When he becomes a blooded member, I am to become his woman before all of the Guide." Rachel returned to walking toward her room. Wolf continued to walk with her and proceeded to reveal the details on the rogue vampire, gathered by the Guide.

Eddie walked into Rachel's room after finishing with Sebastian in the Arena. He stopped the minute he entered. The bathroom door was open and Rachel was in the shower. Eddie was in a good mood and thought he'd have a little fun. He took a pitcher of water out of the refrigerator, poured a glass of the ice water, and headed for the shower.

Rachel didn't know Eddie was there until the ice water came splashing over her as she shampooed her hair. She shrieked out of shock.

Eddie bolted from the bathroom and was stretched out comfortably when a steaming Rachel walked in from the bathroom. She had her robe on now and a towel around her head. "Have a relaxing shower?" Eddie asked as innocently as his laughing would permit.

"Just keep in mind, Lord Laidlaw, that I will get my retaliation."

"But not right now." Eddie extended a hand to her. Rachel took his hand and Eddie pulled her to his side. "I think you should know one thing, Rachel Anne Westchester. I'm in love with you."

"That's not fair. Throw ice water on me and then try this to get out of trouble?" Rachel smiled, thinking how like a childish boy he could be. And such a loving man as well.

Eddie smiled. "But did it work?"

Rachel thought about it a minute. "Yes," she finally informed him.

Eddie opened her robe and pulled her bare chest down against his forehead. Her skin was hot and wet from the shower. He had his eyes closed and just held her.

At first Rachel sat there motionless. "Eddie," she eventually said. She felt him nod his head. "I want you to listen as I tell you about your upcoming mission." Again she felt him nod. Rachel told him of the travel plans that had been made, and that within the hour he would be leaving her. She told him where he was headed and why. Rachel showed him the folder with his wallet, credit cards, and the money. Lastly, she told him about the number in the wallet. "Call it and you will be speaking to a Guide member. If the assignment is too much, call and we'll send someone to pick you up. Also, the number is for relaying information. If there is something you think the Guide needs to know, call." Rachel got up from the bed and dressed. "There is one other thing. I told Gracen how fresh you are at feeding. I have not shown you how to hunt humans in the populace without getting caught. You must know how to hunt the people you would feed from without having them know you've even drank their blood. For that reason, you will not be going alone. Colonel Wolf has promised me he will send someone with you for you to feed from. It will be a human, Eddie. Remember to practice control when feeding, and feed only as you must."

"I'll be careful," Eddie promised. "I guess I need to pack a few things, then. It will soon be time to go."

"I've asked Rita Janel to see to that," Rachel informed him. "There is one good thing about this, Eddie. Once it's over, you won't have to worry about getting into the Guide. The Induction Ceremony will be just a formality."

Eddie could tell from Rachel's voice that she was not pleased about this venture. Worry marred her features. She was desperately trying to hide it from him, so he pretended not to notice her concern. Then there was a knock at the door and it was time to go.

CHAPTER 19

Eddie looked down at the ground as the helicopter lifted off. Far below stood Rachel, Rita Janel, Sebastian, and Gracen. They had seen him off. Rachel waved as the helicopter banked away from Gracen's house, and then she turned and walked away. Gracen started after her, but Rita Janel grabbed his arm.

"Let her be, Orbis," Rita Janel said softly to him.

"I know you think of her as a daughter, Rita Janel, and she thinks me her enemy right now, but do you really think I would do her any harm?"

"It doesn't matter what I think. She needs time--time the membership and you have not been giving her." Rita Janel turned to face Gracen. "One more thing, old friend. Someone is playing games here, and I think you know who."

The three of them stood on the landing pad. Gracen looked from Rita Janel to Sebastian. "There are a lot of games in motion. Some to fool the Guide membership, some to just make fools of the membership. Which game are you talking about?"

"We three go back too far to act like children to each other," Sebastian said to Gracen. His voice was not soft like Rita Janel's had been.

"You've been on your Island a long time my friend, and you, Rita Janel, have been everywhere else but here. The membership is dissolving and the Followers grow stronger every day. All of the things we planned—" He shook his head lost in thought for a minute. "I'm losing control here, and the young members are all so arrogant, they think more like the Followers every day. They do not know the pains so many of us experienced trying to survive up to this point. I'm getting old, too, as are you two, and the young think the stories we tell are cute, but just stories. Too many are not old enough to know the cost of playing God with the world. I think we are all not long for this world, and maybe it is time to stop fighting."

For the first time since they had known each other, Rita Janel and Sebastian both thought how old and tired their friend looked.

"Your vision of a better world was a good one, Gracen. It isn't over. The future has received a fresh breath. It has young arms and a strong heart. It is rising fast and change will follow as it lifts us all up with it." Sebastian pointed to the dwindling helicopter. "Look, Orbis Gracen, look and see the change. Make the future and us bow to him and serve him." Then Sebastian pointed to the form of Rachel just reaching the house. "And see the only thing that has meaning to him. When you think about the future, consider who's future you are thinking about." Sebastian patted his friend's shoulder and headed back to the house.

Rita Janel waited for Gracen to look at her. "Sebastian has always been the romantic of the three of us. I'm the radical, and you are the brains. Decide soon, my friend. Don't make us decide for you." Rita Janel moved off, leaving Gracen to his own thoughts.

Eddie watched out the window as the helicopter touched down. The crewman aboard the aircraft assisted Eddie in getting out and getting his bag. As he stepped away from the helicopter a woman approached, reached out her hand, and smiled friendly enough at him.

"Hello," she called out to him.

"Hello," Eddie replied a polite smile on his face.

"They told you you'd be met, didn't they?" she asked, seeing the confused expression on Eddie's face.

"Yes, but I didn't expect--well, I guess I just didn't expect a woman detective."

The woman laughed, leading Eddie into the airport. "I'm sorry, Mr. Laidlaw, for laughing. I'm not here to help you find the rogue. I'm lunch," she explained with a vicious chomp of her teeth.

Eddie looked at the woman.

She pulled a gold medallion out of her shirt.

"What's your name?" Eddie asked. He shook his head and grinned at his misunderstanding of her arrival.

"Mrs. Laidlaw," she told him with a grin.

"I guess I missed that in the briefing as well."

"I'll brief you more fully on the flight to New York. The plane is due to board shortly. Would you like to make any stops before we get seated?" The woman pointed to the restroom.

"I'm fine, thank you."

She nodded and led the way to the departure gate.

The seating went quickly and soon the plane was at altitude and cruising. Eddie sat back in the seat and watched out the window for a time. The woman sat there quietly, letting him think. He turned to her after a little while. Up to this point Eddie had not really looked at the woman. Now he did. She had auburn hair with a few, very few gray hairs peaking through. She was tan, but not dark, and she had hazel eyes. Eddie noticed her watching his examination of her. It made him feel like a school kid, but her smile was sweet, so he relaxed.

"So, Mrs. Laidlaw, do you have a first name?"

"Dena. Nice to meet you, sir."

"Eddie, but you can call me Master."

Dena laughed and patted his arm.

"Hello. Would you folks like anything tonight?" asked the flight attendant.

"Yes, I'd like a scotch on the rocks please," Eddie told the attendant.

Dena looked at Eddie. "Did you forget Eddie, the doctor told you alcohol was bad for your stomach?"

Eddie looked at her. "He did?"

"Two orange juices," Dena ordered. The attendant nodded and left. Dena gave Eddie a concerned look. "Are you all right? I didn't think members forgot about things like alcohol and what it would do to them."

"No one said I couldn't drink," Eddie told her, as abruptly as she's changed his order.

"How long have you been a member Eddie?"

"Well, technically I'm not yet. This is a test for me--a little something extra before the Induction Ceremony."

Her stare became blank and her mouth dropped open. Dena slowly lowered her head to her hand and sat there very still. "I see why the Colonel asked for me now." She turned her eyes back to Eddie. "You see, it's been about four years since they've assigned me. This is usually left to the kids."

Eddie knew Dena had a couple of years on him, but he wouldn't say she was as old as she made herself sound.

"Hi, I'm mom," Dena said playfully, reintroducing herself.

"Your orange juices," announced the attendant's return to their table. Dena put the glasses on her tray as the attendant moved on.

Eddie reached to the closest glass.

Dena caught his hand. "Let me." With one hand she held his out stretched hand, with her other hand she reached up to Eddie's mouth, slipping her pinky into his mouth and across his tongue. Dena took her finger out of his mouth, wet with saliva. She used his thumbnail to cut open her pinky, which she put into his glass and stirred.

Eddie could see the streaks of blood lace the juice as she stirred. He could smell the blood and surprised himself as he realized the glands in his mouth were making his mouth water in anticipation of the blood.

Dena returned her finger to his mouth and had to pull it out after he got a taste of the blood. "You're not trained Eddie, maybe they should send another?" Dena suggested, handing Eddie his flavored juice. She wrapped her pinky in a napkin that came with the juice.

"That isn't an option for me," Eddie told her.

"Then I'll teach you what I know and what your Mentor should have. How long have you been studying with your Mentor? I guess I should also ask, who is your Mentor?"

"Well, Rachel is, and as for the how long part, about two weeks, just under."

"Why in God's name are they sending you out after a rogue?" Dena implored, raising her voice higher than she'd intended too.

"I told you, it's a test. Half of them want to see me fail because I'm a Lord Vampire, or so they tell me. The rest are undecided but they'll watch and jump to the side that wins," Eddie explained. "You said the Colonel asked for you in particular. Mind if I ask why?"

"I think I'm baby sitting. Drink your juice."

Eddie sipped the juice. "You're very tasty," he told her with a lick of his lips.

"Good enough to eat, so I've heard," Dena commented, throwing the old joke at him.

"I'll agree," Eddie said, looking her up and down.

"Thank you." She inclined her head indicating a bow to him.

"Tell me something. How did you get into this line of work?"

"What do you mean, being food of the gods?"

"Is that what you call it?" Eddie let himself sink deeper into the heavily stuffed first class seat. He felt relaxed with Dena. He wasn't sure why, but he liked the feeling.

"You haven't been around a whole lot of us staff people have you?" Eddie shook his head no. "Yeah, a lot of us call it being the food of the gods."

"We're not gods. We're just people."

"Just people, is what we are. Generally, your people will out live us without aging, not the same, anyway. You are not affected by disease, and you won't die from most things that would kill me." She twisted in her seat to face him better. "As a Vampire, you are affected by fire first and foremost. It will kill you if enough of your flesh and bone is burnt to ash. For example, if this plane crashed you could become internally injured, bones smashed with missing body parts. But if you did not burn to ashes, you would live and heal rapidly. Being ripped apart could kill a member, but it is very hard to tear your kind apart. You can eat arsenic for lunch with no problem, but the alcohol you tried to order would make you sick and incapacitate you for a long period of time. You have to avoid any kind of pastas, and no carbonation at all. You'd think you drank battery acid. Red meats are fine, but you might even find yourself eating them more rare than you're used to. Chicken and pork will disappear from your diet as well. You'll lose your taste for them. A lot of the members of the Guide are even vegetarians, except for their blood supply. Not all are, so don't let it worry you."

"How did you get into this?" Eddie repeated his earlier

question.

"When I was in college I was a journalism student. I got a job working part-time for the local paper. I was supposed to be a 'gofer,' go for this, and go for that--a runner. I worked late one night and the only ones in the building were security and I. The guards knew I was there and didn't care."

"And what happened?"

"One of the hot shot reporters was working on a story about drug trafficking in the area. It was on the rise. He was also working on me," she said with a smile. "I was twenty then, and danger was a kick. Well, to make a long story short I was snatched out of the office that night and it was the beginning of my life among the Guide."

"The Guide grabbed you?" Eddie said, shock crinkling his features.

"No, the drug dealers. They grabbed Clifton, the reporter, and asked him whom he had been talking to. My name came up and he thought to trade me for a clean escape."

"Nice guy."

"I thought so until then."

"So what happened?"

"I got grabbed, like I said, and taken to a place way out in the desert, to a house that the drug dealers maintained for questioning people. Clifton was there already."

Dena nodded. "They had him there and some other guy I didn't know. The other guy looked bad. They had beaten the hell out of this other guy. Clifton didn't have a mark on him. After getting picked up by these guys, he told them anything they wanted to know. They started to cut him apart in front of me and the other guy and then the other guy seemed to come to life. He broke the chair he was tied to and tore into the drug dealers yelling, 'Die, Followers, die.' He screamed at them with such furious angry passion that it was frightening and thrilling at the same time. When it was over the only one standing was this guy. He looked over at me and the rage in his face just disappeared. He asked if I was all right as he cut me loose. After he confirmed I was okay, he called the police. He stayed there with Clifton and me until the sirens could be heard and the flashing lights could be seen, and then he ran off into the desert. When the story broke, I got Clifton's job on the paper, a pay raise, and Clifton slid away like the snake that he was. The other guy, though, stayed in my mind. All I had to go on was what he had yelled as he'd freed us, 'Die, Followers, die.' But that and the dead men themselves were a start, and it did eventually prove worth the effort. It took a year but I tracked the guy down and found that he worked for a company that I was having trouble getting any information on. But I kept digging. One night I walked into my apartment and found my answer sitting there in my living room. His name was Gerald Glass. We talked for a long time and when it was clear to him that I wasn't about to stop digging, he invited me to meet some other members of the club he was in. Being a reporter, I was skeptical, but I was also interested in this guy. He took me to Sebastian's island and after a week there I asked to remain. That was before they told me about the membership of the Guide being vampires. That came the next year, then two years after that Gerald was killed. Colonel Wolf picked me up when that happened. I've worked for him ever since."

"You never had a relationship with him, did you?" Eddie stated. He reached that decision about her and Glass on just an instinctive feeling, and by the tone of her voice more than anything that Dena had actually said. There was also something in her eyes. He wasn't sure, and he certainly wasn't an expert on relationships.

"Never more than to feed."

"And you loved him?" Eddie probed.

Dena nodded.

"Did he know?"

Dena shook her head.

Eddie reached out and took her in his arms. He held her tightly to his chest, wishing there were words he could say to ease the pain of the memory.

As if reading his mind, Dena said to Eddie, "Thank you for your concern, Eddie, but that was over fifteen years ago. I'm much stronger now." She didn't pull away from his grip, though, so Eddie held her.

* * *

Rachel was sitting in her room when there was a knock at the door. She got up and answered it. It was Colonel Wolf.

"I thought you'd like to know. Our contact at the hotel has just reported to us of their arrival. The plan was for them to rest today and get a fresh start in the morning."

"Thank you, Colonel."

Wolf started to turn away but hesitated.

"Something more?" she asked, seeing he was reluctant to walk away.

"I was wondering Miss Westchester, what are you doing for dinner?"

Rachel wasn't expecting this kind of question.

"I'm asking because several of us are going into the city this evening and I thought it might help to keep your mind off of what's happening in New York." When Rachel didn't reply, the Colonel took that as his answer and started to leave.

"What time should I be ready, Colonel?"

"The car will be out front at six-thirty. Would you like to meet us at the car, or would you rather I come by here and pick you up?"

"You can meet me here at a quarter after six if that isn't any trouble."

"I'll see you then. Casual dress, Miss Westchester."

Rachel closed the door, still wondering, what, if anything, was behind the invitation. She'd just have to wait and see.

As a man sat and watched the people, the hunger deep in his gut twisted his insides. It was wrong, he told himself. It was delightful, disgusting, horrible, and exciting all at the same time. He watched the people far below his perch and waited. The struggle inside of him wasn't over yet, but he knew the hunger would win out. It was so hot out. He wished it would rain.

Eddie sat in the dining room of the hotel and Dena was seated across from him. He had his fork in his hand and was staring at his food but not eating.

"Are you all right?" Dena inquired.

Eddie nodded. "Just don't seem to have an appetite."

"I'm almost finished. Would you like to go upstairs and have a bite?"

"No, not right now." Eddie looked up her. "Would you like to go for a walk? Get out of here for awhile?"

"Sure." Dena signaled the waiter and asked for the check. The bill went on Eddie's Guide Visa Card, as did the tip, and was signed for by Mrs. Laidlaw. Then Eddie and Dena left the hotel and started a slow walk, looking at the lights of New York City. Dena had been to New York City before and told Eddie they were in the better part of the city--one of the places where the people with money stayed when in town. She gave him the tour of what she knew and pointed out things and places of interest as they walked. It was distracting, but not much. Eddie knew where he wanted to be, and that was with Rachel. He told himself that to get there he had to see to this matter first, and he wasn't even sure how to start. After walking a while, he told Dena about his problem of not knowing how to even start looking for the rogue vampire.

"Well, I guess we could start with the library. See what we can find in the newspapers and maybe get some kind of a pattern from there."

"The police haven't found one, and neither has Wolf's people. But you're the reporter. If you think that's the place to start, then we'll start there." Suddenly, Eddie stopped walking. He visually scanned their surroundings.

She could see something was wrong. "Eddie, what is it?" she asked.

"Blood, I smell blood, and a lot of it," he told her. A sniff of the air and Eddie had the direction from which the scent was coming and followed it. "Dena, you stay back just a little. All right?"

Dena did as he asked, as Eddie headed for the scent. A half a block further ahead was a side street. The night air was blowing up it onto Eddie and Dena's street. Eddie moved cautiously into the side street and the smell grew stronger. Halfway between Eddie's main street and the next main street that ran parallel, Eddie found the source of blood. Eddie knelt in front of the man and checked his pulse.

"He's alive, Dena, call an ambulance." Dena took off at a run for help. Eddie looked at the injury. It wasn't their rogue vampire--it looked to Eddie like the guy had been mugged. He wore a fine, expensive suit with no identification, no watch or jewelry, and a look of shock on his unconscious face. Shortly, Dena returned and then the police came. After the police arrived and before the ambulance made it there, the man died. He had lost a lot of blood and there was nothing anyone could do. Dena and Eddie spent the rest of the night telling detectives they had just come to town and had been out walking when they had found the dying man.

Dinner had gone well and Rachel found no ulterior motives to the invitation. The company was pleasant--even if it was all the Colonel's friends and not the people she normally spent time with. When dinner was over, they all returned to Gracen's house. Colonel Wolf said good night to his companions at the car, insisting on walking Rachel back to her room. Rachel opened the door to her room then turned to Colonel Wolf.

"It's been a pleasant evening. Thank you for inviting me," Rachel told him.

"May I come in?" Wolf asked her.

"Perhaps another time, Colonel. I'm feeling very tired tonight. We can talk tomorrow."

"I did not wish to talk. As I've told you before, Miss Westchester, you are a very attractive woman. I have been told myself that I am not an ugly man. I was thinking we could explore other possibilities."

Rachel went from tired to angry before he had finished speaking. Rachel stepped into her room, pulling Wolf with her. She slapped him across the face with the same force she used to slam the door closed.

"How dare you? You know I'm involved with Eddie, you selfish pig. To think I would--" Rachel was yelling until she saw the grin on his red face spread.

"That hurt quite a bit, Miss Westchester," the Colonel told her.

"I don't understand. What was with that comment in the hall?"

"It's very simple, Miss Westchester. The Membership is watching you. Even if Gracen were to give his blessing to you and Eddie, that would only undermine his authority here. People would doubt him and soon the foundation of the Guide would fail. I've spent my life with the Guide making it stronger. I have no intentions of watching it get torn apart, especially from the inside. I know, as does Gracen, you want to be with Eddie. The rest of the membership doesn't know. Oh, they think they do, but that is not the same. What I'm telling you is that until Eddie is a blooded member and can claim you as his, you are mine. If not me, you and I will pick someone else, someone that you will be seen with all day every day until that time. I know you have some opinion of this matter, but I can't say I give a damn about it. You will not destroy the Guide. Do I make myself clear?"

Rachel thought about the matter at hand and how to react. Rachel slapped him again, but not as hard this time. She pointed to the couch. "You sleep there." Rachel walked around Colonel Wolf and to the bathroom.

"Exactly what I had in mind, Miss Westchester," Wolf replied.

CHAPTER 20

"I've got an idea," Eddie said to Dena. She was seated across the table from him in the library.

"Oh yeah? So tell me," she replied, not looking up from her newspaper article.

"You're not going to like it."

This made Dena look up. "Are you going to get me killed, Eddie?"

"I hope not."

"What's your idea?"

"I think I know of a way to track this rogue, but I need to test my theory."

"I'm listening."

"I've been thinking about the other day, the morning after we found that man. I found him by his blood, by smelling it. All of these articles agree on one thing about the victims: they're shredded, torn apart. He's feeding on them and doesn't know how to feed the Guide way, or just simply doesn't care. Either way, he's getting covered in their blood. He can't tear them apart like this and not get blood on him."

"I think I see what you're getting at. You want to track him by the blood scent of his victims, but you don't know if it'll work or if you can do it over distance."

"What do you think?" Eddie laced his fingers and rested his elbows on the table.

"Truthfully, Eddie, I don't know. Staff personnel aren't normally this involved in Guide business."

"I'm sorry, I'm asking for too much help from you on this, aren't I?"

"No, Eddie. I'm having a great time. I'd forgotten how much I enjoyed the investigation part of reporting." Dena made her decision right then. "Let's try it." She extended her hand to him. Eddie put three fingernails to her palm and sliced it open. Dena took the handkerchief he offered her and wrapped up her hand. "Got the smell?" she asked, knowing he did.

Eddie nodded. "Okay, couple of other points. If he's covered in blood, he isn't likely to be using public transportation, which means he's walking to and from the crime scenes, or using his own car. I'm betting he's walking. Next, we have to assume we're not going to hear about the victim first. The police aren't likely to call us for assistance, so we'll be at least an hour or two, maybe more, behind them. And there's no telling how far behind the killing they'll be, so you take off and I'll come looking in two hours. Okay?"

"Tag, you're it," Dena told him and left. Eddie looked at his watch, then to her as she walked off. Dena was going to find some place in the city to hide and see if Eddie could track her down. In the meantime, Eddie turned his attention back to the news reports on the killings, hoping for some piece of information he might have missed. Dena was good at this kind of work, and she hadn't found anything. He doubted that he would, but he had to keep looking.

The hunger woke him from his nightmare dreams. He sat up and looked around. He was in an alley but he didn't know where. The smells of rotting garbage and decay permeated the stale air. There was nothing moving in the alley but him, as he got to his feet. The hunger was coming quicker each day. It was getting harder to satisfy it, but he had no choice. The pain from the hunger was too much to take. The pounding in his head only got worse. He walked to the opening of the alley. It was early evening, and the sun was disappearing behind the skyscrapers. He didn't care--all that was important was the hunger. He looked around the street. It was deserted where he was, but he could hear voices in the distance. If there were voices, then there were people, and the hunger could be quieted and the pain stopped for a time. He followed the sounds. On the next street he found what he needed.

The woman felt the hot breath behind her but she was busy. "So what's it going to be? A good time or take a hike? My prices aren't negotiable. And I think I got another hot one behind me here." She pointed to the guy behind her with her thumb. The man in the gray suit looked at the guy behind her. His face went white, his eyes bulged, and his legs quaked with instant fear. That did him no good. Running might have helped, but he froze. The hooker saw his reaction and turned. She screamed and started to run. It didn't help.

He hated it when they screamed, but it also made his blood race. The scream got the attention of others on the street. One strike ripped her throat out. The man in the suit started to turn, to run and was grabbed by the back of the head. He screamed as fingernails cut his scalp and fingers locked onto his neck.

"Police! Freeze!" screamed another man farther up the street. The police officer ran toward the commotion, pulling his pistol as he ran.

The screaming man was trying to get free as the other man was dragging him off toward the alley he'd just walked out of.

"Stop or I'll shoot!" yelled the officer.

The man dragging the other man paid the officer no heed. He dragged the screaming man easily.

The officer fired, hitting the one man in the shoulder. The bullet made the man lose his grip and the screaming man fell on the ground. The shot man looked to the officer and leaped at him. The gun discharged twice more and then fell to the sidewalk. The officer felt the force of the blows to his Kevlar vest and knew the feeling of bones breaking. He crumpled to the ground as the man let go of him. The officer looked through blurred eyes for his weapon, his hope of stopping this man. The other man was screaming louder again. The officer picked up his gun, took the best aim he could and fired again. The recoil of the weapon made his broken ribs tear at his insides. His vision blurred more and he fired again. He took his vow to protect the public very seriously, but by the time his vision cleared there was no public around to protect. It was just he and a dead hooker. Then the screams stopped. He worked his way back to his car and called in the shooting, "Officer down, need back up." He sat in his car until help arrived.

Eddie walked into the Emergency Room entrance and sniffed the air. A hundred chemicals and dozens of sources of blood assaulted his nose. Eddie smelled the air carefully and surprised himself that he could still detect Dena's blood over all of the other blood scents in the air. He started walking the hall. At door six he stopped, pushed it open, and peeked in. Dena was sitting on one of the examining tables, getting her hand looked at.

"Hello," Eddie said to her.

"Excuse me," the doctor said to Eddie. "But this is private."

"No doctor, he's with me."

"All right." The doctor looked to Dena's hand again. "I think you should let me stitch it. But if you don't want me to, I'll let the nurse clean it and let you go."

"That'll be fine, Doctor," Dena told her.

"I'll get the nurse." The doctor left Eddie standing there alone with Dena.

"You're tricky," Eddie told her. "Smearing blood on the side of a bus. I followed that thing for half an hour before I was able to make sure you weren't on it. Then I had to back track to were I picked up the bus and then back through its route to see if I could find out where you met up with it. The pool of blood you left at the bus stop was easy to follow after I found it."

"You liked the bus, though?" Dena asked with a smirk.

"Nice touch. I can track you but I'm wondering if some of that is because I've tasted you. I'd like to do it again on someone I haven't tasted. But without another staff here, I don't see how."

"I'll call the Colonel tonight. We'll say--" Before she could continue, the nurse walked in and the doctor followed. The group fell into conversation about the injury and how it occurred as the nurse dressed the cuts. The door opened again.

"Doctor, we have a cop coming in and two bodies. Torn up by our maniac from the sounds of it. It's all sketchy at this point. Five minutes arrival time."

"I'm coming." The Doctor looked to Dena. "I have to go. You people have a pleasant time in New York and be more careful."

"Promise," Dena replied. "Eddie, let's go." Dena got up from the table. She knew Eddie would have to get moving if he was to track the rogue. They stopped at the front desk to pay her medical bill and listened to the reports coming in over the dispatch radio of where the attack occurred.

After putting Dena in one taxi headed for the hotel, he then took a second to the crime scene. From there Eddie would see if he could track the rogue vampire. He got out just short of the location where the attack had taken place. There were police everywhere and they had the area roped off, but that didn't concern Eddie. He knew the rogue wasn't in the roped off area and he could smell the powerful odor from where he stood. The scent split, from what he could tell. Part of it, the stronger part, was headed back in the direction he'd just come from. Eddie figured that was the direction in which the coroner had taken the bodies. That left the other direction and hopefully the rogue. Eddie started walking slowly and sniffing the air. The streets were unfamiliar to him, but that didn't matter. He was confident that he could handle anything that might come up. That was one of the things he did like about being a Vampire--his self-confidence was building and he felt good about that. Rachel crossed his mind. She was so much the reason for the changes in him. Anything he had to do to be with her was worth it. Eddie wondered what she was up to as he walked and tried to look at everything around him at once. The scent wasn't proving that hard to follow. He told himself that the rogue must be covered in blood. At first, Eddie was finding droplets of blood on the ground. The droplets and the scent took him several blocks away to the site of the second body and the police that were there investigating it. He almost walked into the police blockade before he realized it was there. He skirted the rim of the yellow police line tape, listening intently to the police discuss the crime and their suspicions about the killer. The injured cop had reported it to be a man in his late thirties to forty, with dark brown hair, cut short, but that was all the cop had remembered. He had fired at him three times, hitting him at least once. Eddie was listening to the conversation and did not notice the other man approaching him.

"Can I help you?" the man asked.

Eddie looked at the man. He was black, a little over weight, and slightly taller than Eddie. Eddie's eyes dropped to the gold shield hanging from the pocket of the man's coat.

"No." Eddie didn't want to sound too interested in the conversation. He hoped the detective would take him for just a curious on-looker.

"You seem very interested in their discussion. Are you one of those lip reading reporters?"

"Do I look like a reporter to you?"

"They come in all shapes and sizes. Who are you?"

Eddie looked at the man. "Laidlaw, Eddie Laidlaw."

"What are you doing here, Mr. Laidlaw?"

"Watching." Eddie indicated the rest of the onlookers. "Is that a problem, Detective--?" Eddie strung the last word out inviting the man to give him his name.

The man smiled. "That depends on if you get in the way of my investigation."

"Wouldn't want to hinder that any. I'll just move along." Eddie sniffed the air and caught the scent again and headed off. As he did, the Detective located one of his men and assigned him to follow Eddie from a discreet distance, to see what he was up to. He almost laughed out loud as he heard the Detective giving his orders. Eddie moved off, following the smell of the blood. He moved slowly to make sure he stayed with the scent. Even with his cautious approach, he lost it once and it took twenty minutes of backtracking to find it again. Then, an hour into his search, the rain started. A light drizzle, at first, but it steadily continued. Before long, Eddie was soaked and had no scent to follow. He hailed a taxi and headed back to his hotel.

In the morning, Rachel rose with the sun. She looked at the still sleeping form of Colonel Wolf. He looked uncomfortable in the chair he had slept in for three nights in a row. She had heard whispers of her and the Colonel, and Rita Janel pinned her to the wall for answers the day before. She gave the right answers that sent Rita Janel off in a fit like she'd told the Colonel she'd do. If Rita Janel thought there was something going on between them, then everyone would believe and Eddie was safe. Rachel got out of bed, collected her clothes for the day, and went over to the Colonel. She knelt beside his chair. "Wolf," she said softly.

"What?" he asked groggily.

"Why don't you crawl in the bed and get some proper sleep? I'm up for the day and going to get a shower."

"You're sure you wouldn't mind?"

"Go get in the bed," Rachel told him and went to the bathroom.

Wolf pulled off his clothes and took her advice. In no time he was fast asleep and much more comfortable.

Rachel was in the shower when she thought she heard voices in the bedroom. She turned off the shower, and did, in fact, here voices. Rachel pulled on her robe and walked into her bedroom to find Colonel Wolf sitting up in bed. Gracen and Sebastian were there.

"What's going on?" Rachel demanded to know why their privacy was being interrupted.

"We received a message from Eddie. He thinks he can track down the rogue," Gracen told her.

"Well, that's good. I told you he could handle the matter." Rachel's pride showed on her face.

"Tell her the rest," Sebastian told Gracen sourly.

"Tell me what?" Pride was quickly replaced by concern.

"We have a report that Followers might be in New York, either after the rogue or after Eddie. We're not sure which."

"I'll be dressed in a minute. Get me a flight to New York at once," Rachel said, turning to go back into the bathroom.

"There is a meeting scheduled in two hours for my advisors to discuss intervention," Gracen explained to her. "You as Mentor, are welcome, and Colonel, I expect you there." Gracen left the room. Sebastian gave Rachel a smile of support and followed Gracen.

"Discussion? What's to discuss? We can't take the chance they're after Eddie," Rachel said to no one in particular.

"They do not see it that way." Wolf got out of bed. "May I use your shower?" he asked, collecting his clothes from the end of the bed.

Rachel nodded. She followed him into the bathroom to get her things to finish dressing.

* * *

"What is the source of this report that the Followers are in New York?" asked James Anders.

"That is not important, or the issue here. The report is reliable," Colonel Wolf told the man.

"The matter before this advisory board is what to do about it. So far, you all seem reluctant to get involved," Gracen, pointed out.

"We are involved, he is one of us. A member of the Guide," Rachel said angrily to the group.

"No, right now he is just a new member. He has not been made a blooded member as of yet," Becky argued. "Do we want to use up resources on someone we're not sure of?"

"Or risk open war with Delvar and his people for that matter?" Montgomery agreed.

Colonel Wolf got to his feet. "I have sat here all afternoon and listened to your pathetic excuses for not going to help the boy. Let me remind all of you of a few times from the past that this advisory board has met." Wolf looked from one member to the next, then continued. "We met and dispatched a team to help a young courier that was picked up for smuggling in Africa and was to be tortured to death. Remember, Becky?"

She looked down at the table, remembering the way she had been treated and the relief she felt as the membership of the Guide came to her rescue.

"Or the time that the Followers of Delvar had a member trapped in Rome because of his own stupid mistake," Wolf said, looking to Anders. "Or a brash young officer, and at the time a young member, engaging in matters better left to those more experienced in the ways of the Guide, and all of the trouble that caused. None here then debated whether or not to send help. It was accepted that this membership swore oaths to each other and to the Guide, to help and protect one another."

"Sit down, Colonel," Gracen said to him.

Wolf nodded and resumed his seat.

"I think it is time for all of you, except my advisors, to step out. We will let you know what is decided." Gracen looked to the rest of the people at the table. All but the advisors left.

Rachel was waiting for Wolf as he exited. He stopped as she

approached him. "I wanted to thank you for trying to remind them of their obligations to the Guide," Rachel told him. "Although, I think I know the outcome before their meeting is over."

"You can never be sure of people, Miss Westchester," Wolf told her. "Take us for example. Who would have guessed we would be fighting together to save anything?"

"I think, Colonel, that I might have to change my opinion of you."

"I certainly hope not," Wolf said. He walked off after flashing a quick smile to Rachel.

CHAPTER 21

Eddie was watching the television when Dena woke up and came into the living room. He glanced at her and smiled and she returned it. "Sleep well?"

"Fine, yourself?"

"Didn't. I've been up watching T.V. News and an old Christopher Lee movie."

"Dracula?" Dena asked rolling her eyes.

"Yeah, I thought I might learn something."

"From Dracula?"

"No, from the news." Eddie watched her as she sat down next to him. "How's the hand?"

"It needs your attention." She removed the hospital bandage and extended the hand to him.

Eddie could see the redness in her hand and he figured it must be sore. He still found it amazing that the saliva glands in his mouth, in a vampire's mouth, could help heal minor cuts, and heal them without scarring. He took her hand in his and brought it to his mouth. Eddie could taste the medication the hospital had used on her as he moved his tongue over and through the cuts. At first, she flinched at the touch of his tongue, but after the saliva began to get into the wound, it numbed the area and Dena relaxed. Eddie stopped and looked at her. "After the blood loss yesterday, I'm afraid to push it, but may I feed?"

"Yes, my Lord Laidlaw. I will need to rest today, though," Dena told him. She decided that she liked working for Eddie and was going to ask the Colonel if he would mind her transferring to Eddie's staff. That wasn't likely to happen until he was a blooded member.

Eddie sucked the blood through the cuts in her hand and licked the cuts clean when he finished. "I hope that won't bother you too greatly today. If it does, you have the day and more to rest, as much time as you need."

"I'll be fine, Eddie." Dena knew how fresh Eddie was at this life, so she decided to educate him a little. "You see, Eddie, when a medallion wearer is the menu for the night on a Guide property, you might have a dozen or more Members feed that night. None of them feed heavily, it isn't needed, but that many does drain a body. That is why there is a long time between medallion wearers being fed on from one time to the next. But a lone member could feed in small amounts daily, or larger amounts weekly without affecting the staff person. I'm fine, Eddie, really," Dena assured him.

A knock at the door stopped their conversation. Eddie got up and went to the door, opened it and found the detective from the night before. "I didn't order breakfast yet," Eddie said to the cop.

"Mr. Laidlaw, can I come in? We need to talk."

"Whom am I talking to?" Eddie asked directly this time.

"Lieutenant Paul Weaver, New York City Police Department."

"What can I do for you?" Eddie asked, swinging the door open to let the officer in.

Lieutenant Weaver saw Dena, and then looked to Eddie.

"You can speak freely, we don't have any secrets," Eddie told Weaver.

Paul Weaver pulled a picture out of his pocket and handed it to Eddie. "Do you recognize this man?"

Eddie looked closely at the man in the picture but didn't know him. He shook his head.

"You don't know him, you're telling me?"

"That's right, Lieutenant, I've never seen the man before. Should I have?"

"He was assigned to follow you last night when you were out at the crime scene. I assigned him."

"Then the man had a boring night. All I did was walk until it started raining, then took a taxi back here."

"Not as boring as all that. You see someone killed him just like the other murders of recent weeks. Tore him limb from limb. He reported his location as an alley he was following you into, then he was found there dead." Paul Weaver did not consider himself an easy man to trick and was very confident that he could tell when someone was lying to him. He watched

Eddie's reaction to his statement.

Thoughts of the rogue filled his head. He should have stayed out last night looking for the killer, but then it struck him that this wasn't the work of the rogue vampire. Their rogue had gorged himself only hours earlier, and he wouldn't have been back out hunting that quickly. If the officer was following Eddie, then he didn't trip across the sleeping rogue vampire until after Eddie had gone. But wouldn't he have called for backup before going after the suspected killer? Lots of questions, and Eddie was sure Weaver had more of his own. "I'm sorry to hear about your man," Eddie told him.

Dena joined the two men near the door. "Eddie, he thinks you did it."

On important matters, Dena could slip into and hold a reporter's tone in her voice. Eddie could see her words hit home as Weaver's expression changed for a second, then became neutral again.

"Why was your man trailing Eddie anyway?" Dena asked. Her voice was sharp with accusations of her own.

"I didn't get your name, Miss?" Weaver asked.

"Laidlaw, Mrs., like you didn't check the register before coming up."

"Oh, I did. I also ran a background check on Mr. Laidlaw here. Interesting reading. You just arrived in our city and this is the third police report that your name is going to be involved with, in as many days. A mugged man dies and you two are there. Two people killed and one officer hurt and you are there, Mr. Laidlaw. And now one of my men dies while following you. Yes, Mrs. Laidlaw, your husband is on my suspect list. And do you know what the topper is? The mysterious company that, all of a sudden, you work for. Until a few days ago, you were listed as unemployed and broke. Now you're in my town with money to burn, from what your bank account says."

"I married well," Eddie told the officer.

"You better come up with better answers than that or your ass will be in a jail cell."

"You want to talk to Eddie or me, Mr. Weaver, you shall now do it through our lawyer."

"Relax, Dena, he has a job to do." Eddie led him to the living room. He knew there wasn't much of the truth he could tell Weaver, but he'd tell him what he could. The three of them sat in the hotel room and talked for an hour. Dena's reporter's edge grew sharper as she hacked information out of Weaver, for what little information she and Eddie could give him. Weaver wasn't happy when he left and told them so, but he also told them he would be in touch. At least he left without dragging them down to the station house.

"Go find a pay phone, Eddie, right now, and call in. The Guide needs an update."

"I called this morning, a couple of hours before you got up. There is one thing that does bother me. If it wasn't our rogue, and I doubt that it was, then who killed the officer?"

"I wish I knew, Eddie."

"Do you think it could be the Followers?" he asked her.

"Who knows? What I do know is that we're going to have to move more carefully."

"No. You're out of this. You've been a big help up 'til now, but you're back to just being the menu."

"Why?" Dena demanded, shocked at his reaction.

"Because I'm not going to your funeral, Dena," Eddie told her firmly. With that answer, she decided not to argue, but would still help and not let him know about it.

"I'm going to go wash up, Eddie."

He nodded, leaned back deeper in the sofa, and thought about what to do next. If the Followers of Delvar were here, was it because one of them had been mind-touched by the rogue? Or were they after Eddie himself? The Guide claimed the victory on the Island was due to him. Did the Followers of Delvar see it the same way? Eddie ran this thought through his head for a minute, and then grabbed the phone. He didn't care if the phone had been tapped. His call wasn't long. Eddie then got up and headed into the bedroom. "Dena!" Eddie called out, walking into the bathroom. She was in the shower. "Dena!" he called to her again as he opened the shower door. She was surprised by his walking in on her and jumped back from him. "Could you finish up and come out here, please?"

Eddie was sitting on the bed when Dena came out of the bathroom. "I've been thinking. I called the Guide and they don't like it, but I'm sending you home. I'm going to feed heavily on you this morning and you're going to rest this afternoon. Then tonight you're out of here. If the Followers are after me, I don't want to worry about you."

Dena stood silently listening to him. His tone of voice told her he was serious. "I agree with you feeding heavily, you'll need all of the strength you can get, but I'm not going anywhere. I'm the only help you have. I won't go."

"Don't you even care what happens to yourself? What if I can't protect you?"

"I made my choice to be with your people a long time ago. I've made my choice to be with you, and you're not changing my mind, Lord Laidlaw. I am here to stay." Dena sat down on the bed with Eddie. "Eddie, I know you're new at this and I'm not a vampire, so that worries you. But believe me, if I thought I wasn't safe with you, I'd leave."

Eddie looked at her. Dena's robe was wet from the shower and clinging to her body. She hadn't dried off. "Go finish your shower," Eddie told her.

"Give me a reason to need one." Dena opened her robe and pulled Eddie down onto the bed with her.

Eddie started to respond, for Dena was a beautiful woman. He ran a hand over her, then stopped and sat up.

"I can't. I'm in love with someone. I just can't." Eddie got up from the bed and left the room.

Dena turned over and buried her face in the pillow. She lay there until she heard the front door open and close. Wondering if the Lieutenant had returned, she looked out into the living room. It was empty. Dena looked around the suite and found Eddie wasn't there.

Eddie walked out to the street and grabbed a taxi back to the crime scene of the night before. He wanted to find something, some clue. He had to clear his head and the only way to do that was to get out of the hotel room. Besides, if Followers were out, he didn't want to be around Dena. On the street corner after the taxi dropped him off, Eddie made another phone call to the

Guide.

"Yes, that's what I want," he told the Guide operator. "She's refusing to leave so I want someone sent here to make sure she remains safe. To protect her while I'm out hunting this rogue." Eddie was getting tired of telling this operator the same thing over and over, so he stopped. "Just do what I've told you." Eddie hung up the phone. He started walking the streets looking at the area. As he did, he thought how different the place looked from the night before. Eddie noticed that it wasn't different to his nose, though. There were new smells, smells of decay mixed with last nights rain.

The sun was up and promised a warm day. Eddie looked up at the fireball, ninety three million miles from the Earth. He looked at the buildings around him, apartments, stores and shops, half of which were boarded up. That's when Eddie thought of his next idea. He smiled, found the tallest building around him, and entered it. Maybe from a rooftop, Eddie could see more than from on the ground.

He took the stairs to the top of an abandoned and walked out on the roof. Eddie was surprised to see that the roof was almost as cluttered with debris as the alleys and streets below. He spent an hour on the first rooftop watching the street and the people below. Then he moved to a different one and then a third one, each time changing rooftops to get a different view of the area. Eddie spent half of the day in the alley, before changing locations to a section of the city where the killing had taken place a week earlier.

It was a residential area, with homes and families. He thought of Frank, Debra, and Marsha as he walked these streets. From what the newspaper article had said, the killing here had been some old lady that lived by herself and did nothing except play bingo and go to Church. A daughter and three grandchildren had survived her.

Eddie was reflecting on the old women when he saw something on the ground that caught his attention. He picked up the piece of cloth and sniffed it. Blood had dried on the cloth and last nights rain had not washed it out. The blood scent was weak, but he could still smell it. The cloth was torn in half.

Why did the cloth catch my attention, he asked himself as he stuffed the cloth into his pocket?

Eddie continued his walk of the area, and then backtracked to the murder site again. He found nothing there. He went back to the street, to the alley that the cop had been killed in, and sat down. "Where are you?" Eddie yelled at the empty alley. He sat there for hours, staring into space.

The sun had set, the night had grown cold, and before he knew it the sun was back up. Eddie started his search again. This time he went and looked over a parking structure, also a murder site. From there he went to the park, and then to the next residential area. He found nothing new and each night he made his way back to his alley. He told himself it was safer.

Eddie would sit and listen to the police calls on a scanner he had picked up and waited for the next report of a murder by his rogue. He had not returned to the hotel in three days but now he needed to, for fresh clothes and to feed. He was getting a small taste of the hunger he had felt before he knew what it was.

The morning of his forth day out, Eddie was sitting in his alley listening to his police scanner, when it came to him why the cloth he had found days earlier was important. He looked across the alley and there was his answer, or part of it.

Eddie pulled from his pocket the piece of cloth found earlier, crossed the alley and compared it to the piece he'd just noticed. They matched each other, but one thing that didn't match was the bloodstain. Both had them, however, the newest piece was totally saturated in blood. Eddie smelled it but got no scent from the blood. The new piece told him more than he wanted to know. He stood up and left the alley, flagged down a taxi, and returned to the hotel.

"Where the hell have you been?" Rachel yelled at Eddie the minute he entered the suite. He had a welcoming committee waiting for his return. Rachel was in his face.

Eddie kissed her forehead. "Nice to see you, too." He looked to the rest of the welcoming committee. Gracen said nothing, nor did Colonel Wolf, but Eddie could see Sebastian was going to light into him. Probably Dena would, too. Eddie didn't think he'd hear anything from the other two vampires with the group. He didn't even know them.

"Well, answer me!" Rachel ordered harshly.

"I need a shower and a bite to eat." Eddie took Rachel in one arm and grabbed Dena with the other as he walked straight to the bedroom.

"I think, Sebastian, your Young Lord has reached maturity," Wolf commented and took his seat again.

"I think we have a dragon among us wolves," Sebastian agreed.

"What do you think he'll tell Rachel?" Gracen asked.

"That isn't the question. He'll likely tell Rachel everything. The question is what will she tell us?"

Eddie put Dena on the bed and took her arm. "Rachel and the others will take care of you."

Rachel stood back watching as Eddie cut open Dena's arm and fed.

Eddie fed heavily from her and told her to rest there. He took Rachel into the bathroom. As Eddie showered, he told Rachel what he had been doing and where he had been. He told her about his findings and his thoughts on who they were looking for.

Rachel listened without comment as he talked.

Eddie toweled off and put on fresh clothes. "So you see, I can't stay. There are a lot of places to check. Maybe you and the others can cross reference some of them and narrow the search down some."

"Perhaps," Rachel agreed. "But, Eddie, you can't go out alone again. We came to help, so let us."

"If I get help now, it blows this test. No, I have to bring in my rogue, stop the killings, and keep the Guide out of it." He pulled Rachel to his chest and held her. "You understand that, don't you?"

"No, but I'll let you try if you agree to stay in touch. Several calls a day and a phone call every time you find out something." Eddie kissed her and entered the bedroom, where Dena was fast asleep. He and Rachel went into the living room, prepared to fight the Guide and its leaders' wishes to do this their way.

"Of course, Eddie. If your Mentor thinks you can handle this matter, we'll let you see to it. Just let us know if you need anything," Gracen told Eddie and Rachel. They had told Gracen, Sebastian and Wolf next to nothing and got the approval to proceed. Eddie gave Rachel a second kiss and left the hotel room. The minute the door closed Gracen turned to Wolf. "Set your men about their work, Colonel."

Wolf turned to the two Guide members across the room from the group. "Follow him, keep us informed, and him out of danger." That was all the orders he gave, and the two men left the room.

Rachel looked to Gracen. She then looked to Sebastian.

"You didn't think we would come here and let him roam unwatched if there might be Followers after him or this rogue, did you?" Sebastian asked. "You did, after all, argue for us to come to his aid."

"This test is for his membership. If you interfere with his completion of it, it will be listed as a failure."

"No, Rachel, this is not for his membership. We can't do anything official about his membership until he completes the Induction Ceremony. We will not interfere with his finishing this assignment unaided, as long as no Followers show up." Sebastian knew the agreement Rachel had with Gracen. After this job, Eddie would be treated as a blooded member. He knew and hoped she knew that even their agreement would not make him a blooded member, even if he were treated like one in some ways.

"Eddie's membership is not in jeopardy." Gracen looked to Sebastian. "I may have had to be reminded of the reasons for the Guide and that we protect our own but my mind is not so far aged that I don't know a good thing when I see one, or know when someone or something is wrong." Gracen walked the two steps to Rachel that separated them. "Your man, our young lord, is a good thing for the Guide. He shakes us up and makes us remember our youth and our duties. I informed my advisors that his membership will be seen to quickly after this assignment. He will be blooded and active if he will accept membership in the Guide. I told them that before I disbanded my advisors."

"Disbanded the advisors?" Rachel gasped.

"For now," Gracen replied. "I will still seek out members and their opinions, but for the time being, there are no advisors."

"I told you there would have to be changes and they were coming soon," Sebastian said to Rachel.

"Changes indeed," Rachel replied. She looked from one man to the other and back. "Are there more changes I should know about?" she asked with a cautious tone to her voice.

"There are always more changes coming Rachel, always more changes," Sebastian informed her.

CHAPTER 22

Rachel and Sebastian were seated in Eddie's suite. It was a silent contest of wills as they stared at one another until a knock at the door ended it.

"I'll get that. Check on Dena again, would you?" Sebastian asked.

Rachel nodded as Sebastian headed for the door, and opened it.

"Lieutenant Weaver, New York City Police Department," Paul told the man with the braid. He held his badge up for the man to see.

"What can I do for you?" Sebastian inquired.

"May I come in?"

Sebastian opened the door, letting Paul enter.

"Is Mr. Laidlaw in?" Paul asked.

"I'm afraid not."

"Who are you?" Paul asked next.

"A friend of the family, and Eddie works for me," the man replied. "But I imagine you want a name. Sebastian Smith."

Paul looked up at Sebastian.

"It's quite true, Lieutenant. Would you care to see some identification?"

"No, that won't be necessary. Not just yet."

Sebastian shrugged his shoulders.

"Is Mrs. Laidlaw in? I'd like to talk to her, if I could?"

"I believe she's resting," Sebastian told him.

"She is?" said a voice from behind Paul. He jumped in spite of himself. As he turned around, he found what he decided was the most beautiful woman he'd ever laid eyes on.

She smiled.

"And who are you?" Paul asked, forcing his mind back to business. His wanting to know who she was had nothing to do with official police business.

"Mrs. Smith," Rachel replied, pointing to Sebastian.

"I suppose you have I.D. as well?" Paul asked.

"As a matter of fact, I do."

"I'd like to ask you two a few questions, if that would be all right?"

"If it isn't all right, will you leave?" Rachel asked.

"Yes I will, to obtain a warrant and take all three of you down to my office to answer some questions."

"What are your questions?" Sebastian asked. He gave Rachel a stern look.

"What does your friend, Eddie Laidlaw, have to do with the recent killings?" Paul asked bluntly. He desperately wanted to see their reactions.

"What killings?" Rachel asked stepping closer to Paul as if suddenly interested in what the man had to say.

"I don't believe he has anything to do with any killings," Sebastian told Paul. Both men stared at one another for a long time. Each judging and sizing up the other's expression.

"What killings?" Rachel asked again, with a touch of irritation in her voice.

"The unusual ones reported on the news? Those are the ones you're talking about, aren't they?" asked Sebastian.

"When was the last time you spoke to your friend, Mr. Laidlaw?"

"What did your officers report?" Sebastian asked.

"All right, this place has been seriously watched for several days now. Mr. Laidlaw has been tripping over bodies since his arrival in New York, then he up and disappears until this morning. He breezes in, and then back out. What does he have to do with the murders? Does he know who the killer is?" Paul decided to push a little to see what would happen.

"Should I send for my lawyer, Lieutenant?" Sebastian asked smoothly.

"Do you think you need one?"

"When you ask me questions like your last ones, I think he would tear you apart."

"Interesting choice of words, Mr. Smith, considering how the victims were torn apart."

"Now he's accusing you, Sebastian," Rachel said, a wide smile covering her face. She turned to the Lieutenant. "Accuse me as well. I hate to be left out of anything."

"I don't accuse people, Mrs. Smith, I arrest them. Would you like that?" Paul quizzed, deciding although she was beautiful, he would be wasting his time talking to her. "Mr. Smith, I really don't want to make this situation any more difficult than it already is. I think Mr. Laidlaw is tied to these murders. I will find out how."

"He is not tied to your murders. As hard as it must be to accept that, it is the truth. He is here on business. Eddie recently entered my employment and I have him researching zoning documents for the project I am considering. When you check, you will find the documents were filed months ago. I can see how our arrival here and the misfortune of Eddie and his wife finding that mutilated man, would look suspicious, but it is just bad timing."

Paul studied Sebastian Smith. The man was either the smoothest liar Paul had ever met, or he was telling the truth. "I'll consider what you've told me, but I do have more questions."

"Please ask them," Sebastian encouraged. He led the group into the living room were the questions began anew.

Paul, Sebastian, and Rachel talked for over an hour. Paul's opinion of these people did not waver, as he did not get many informative answers to his questions. He did change his mind about the woman, Rachel Smith, though. His first impression of her being a waste of time to talk to, he decided, was wrong. She had a sharp mind behind her devastating eyes and disarming smile. Paul eventually came to the conclusion that he would get nothing more from these two, so he excused himself and left.

All the time Paul had been with Rachel and Sebastian, she kept thinking about the rogue and Eddie being out there alone after it.

"Sebastian, if Eddie's right about this rogue, about who he suspects, I'm worried he won't be about to stop him. I mean, normally by the time the Guide comes across a rogue he's been running uncontrolled too long and we have to destroy him."

Sebastian raised his hands. "I would love to try and ease your worries, sister, but without knowing who Eddie thinks is responsible, I can't. This rogue has run wild for several weeks--at least ten days since the first murder. That isn't much time at all for a rogue. We might be able to return him his sanity before the blood lust drives him completely mad, but only if we find him soon. Eddie discussed the matter with you and you alone, so tell me what he said and I will try to help."

Rachel thought about talking to him. She had put her life in Sebastian's hands many times, but it wasn't her life they were discussing. Eddie's blooded membership was not at stake, according to Gracen, but his pride could be, and most certainly other members' faith in his abilities would be judged. She considered telling Sebastian Eddie's theory. "I wish I could, brother. I think I need some air. A walk might loosen my tongue." Rachel stood up and Sebastian got to his feet as well.

"I will join you. If you do feel like talking, I'll be close at hand."

Rachel shook her head and stopped him with a raised hand. She headed downstairs, out of the hotel, picked a direction and began to walk. Her thoughts were so far inside of themselves she didn't notice a certain black lieutenant following her.

Rachel had been walking for some time when she reached the decision that it was time to return to the hotel. She knew this part of town backward and forward, the alleys and cross streets, because the upper class shops and boutiques were here. Rachel had shopped here plenty and knew that at this time of the afternoon, the next street would be deserted, but it was the quickest way back to the hotel. She turned onto the street. It was long and quiet, but well lit. Even with the streetlights, at first she didn't seem to notice the approach of four people from the opposite direction. When she did finally notice them, they rapidly closed the distance between themselves and Rachel. She and the four people were talking in loud voices, arguing. Rachel couldn't miss the stares of the people in front of her, as they all looked right past her. She glanced over her shoulder to see Paul Weaver as he poked his head around the corner. Rachel turned back to the group and caught a backhand across her jaw from the closest of them to her.

Paul pulled his pistol as he raced toward the group.

"Freeze!" he screamed, reaching them. "Police! Everybody just freeze." He had his .357 Magnum pointed at the one that had hit Rachel. He gave her a quick sideways glance. There was a little blood at the left corner of her mouth, but she looked all right other than that.

The man Paul was holding the gun on laughed. "Who is this imbecile?"

Paul thought about shooting the man right then. Instead, he cocked the gun. "Lieutenant Weaver, N.Y.P.D., and you're the meat going to jail."

The man was quick. He started to pull something from his coat. As he did, Paul fired. The bullet tore into the man's shoulder, spinning him around. Before Paul could bring the powerful handgun to bear on the next of the four assailants facing Rachel and him, the gun was snatched away.

Rachel was ahead of Paul in that same instant. She put a kick into the gut of the person closest to her, and followed up with an elbow to the base of their head as they doubled over from the kick. Before he could think, Rachel had Paul by the shoulders pulling him back up the street in the direction they had come from. "Run!" she was screaming over and over. The three people standing started to give chase, but they stopped almost as quickly as they had started. Paul and Rachel noticed that ahead of them, coming from the other side of the street, there was a second group of people. They had just exited a car parked at the end of the alley. Now there were six on one side of them and four on the other. Three, Paul corrected himself--he had put a bullet in one of the first four. That's when Paul realized his hand hurt. Looking down toward his hand, he saw three deep gouges along his forearm, wrist, and on the back of his hand. Blood had already soaked his clothing.

"You have nowhere to run, Ms. Westchester," one of the group said.

"What do you want?" Rachel asked the group.

A man stepped forward. "We'll start with you," he informed her. His eyes then moved to Paul. "Well, maybe you'll be second."

"He has nothing to do with this. Leave him be."

"They want a piece of me, let'm try," Paul informed them with as tough a pretense as he could muster. He was feeling extremely weak, like he was going to pass out. Whatever they cut him with, it must have nicked bones as well as slicing open a major vein or two.

"Let him be!" Rachel demanded of the man again.

"On one condition. You come along without a fight and I'll let him live."

"I'll tear your head off," Paul growled.

Rachel rapped Paul Weaver on the side of the head. He was unconscious as she caught him and lowered him to the ground. "Let me tend to his arm before we go, and I won't fight you."

"In the car. Now!" the man ordered her. Two of the group grabbed her arms and took her to a waiting car. Two more of the group picked up Paul Weaver and carried him away as well.

Rachel watched as Paul woke to find himself in total darkness. He touched his right forearm gently with his left hand. It was tender, a little numb even, but the gashes felt scabbed over, dried blood most likely.

"How's the arm?" a voice in the dark asked. It sounded to him like Rachel but the voice was very weak.

"Rachel?"

"Good guess, Lieutenant."

"The arm feels fine, but I've got the mother of all headaches."

"Sorry about that. I thought they would leave you behind. I guess I should have known better."

"Where are we?"

"I don't know I didn't get a window seat."

"What?" he asked, confused by her remark.

"They put me in the trunk for the ride here and from the trunk straight into this room. They brought you in an hour or so after I was put in here."

"Who are they, and why did that one man call you Ms. Westchester?"

"They are old enemies of mine and my friends, and that is my name. Rachel Anne Westchester, at your service."

"Are you all right? You don't sound good."

"I've had better days."

"How long have we been here?"

"Ten or twelve hours. I'm not sure."

"Why are they holding us?"

"Lieutenant Weaver, I hate to be rude, but I think it's better for both of us if, for now, we sleep. I get the feeling that we might be here a long time."

"Not that long. The N.Y.P.D will be looking for me before too long, and when they find us these friends of yours will be sorry they kidnapped a police officer."

Before Rachel could comment, the door to the room opened and a bright overhead light came on. Paul and Rachel covered their eyes from the sudden light.

A man and woman entered the room. "On your feet, Ms. Westchester," the woman ordered.

Paul blinked tears from his eyes as Rachel got up and moved to the door. The woman turned Rachel around, pulled her arms behind her back, and Paul heard the unmistakable sound of handcuffs snapping closed.

"Just try to relax and rest, Lieutenant," Rachel told him, as the woman and man took her out of the room. The minute the door closed, locked, and the lights went out, it again plunged the room into total darkness. Paul sat there at first, and then started feeling his way around the room. He found four barren walls with one door leading in and out of the room. He wasn't sure how long after they had taken Rachel they brought her back, but she didn't talk to him much more than to say, "For now, just stay back and leave me alone." She sounded very weak--weaker than before she'd left. Paul wondered what they had done to her and what they had in mind for him.

Eddie had hit pay dirt early in the day and headed into a low rent neighborhood, home ground for his rogue, if he was right. Finding the address of the building was easy. It was one of the few well-kept houses in the area, an old brownstone, if Eddie's library research was right. This was a rich part of town over a hundred years ago. He thought maybe he'd ask Rachel what she knew about the area from personal experience. She could have been here back then, but for now, though, there was business to see to. Eddie walked up to the door of the building. It was a security building with an intercom to buzz the apartment of the person you'd come to see. Eddie looked over the names listed and touched the button under the name, "MICHEALS." There was no answer. He waited, and then buzzed the apartment again. There was still no answer. Eddie touched the button marked, "MANAGER."

"Yeah," replied an older female voice.

"I'm trying to reach Walter Michaels. His door buzzer seems to be broken," Eddie told the woman.

"Maybe he ain't home. Try work."

"Well, that's where I'm from. He hasn't been to work in a week, and we were kind of concerned." Eddie lied to the woman. The security door buzzed, as the lock released.

"Top of the stairs, last room down the hall on the right," the woman informed him.

"Thank you." Eddie entered the building and headed upstairs. Finding the apartment was easy and the doorknob confirmed his suspicions. It had dry, dark stains on it, and a sniff told Eddie it was dried non-vampire blood. Had it been vampire blood, he would not have been able to detect a scent. Eddie tried the knob. It was unlocked. He pushed the door open, entered, and shut it firmly closed. "Michaels!" Eddie called out. "Hello?" Eddie called out again and waited for a reply. When no one answered he started looking around the apartment. The place had simple furnishings. It wasn't large and it was a mess, but Eddie would have bet that before the change, the place had been neat as a pin. There were several pictures on all the walls, along with degrees and awards for community service. "It must have been one hell of a fall for you, huh, Michaels?" Eddie said aloud, talking to himself.

Behind him the bathroom door flew open and out rushed Walter Michaels, rogue vampire. He slammed into Eddie, with both men hitting the wall. As Eddie's face smashed one of the pictures, he felt the broken glass slice him open. Michaels' claw-like nails tore at Eddie's back, cutting deep gouges in his flesh.

Eddie twisted around and pushed him away. Michaels charged him again but Eddie was faster and more experienced at fighting, thanks to Sebastian's training. He got a grip on Michaels, swept his legs and took him to the floor with a thud. Grabbing Michaels by the hair and bouncing his head on the floor twice, Eddie tried to stun the man long enough for him to get a better position on him. Michaels was stunned, but got a foot against Eddie's chest and pushed him backward. He crashed into the dining table. Eddie and the table went in two different directions. Michaels charged after Eddie again. Eddie grabbed him again as Michaels reached out. He twisted Michaels around and locked a chokehold on him. Thrashing as hard as he could, Michaels couldn't break free of Eddie's grip. Eddie forced him against a wall to restrict his movement even more, and then he reached to Michaels' left rib cage as Rachel had taught him. Eddie punctured a hole from just under the rib cage, up to Michaels' heart. Michaels' reaction was almost immediate. He passed out. Eddie carried the unconscious man into the bathroom, dumped him into the tub and turned on the water to carry the pooling blood away. Eddie pushed his finger into the chest cavity once more to make sure the path to the heart was open and would stay open. With any luck, the madness would drain away with the blood. If the madness didn't subside, Eddie hated the thought of having to kill this man in order to stop him from killing again.

Walter Michaels woke up and found himself in his own bed. The nightmares that had been his life seemed distant, but not gone.

"You awake?" someone in the room asked him.

Michaels nodded. He tried to raise his head and look around, but found he was to weak. The owner of the voice came into view, and then sat down on the bed next to him. Walter did not know this man before him.

"Who--" He couldn't make his voice work to finish the question. His throat was so dry.

"Believe it or not, a friend," Eddie told the man.

Walter tried to talk again but his voice just cracked.

"Don't try to talk. You'll feel better later. Can you listen? Do you understand me?"

Walter nodded.

"All right. I'm Eddie Laidlaw. I was sent here to find and help you. For now, that's all I'm going to tell you. After you get some of your strength back, we'll talk. For now, though, just go back to sleep."

Walter looked at the calm expression on this Eddie Laidlaw's face and felt like maybe his nightmare was ending. His eyes drifted closed and sleep returned quickly.

When Eddie was sure that Walter was unconscious and was not getting up for a time, he took Walter's keys and headed out to the closest market he could find. After a bit of shopping, Eddie returned to find his charge still sound asleep. He watched him the rest of that day and most of the next, before life and thought returned to Walter.

When Walter woke the next time, he sat up in his bed. His throat was so dry it almost hurt. Eddie was standing over him.

"This will help." Eddie handed Walter a tall glass of orange juice. Walter sipped it, and then drained the glass.

"Who are you again?" Walter asked.

"A friend that's here to help."

"There is no help for the damned," he told Eddie. "Best you leave before I hurt you, before I lose control."

"As far as the damned are concerned, I wouldn't know, but all you get is me. You've already tried hurting me," Eddie told him. "Two and a half days ago. The wounds Eddie had received from fighting Walter were healed.

Walter looked to Eddie. "I don't remember."

"I know. It doesn't matter if you did."

"I don't know what's been wrong with me lately." Walter looked to Eddie like he was on the verge of tears.

"I do know, but it will be hard for you to hear and even harder to believe. Are you up to listening, Priest?" Eddie asked.

Father Walter Michaels looked at the stone like face of the man before him. Something in Eddie's eyes told Father Michaels that the man before him knew what he was feeling. He nodded and listened as his life fell apart.

CHAPTER 23

"Hello," Sebastian said, picking up the phone.

"I got him," Eddie replied.

"My God, Eddie, where are you?" Sebastian demanded.

"With the rogue, I mean, Father Michaels."

"Is Rachel with you?"

"Rachel? No, why would she be here?" Eddie inquired, a touched confused.

"A lot of things have happened, Eddie, since you were last here."

"Like what?"

"Rachel went for a walk the other day, a couple of hours after you left, and hasn't been seen since. She is missing along with that police lieutenant. The two Members we had tailing you turned up dead, as did two plainclothes police officers. All the killings are being blamed on the rogue."

"Missing, missing how, she doesn't answer her cell phone, she hasn't checked in, what? And it's not the rogue--he's been with me. Unconscious for the last three days, well up until about an hour ago."

"Then it is as we suspected--Delvar and his Followers. Give me your address there, Eddie, and we'll come and get you and your rogue."

"Sebastian, if Rachel was in trouble why wouldn't our bond let me know? I felt her danger on the island and at Gracen's."

"I have no answer Eddie. Perhaps the distance is to great for such a new bond or perhaps she is not in danger but she is definitely out of communication with the Guide. Now give me your address there so at least this part with the rogue in done."

Eddie gave Sebastian the address, Sebastian told him to sit tight and that the Membership would be there within half an hour. Eddie turned to Father Michaels as he hung up the phone. "My friends are coming to pick us up. You don't really need to worry about packing. You'll be back and the Guide will have someone keep the place up for you until you do return. I know they're doing that with my place right now." Eddie looked down at what the priest was staring at. He then looked over at Eddie.

"I've spent my life working toward a belief that one day things will be on Earth as it is in Heaven. Now what?"

"That doesn't have to change, Priest. You just have more time to help people once you learn what the Guide will teach you." Eddie picked up the crucifix and handed it to the man.

"I've broken some of the most sacred laws of God. Thou shall not kill. How do I make amends for that?"

"Think of it as a type of insanity. You didn't just go out and kill. The changes that you had no control over made you react the way you did. If a man walked into your church and told you what you found out today, what would you do? Would you condemn him? Would you shun him? Or, would you try to comfort him?" Eddie stood there and as the priest fought his faith and convictions against the truth of what he'd become, Eddie searched his own mind for all of the arguments that Sebastian and Rachel used on him when they first told him about who and what he was. They were so much better at this than he. They had the experience from so many years of dealing with this sort of thing. All Eddie had were words from them.

"I'll meet with your friends, Eddie. You've helped me, but I have much to think about." The Priest put the crucifix in his pocket and picked up the two pieces of cloth that led Eddie to him. Together, they were the collar that he wore when dressed as a priest. Now the two pieces were torn. Half was torn off by one of his first victims--his last victim tore the rest from his throat, the night the officer shot him. Walter reached to his neck. "I was shot in the throat and shoulder." He looked to Eddie. "I cannot die. How does one reach the Kingdom of Heaven if one cannot die?"

"Vampires can die, Priest. But we're very hard to kill I know that. When I found out I was a monster, I jumped off of a cliff, but the love of a woman and the need to help her did not let me die. You deal with it. You say, 'Okay, I'm a vampire and I'm here for a while.' The Guide and its members are trying to help mankind. A priest might be a great deal of help." Eddie touched the priest's shoulder. "If not today, maybe tomorrow." Eddie walked away from him and went to the window. He decided to let Walter contemplate what they had talked about, and hopefully, Sebastian would be there soon.

The street below wasn't a busy street, but it had traffic and people moving along it. Eddie stood there lost in thought as Walter moved through the apartment collecting things from here and there.

"This place was a mess," Walter told Eddie.

Eddie didn't respond at first. When it dawned on Eddie that Walter was talking to him, he turned half away from the window. "I didn't catch that," Eddie told the Priest.

"I said this place was a mess. Thank you."

"I had time on my hands while you were sleeping. We kind of tore the place up a little when we fought."

"Fought?" Walter said surprisingly. "I didn't know we fought." He looked down at the ground. "I'm sorry. I hope I didn't hurt you."

"I'm fine. You see, at the time of the change, if the blood isn't drained from the body it causes a type of madness. Caught in time, like with you, your sanity returns. The change to a vampire doesn't have to change your personality, just your physical body." Eddie stopped. "I'm not going into a lot of detail about that right now. Your Mentor will do that. They'll assign someone to you when you get back to Gracen's house."

"What is this Mentor?"

"The person who will teach you how to live as a vampire, whether you choose to be Guide or not."

"But that will not be you, I take it?"

Eddie almost laughed. "No, not me. I have much to learn myself, first. They'll give you someone wiser than me."

"You seem to know this Guide business rather well."

"I have good teachers." Eddie looked out the window again, but this time noticed something strange—two men on the street that he thought were looking up at the window, moved off into the alley across the street from the Priest's building. Eddie would have thought nothing of it except that he could see the shadow of one of the men even after they supposedly left. That told him they were watching the building and probably had followed him there. Dead cops, dead Members, a rogue vampire-priest, Rachel missing and now the Followers. He moved back from the window so no one on the ground would be able to see him. Eddie took up a position so he could still look out the window. Watching them seemed advisable until Sebastian arrived.

"What's out there?" Walter asked.

"Trouble, if we're not careful," Eddie told the priest. "Let me know when you're done packing."

"My duffle bag is packed. What's down there?"

"One thing I haven't touched on is that although the Guide is a collective of good vampires, there is also a cell of what you would call not so good vampires. They're the Followers of Delvar. And they're downstairs." Eddie watched as a car pulled into the alley. The men he knew were there went to the car--with a quick glance up to be sure he wasn't in the window. They didn't know that he had seen them. The two men didn't get in the car. Instead, four other men got out, the car turned around and pulled in front of the building. "Priest, we're in trouble." Eddie changed positions and walked back to the window like he'd just gotten there. He opened it and leaned out. "I knew Sebastian said he had people close, but you got here a lot faster than I expected," Eddie yelled down to the group of men. "I'm going to need some help moving Father Michaels. A couple of you come on up and give a hand." Eddie waved to the men.

They all looked at one another, then smiled and waved back. Three of the six men nodded and headed into the building. When they reached the security door of the building, they touched the buzzer.

"Buzz them in, Priest."

"If they are these Followers, as you called them, why are we letting them in?" Walter asked, hitting the door buzzer.

"Divide and conquer, or at least divide. Be ready to leave in a hurry." Eddie moved toward the front door. "Feel like fighting, Priest?"

"I'm not a violent man."

"You could have fooled me. What do your rules say about just holding one of them until I can get to him? Even the odds a little?"

"They are not my rules, they are Gods laws," Father Michaels pointed out.

"Just grab one of them and hold him. I'll do the rest." Before the priest could comment there was a knock at the door. Eddie looked in his direction, reached for the doorknob, turned it and opened the door. The Followers walked in. Eddie smiled and let them walk past him. The three men thought they were fooling him. As the last man neared Eddie, Eddie grabbed him by the head and twisted viciously. The priest was more stunned than the two remaining Followers. Their companion dropped to the ground, all of the bones in his neck broken. Eddie grabbed the second guy, trying to get a similar hold on him. The priest stood staring at the body on the floor.

Eddie was quick but so was this second man, managing to get a grip on Eddie's arms. They both were struggling for position and better holds as the last of the three men threw himself at Eddie. The two Followers and Eddie went to the floor. "Help me!" Eddie screamed, as the priest just stood there watching. Eddie felt a clawed hand rake his face, pain exploding through his body from the hardened nails. He was fighting with all of the strength he had, but two on one and him on the bottom made things difficult.

The Priest stood there as if frozen. The look of horror on his face told Eddie he'd get no help.

Maneuvering his left foot between him and the Follower pounding away on his stomach, Eddie pushed up, kicking the Follower off. The other one was trying to keep his hold. Eddie reared up from the floor, head butting that Follower. It stunned the man but it hurt Eddie's damaged face as well.

The Follower that had been kicked off was back at Eddie. He reached out for the face, thinking to attack the injury Eddie had already sustained.

Eddie grabbed the Follower's hands, now that his own were free from the head butt, and twisted the man's wrist.

The man screamed as bones broke.

Eddie twisted harder then pushed the man away. He got to his feet just as the second Follower grabbed him again. He and this Follower got a grip on each other's wrists and throats and both men were applying all of the pressure they possibly could.

It was almost a struggle of wills more than strength. Eddie could only think of one thing--can't breathe, can't breathe, kept going through his mind, when a second thought joined it. Someone had told him once, he couldn't remember who, "Eddie, you're a Vampire. You can do without air for a very long time." Eddie remembered the conversation and smiled at his opponent. He found new strength in the thought and applied it. Neck bones snapped like old twigs.

The Follower's eyes bulged and Eddie grinned, pushing the man against the wall. He abandoned his grip on Eddie's throat, which might enable him to tear Eddie's hand from his own throat. He held out thirty or forty seconds longer, then Eddie closed his grip even more.

Eddie released the Follower when he was certain the man would be no more trouble to him. He turned to the last Follower nursing his broken arm. He smashed his fist against the man's head as he looked up at him. Blood-covered and in pain, Eddie turned to the Priest. He looked at him with his still good eye. "Come on, Priest, time to move before we have to go through this again." Eddie grabbed a dishtowel from the kitchen before heading for the door. He had to take the Priest in tow.

Walter was in shock, and Eddie understood that.

Eddie remembered all too well the night that the Followers of Delvar attacked the Island. He remembered the horrible fighting he saw and how he did not understand then. He had been in this man's position, then, and Rachel had seen to him. It was his turn. "Is there a back door out of this place?" Eddie asked, leading the way to the stairway.

"Back door," the Priest repeated. He shook his head trying to get the images of the fight he'd just witnessed out of his head. The man before him had killed two of the three men, and had injured, possibly crippled, the third. But he had not escaped unscathed. Half of his face had been ripped apart. He held a towel to it but blood was soaking through the cloth. Sweet blood, Walter's mind told him. He threw up at the thought.

"Are you all right?" Eddie asked.

"Have to rest, don't feel good," Walter told him.

"No time, Priest." Eddie pulled the half-doubled-over man along. When they turned the corner and found the back door, Eddie stopped. "We'll take a few seconds here. Got to get myself together in case they have people out back."

"I'm sorry I couldn't help you back there. I--" The man stammered for the words. "I'm a man of the cloth, not a man of violence. I'm sorry."

"Nothing to be sorry about. I shouldn't have asked or expected you to help. It was wrong of me."

"You killed two men."

"We'll discuss it later, Priest. We have to go. Are you ready?" Eddie moved to the back door. "If we get into any trouble out here or if we get separated, go to the Ritz Hotel, that big one near the airport. Ask the desk clerk for Eddie Laidlaw's room. The people there are my friends and can help you. Just tell whoever you find there that I sent you and that you are the rogue. They'll understand. Just do as they tell you."

The priest nodded his agreement.

Eddie pressed the locking bar on the fire door and pushed it open. He looked outside. A group of Followers, men and women, raced toward the half open door. Eddie pulled it closed, slamming the locking bar into place. "Not that way, I guess." The two men left through the back door and headed back the way they'd come.

"There are only two doors to this building," the Priest told Eddie.

"I thought you Priests had secret tunnels to escape through?" Eddie said, as they heard pounding on the back door.

"Only secret tunnels in the church, not in our homes," the Priest jested. They headed upstairs. The Priest glanced into his open apartment door as they walked by. "Eddie!" he called out.

Eddie came back up the hall.

The Priest pointed to the first man Eddie had fought. He was getting up, his head leaning to one side from the broken neck that hadn't had time enough to heal.

"Too quick." Eddie stepped into the room and booted the man in the head. His already broken neck didn't give the man any support against the kick at all. His head spun around on his shoulders. He dropped back to the floor. Eddie grabbed the Priest and took off running, again. He could see the look on the Priest's face. It was a look of confusion. Not too surprising, Eddie thought. "The Followers are Vampires like us, Priest. Thought I mentioned that."

"You mean those men will recover?"

"Yes," Eddie told him. "How do we get to the roof of this building?" They headed upstairs.

The Priest took the lead and showed Eddie to the attic door which he proceeded to bar after they entered. With a quick look around, he turned to the Priest. "The roof?" Eddie asked, not seeing any doors or windows out of the attic.

"This way. It's blocked from this side and you can't tell what it is from the outside. The owner had it made for the maintenance people to have access to the roof." The Priest went to a stack of boxes and pushed them aside. Assisting, Eddie grabbed boxes with both hands, tossing them away. That was the first time the Priest actually saw the extent of his injury, with some of the blood wiped away. "My God, your eye!" the Priest exclaimed.

"I know, but we can't worry about that right now."

The Priest could hardly keep from staring at it.

Eddie reached the doorway the priest had shown him. The door was stiff and obviously had not been opened in a long time, but it did open. Eddie peeked out and saw no sign of the Followers. He opened the door a little more and moved out onto the ledge that was the lowest section of the roof.

The Priest was right behind him. "Eddie, look!"

Eddie followed the Priest's indicated direction. It was the front of the building. The door had let them enter onto the roof to the left and just a few feet back from the front. They could see the car and the people around it. Eddie recognized some of the people as those being at the back door. He guessed they had gone around front to tell the people in the car. "Here's what we're going to do. We'll head for the back of this place, then try to cross to one of the other buildings and get out of here."

"All of the surrounding buildings are taller than this

brownstone," the Priest pointed out.

"One problem at a time," Eddie said with a scowl. Moving quickly, Eddie took off along the ledge but stayed low and kept as quiet as possible. As he and the Priest neared the back of the brownstone, they saw nothing even close that they could jump to. They traveled to the back of the building across the backside and along the right side. This put them in the exact same place on the brownstone except on the opposite side of the building.

"Now what?" Walter asked Eddie.

"I'm thinking."

"If it's me they want, then I'll go down to them. I want no more blood on my hands." The Priest started around Eddie.

Eddie grabbed him. "Don't flatter yourself, Priest. I get the feeling they've known your whereabouts a long time. Maybe you mind-touched one of them and for some reason they chose not to respond, to sit back and watch you."

"Mind-touched?" Walter asked.

"Tell you later, Priest. For now, though, let's get back from this edge."

"Look! On the roof!" someone below yelled.

"Too late." Eddie pushed the Priest backward. "You stay here no matter what. My friend, Sebastian, is coming. He's a big man with a gray ponytail. When you see him, stay with him." Eddie returned to the edge of the building and turned his back to the street. He was weak from a loss of blood due to his injuries from the Priest and from the Followers. He also hadn't fed in three days. Normally, not feeding wasn't a problem, but injuries and not feeding didn't go together. He couldn't even use his vampire magic to heal his injuries because it made him weak as a kitten for hours. Eddie smiled at the Priest. "Tell Sebastian to tell Rachel I love her." Eddie leaped off of the edge arcing his back. His arc took him out from the building side then brought him back close. He reached out his hands, his nails scraping the bricks of the building until he got his grip. He hung on the wall a minute, not far from the ground. Eddie made a second jump, landed hard, and rolled across the ground.

The Followers were too stunned to react at first, but that didn't last long. They moved forward, closing in around Eddie.

He got up slow, but stood to face the group.

"Quite a trick you have there," said the closest person, a woman. She moved forward cautiously. "Someone keep their eyes on the roof. We don't want any surprises raining down on us, now do we?" She watched Eddie as she voiced her instructions.

Eddie watched her first, but also tried to watch the rest of the Followers. There was a screeching sound and a smile spread across Eddie's face. The Followers looked from him to the noise. Screaming around the corner came two dark colored vans. They locked up their brakes and stopped just short of the Follower's car. The doors flew open and members of the Guide poured out like ants, with Sebastian at the head of the group. The Followers raced to their car and drove away even before all of the Followers were completely in.

"After them!" Colonel Wolf yelled at the drivers of the vans. Both vans left in hot pursuit.

Sebastian reached Eddie first. He almost collapsed right into his arms, but Sebastian caught him. He led Eddie to the curb and sat him down. Sebastian said nothing, but started looking over Eddie's injuries.

Gracen knelt beside Eddie. "My God boy, you look terrible."

"Your injuries will heal, Eddie, but that eye that's torn out will take some time to repair." Sebastian was genuinely concerned about Eddie's condition.

"I'm so damn tired, Sebastian."

At first, Colonel Wolf stood back and watched in silence. Then said, "On the phone, you told Sebastian you had the rogue with you. Is he still around?"

"Yes, I left him on the rooftop," Eddie told them. Colonel Wolf and two of the men started for the brownstone.

"It might be better if I go. He knows me." Eddie started to get up but Sebastian stopped him.

"You rest."

"Then you go, Sebastian. I described you to him." Eddie relaxed after Sebastian nodded in approval of his accomplishment.

As Sebastian started for the brownstone, the front door opened and Walter Michaels walked out and met him. Eddie was watching and waved Michaels over.

"Pull up some concrcte, Priest," Eddie said, patting the curb.

"These are your friends, I take it?"

"Father Walter Michaels, these are members of the Guide. Members, this is Walter Michaels, rogue vampire."

"Ex-rogue, I would say, thanks to you," Gracen commented. Eddie did the introductions after that, and a few minutes later the vans returned.

"We lost them, Colonel," reported the first driver to reach the group.

"Then our chances of finding Rachel are gone as well," Gracen said. He, Sebastian, and Wolf looked to Eddie. "We're sorry, Eddie."

"Upstairs. Three Followers. I don't think they will have left yet."

Colonel Wolf and a handful of members headed off for the building. As they turned to go, Father Michaels tossed Colonel Wolf his key to the security door of the brownstone.

"Will they tell him where this Rachel person is?" Father Michaels asked.

"If they know, they'll tell him. But in the mean time, let's head back to the hotel. It will be better for you two to rest there, and we can debrief you both more securely there," Sebastian said. He reached out and helped Eddie to his feet. They took one of the vans and headed off.

CHAPTER 24

Rachel felt his touch first. She was half asleep, but the warm hand woke her. "Eddie?" she said into the darkness.

"No," Paul told her. "It's Paul Weaver."

"Oh." Rachel tried to sit up. It was too much of a chore in her weakened condition, especially with Paul's hand still on her forehead.

"Just lie still," Paul told her.

"I'll be fine," Rachel replied, but she stopped trying to get up. She could smell blood--Paul's blood. She forced her mind closed to her hunger.

"What have they been doing to you when they take you out of here?" Paul asked.

"You would not believe me."

"I'm a New York cop. If it's been done, I've seen it."

In the darkness, Paul could not see Rachel smile at his comment as she thought of how wrong he was.

"Let's just say I know how a milk-shake feels."

"Would you like to explain that?" he asked.

"No."

"What do they want?" Paul asked.

"They haven't asked any questions when they've taken me, if that's what you're asking." Rachel drew as deep a breath as she could. Paul felt her shudder.

"You're cold to the touch," he informed her.

"I know. Now, as I was about to tell you, they are either using us, me, in particular, as bait to get Eddie here, or they're just going to kill us and are taking their time." She decided not to mention that they might also be waiting to see when or if she loses control and rips Paul's throat out for the blood that would make her strong again. Rachel had thought about explaining to him about vampires and asking for his blood, but she knew that would only start this all over again. And even completely healthy, she couldn't get the both of them out of this cell. The Followers hadn't fed either one of them. They both were growing weaker by the day. How many days had it been?

"Why you? Why not Mrs. Laidlaw?" Paul asked.

"Detective Weaver wants to know?"

"If I'm going to die, I think I have a right. Don't you agree? Or perhaps you think we'll get rescued?"

Rachel lay there thinking a minute then answered. "I think nothing of the sort, Paul. May I call you Paul?" she asked.

"I think cellmates should be on a first name basis," Paul said.

"I think you and I are dead. I think we are going to just disappear, never to be seen again." Rachel forced herself up. "That is the truth of the matter."

"And I'm telling you that the New York Police Department will find us. Then those people out there will--"

"Have them for lunch," Rachel said, cutting off what Paul was going to say. "Those people out there are nothing like what you have ever dealt with." She knew she could not argue with him without telling him about the Followers and the Guide, or about herself.

"Whatever it is you think I can't handle, I can."

Before Rachel answered or was sure what she would tell him, the bright overhead lights came on. The door opened just after that.

"Good afternoon. How are we all feeling today?" The voice was pleasant but not familiar. Neither Rachel nor Paul could see who was there. They heard footsteps, and then both found themselves grabbed by each arm and led from the cell. As their eyes adjusted to the light they realized they were being taken in two different directions.

Rachel smiled weakly at Paul as he was brought into the dining room. She knew she was as pale as a ghost. Her face was drawn like a person starving to death. Rachel knew it couldn't make sense to him. Hopefully it never would, she thought. Paul was likely to blame her present condition on whatever had been done to her by these people the times she had been removed from their cell.

"You look like hell, Rachel."

"That's funny, I feel like hell, too. But you look very good."

"Does he look good enough to eat, Ms. Westchester?" asked the person seated on the other side of Rachel.

"I should. Two of your guards shoved me into a bathroom to shower and shave, and then handed me this suit to wear," Paul commented.

"No, I'm not very hungry, thank you," Rachel answered.

"What do you people want?" Paul asked.

"Lunch first, Mr. Weaver," the man to Paul's right told him. After this man spoke, stewards entered the room carrying trays of wine. A glass was put at each person's place, except Rachel's. Paul watched as the stewards left and then returned with trays of roasted chicken, and steaming vegetables. Like the wine, food was delivered to all but Rachel. One thing Paul noticed about the stewards was that they seemed nervous. Their eyes were trying to watch everyone at the table at once.

Rachel sat there staring at the person straight across the table from her.

"Okay. Why aren't you getting served?" Paul asked.

Rachel looked around at him. "Eat, my friend, before it gets cold."

"No." Paul pushed his plate away. "Not until you eat as well."

"I was on the guest list, Paul, but not invited to dine." Rachel pulled up with her arms and Paul, for the first time, saw she was strapped to the chair as he was. But with Rachel, they had strapped her arms to the chair giving her only enough room to lift them three or four inches from the armrest.

"This is bullshit." Paul started trying to remove his straps but was quickly stopped and a minute later he found himself tied as Rachel was.

"You should have eaten," Rachel told him.

"I don't eat with people I don't like."

"You are something, Mr. Weaver. Benny told us how you ran to Rachel's rescue. Did you think it the right thing to do? Or was it the policeman in you?"

"I don't see any difference," Paul replied.

The man he was talking to laughed.

"You should know, Mr. Weaver, that Benny is extremely

mad about you shooting him, also. It took a great deal of talking to stop him from shooting you back." The man sipped his wine. "Very good vintage. Well aged."

"Am I supposed to feel grateful to you for that?"

"To me? Heavens no. Rachel talked him out of it."

Paul looked around at Rachel.

"I didn't want you bleeding all over our cell," Rachel told him.

"Thank you," he replied.

"Steward. At least give our police friend a taste of his wine."

The closest steward picked up Paul's glass and brought it to his lips. Paul sipped the wine. It had a strange taste to it. Not bad, just strange--a weak aftertaste. Paul wondered if it was drugged. It didn't make any sense to drug him. As it was, they had the muscle to make him obey.

"So what do you think?"

"I think you people are going to wish you never met me when I get loose. But if you mean the wine, it tastes funny."

"I would have thought that once you reached a higher rank they would have taught you not to mouth-off," said the woman across the table from Rachel.

"Quiet, Augustine," the man that had done most of the talking up to this point, told her.

"You think with Delvar not here yet, you're running this place. Well, Nigel, you're not," Augustine told him.

"Delvar is not here?" Rachel asked.

"Not at the moment. He was informed that we have a surprise for him. Delvar is a very busy man, right now. But he did say he would make a trip here as soon as he could."

"Who's this Delvar?" Paul asked.

"Their Master, you might say," Rachel told him.

"Master, indeed. Think that if you wish, but I assure you, you are mistaken," Nigel corrected her.

"I know what I've been told," Rachel said, not arguing with him.

Paul took another sip of the wine as the steward again brought the glass to his lips.

Lunch continued with pleasant conversation and veiled

threats. Some threats were not as masked as others. After a time, the plates were cleared away but no one left the table.

"Now, we've had this discussion before and you seemed reluctant to help us. Perhaps with your human friend here, you will be more cooperative?" Nigel said to Rachel.

Paul looked to her. Now he knew more about this situation. She had something they wanted and they were threatening him to get it from her. But their words didn't make sense, like he'd missed something. "Human friend," they had said. He looked around at the people seated at the table, then to Rachel. She was looking at him and waiting. He knew she was waiting for him to ask.

"So tell us about Eddie Laidlaw," Augustine invited.

"I'm sure you'll find out sooner or later. Next question?"

Augustine stood up, leaned across the table, and backhanded her. Paul heard Rachael's head hit against the high back of the chair.

"You're going about this wrong," Nigel told Augustine. Nigel reached to Paul's shirtsleeve and pulled it back. With his thumbnail, he cut the surface of the skin open.

Paul grimaced at the sudden pain, but it wasn't a deep cut.

Rachel looked to Paul. "I'm sorry about the pain they will inflict upon you, and they might even kill you, but I can't tell them the things they wish to know."

"So touching. Gets you right here." Nigel poked a fingernail into Paul's chest. Blood covered the area quickly--Paul tensed against the new pain. He set his mind to the fact that it was going to be a long day.

Eddie had sat down to rest a minute and fell asleep. That had been hours ago. He gingerly touched the bandage around his eye but felt no pain. Slowly, he started to undo the wrappings.

"Do you think you should be doing that?" Dena asked.

"I'm sure Sebastian would advise against it, Rita Janel would yell at me, and Rachel would beat my hands down. But they're not here." Eddie looked at Dena with his one good eye. "And if you try to stop me, I'll just bite you."

"Make me offers like that, and I might have to try," Dena

told him.

Eddie laughed and shook his head.

"Eddie, now that you're a Member of the Guide, you'll be putting together a staff of your own. All Members do. I'd like to be on it. I told Colonel Wolf and he said he'd let me go if you'll pick me up."

"I haven't given any real thought to the matter. I have enough trouble watching out for myself, let alone other people." Eddie pulled the rest of his bandages off and blinked. The eye that had been torn from his head had healed. It felt strange to him knowing that an injury like this healed in just half a dozen hours. Strange, but he didn't mind a bit. "Do you need an answer right away?"

"No. I can wait," Dena told him. Her voice told him she lied.

"Let's do this. I'm going to say yes, to picking you up, but you'll have to wait until I know a little more about what I'm doing as a member. I have a small apartment and no room for a staff right now. Okay?" Eddie asked.

Dena smiled but did not reply.

"Where is everyone?" Eddie asked her.

"Colonel Wolf questioned the prisoners you caught. I believe he, Sebastian and Gracen are working up a plan of attack. Gracen had that Priest of yours taken to his house. The Priest seemed reluctant to go, at first, but Sebastian talked him into it."

"Where are they planning their attack?" Eddie inquired.

"Gracen's rooms. The next suite down." Dena reached out to Eddie, barring his way, as he started to get up. He remained seated. "How are you feeling?"

Eddie thought about the question a second. "Hungry," he replied.

"Stay here then and I'll call room service. What sounds good?"

"Type O," he told her jokingly.

"Well, we're fresh out of that. How about a nice AB negative on the rare side?" Dena asked, holding her arm out toward Eddie.

"With all of the members here aren't you a little drained?"

"Not at all. Sebastian asked that the rest of the blooded members here not feed from me, that for this trip, my use, for lack of a better term be restricted to you and you alone," Dena told him.

"Oh really," Eddie said. He took hold of her arm, licked it near the elbow, and then cut it open with his thumbnail. Eddie watched the blood well up. He slipped his mouth over the cut before any blood ran and sucked on the sweet tasting liquid for several minutes. His body had been damaged, healed, left unfed after the healing process, and damaged again. He was healing again, but he was weak. He knew it was from a lack of feeding. This would restore his strength and speed up the rest of his healing process. Eddie ran his tongue through the cut, and then pressed it closed with his lips and sat up.

Dena sat there watching him.

For an instant, he felt very strange about feeding. "Does it ever bother you?" he asked her.

"No. The incisions heal without a scar."

"I don't mean that. I was just wondering if people living off of you ever bothers you?"

"The feedings?" she questioned. "No, Eddie, it doesn't. Unlike the Followers, who kidnap and eventually kill the humans around them, no one forces me to allow this. I think of it as helping mankind, in a small way."

"It's no small way. If the Guide didn't have humans that were like you, we'd have to grab people against their will as well. Even if we didn't kill them, we'd be hardly better than the Followers." Eddie realized right then how important medallion wearers were to the Guide and its members. "I'll tell Colonel Wolf that you're on my staff as of now." Eddie got up and headed out of the suite.

Eddie knocked on the door to the suite and was let in by a member he did not know. He walked in, saw Sebastian and the others, and joined them at the table they all stood around. Eddie was surprised to see Rita Janel. He put an arm around her and hugged her to his side.

"Are you feeling better?" Sebastian asked Eddie.

"Much better. So how are the plans coming?" Eddie asked. He knew something was wrong when all that he received for a reply was silence and the people at the table looking from one person to another. "Somebody tell me something," Eddie demanded, fear creeping its way into his thoughts.

"There's a problem. One we don't seem to have an answer for," Colonel Wolf told him.

"What?" Eddie could feel ice encircle his heart.

"We can attack, of course, but we can't get in so quickly that we could keep the people inside alive," said Gracen.

"Our attack will get us in, but the attack is pointless if the people we are trying to rescue die before we can save them," Wolf explained.

"We need to be in there and near Rachel before we take the rest of the place apart," Rita Janel said to Eddie. "Even knowing where they keep her doesn't help."

"It's an access problem?" Eddie asked.

"Yes." They all answered almost simultaneously.

"I'll go," Eddie told them, staring down at the blueprint of the house and the surrounding area.

"It's not that easy, Eddie."

"We can work our way through the woods around the house easily enough and do it without detection. We worked all of that out already, but that place is mostly rock. It was built to be defensible. The Followers have two types of guards--Followers themselves and a force of mercenaries that they employ to handle the humans they keep as a food supply. We worked out how to neutralize the guards on the approach to the house, but we still have to get in. That's where it will take time. Enough time to fight our way in, which gives them time to kill Rachel, or we blow a hole in the place. But they still have time enough to kill her," Sebastian explained.

"If I'm inside, I can protect her."

Rita Janel forced a smile. "We appreciate your concern, Eddie, but you've only just started healing from the last few days. Even at your peak of health you'd be overwhelmed by sheer numbers."

"How would you get in, Eddie?" Colonel Wolf asked.

"The front door. Walk up and knock," Eddie told them.

"That's crazy, Eddie. Not to mention that if you showed up at the front door, they would know we were coming."

"Not if you attack twenty-four hours after I enter. They would expect an immediate attack. Their guards would be up all night watching for you. When you did attack, they would be completely fatigued, the human ones anyway." Eddie looked over the blueprint more closely.

"You can't use that plan, Eddie. It just won't work," Gracen told him.

"Where in here is Rachel being held?" Eddie asked.

Sebastian pointed to her cell.

"And you know this for sure?"

Sebastian nodded.

"The Followers we caught gave us all the information we needed."

"I'm surprised they talked that quickly, or at all."

"There really isn't anything Wolf doesn't know about making vampires talk," Rita Janel told Eddie.

Eddie looked to Colonel Wolf.

Wolf didn't smile or comment. He had a look on his face that told Eddie it was an education that had been hard learned. There was no sign of satisfaction or shame about the knowledge. It was just something he knew, and knew well.

Eddie listened from that point on as the people at the table tossed out ideas to see what sounded best. Eddie listened to all of the ideas and knew it sounded hopeless.

Night was now upon them, and still no rescue attempt had been formulated.

"Eddie, are you all right?" Rita Janel asked. "Eddie," Rita Janel grabbed his arm and steadied him.

Everyone was looking at him.

Gracen held Eddie's other arm. "You're weaving, my boy."

"You're still too weak to stand around here all night. Go lie down, we'll wake you in the morning," Sebastian told him.

"I should stay," Eddie told him.

"Go rest. When we need you we'll come and get you. You want your strength back to go after Rachel, now don't you?"

Sebastian pointed out.

"Do you need help to your room?" Rita Janel asked.

"I'll be fine." Eddie turned and walked to the door. He left their suite. Outside of the suite, Eddie's slow pace changed to long, purposeful strides. Dena jumped at his brisk entrance to the suite. "I hate to do this to you, but I'm going to have to drain the cup you might say." Dena got a guarded look on her face but let Eddie take her into the bedroom. He took a pad from the nightstand and scribbled a quick note. This he folded and put in Dena's shirt pocket. "When they start looking for me, give this to Sebastian, not before."

Dena nodded.

"Eddie took Dena's arm and fed as heavily as he thought was safe for her. Eddie then slipped out of the hotel.

CHAPTER 25

The evening was cool, the seasons were changing, and this was the first Eddie had really noticed. He had a lot to do and not much time to see to it. He headed straight to a nearby mall he'd passed a dozen times going to and from the hotel. He only needed a couple of things and he was back out on the street. After that, Eddie found himself the nearest motorcycle shop in the yellow pages and stopped there next. He thought how this could be fun to have money, even if it was plastic money, but money enough to walk in and buy what you wanted, right then and there. After they'd run a TRW and credit check on the Visa Card the Guide had given him, it was "Mister" this and "Sir" that. Eddie was getting used to that, too, as well as "Lord Laidlaw" from some members.

"You're sure this is the bike you want. We have much nicer models just over here," the salesman told Eddie.

"No, this is fine," Eddie replied, thinking to himself that it would be a waste of money to buy the prettier bike when this one would get him to Rachel just as well and just as fast.

The salesman pushed the bike out to the street for Eddie and released it to him.

Eddie climbed on and started it up. He took the map he'd bought at the mall from the pocket of the thick jacket he'd bought as well, and looked it over. With some idea of where he was headed, Eddie had one more thing to find before starting out. He put the bike in gear and pulled away. It took him an hour to find what was needed. He switched the bike off, left it in neutral, and coasted to a stop behind a trash dumpster.

The car was quiet, its driver watching traffic and listening to the radio. It had been a slow night so far, and that was good. After the last couple nights of long hours and no real sleep, he was tired. He watched the drunk stumble into the alley entryway. This old guy had enough to drink for one night, but the bottle in his hand didn't waver. The cop wondered if he should run him in for his own good. Would a night in jail stop him from drinking? Not likely. The drunk staggered over to the patrol car and fumbled out a pack of cigarettes.

"You got a light?" Eddie asked the cop.

"Don't smoke," replied the officer.

"What's that?" Eddie asked, pointing to the pack of smokes on the seat next to the cop.

"My partner's," replied the cop.

"I don't see a partner."

"Move on old man," the cop told Eddie.

Eddie hit the cop before he knew the punch was coming. Opening the car door, Eddie pushed the cop to the passenger seat and climbed in with him. "Sorry about this, old buddy, and I'll try to see you get it back, but I need this for now." Eddie finished and exited the car. He locked the car with the sleeping officer in it. After that, he was back on his bike and on his way to Rachel.

Paul hit the ground hard when he was tossed back into the cell. Rachel was pushed in behind him and then the door was locked. The lights were out as quickly as the locks clicked home. Paul didn't care. He had spent his afternoon being tortured, as strange questions were asked of his cellmate. Paul hardly noticed Rachel helping him to lie down and trying to make him more comfortable.

"Can you hear me?" Rachel asked. "Do you understand what I'm saying? I can relieve some of the pain, not all of it, but there is a risk involved. If I relieve the pain, they may injure you again, and more permanently. Do you wish me to aid you?" Rachel asked.

Paul laid there listening to her voice in the darkness. His body hurt everywhere. He didn't realize cuts could hurt so much. And they were just cuts, deep cuts. Even his throat hurt from screaming. Rachel sat there with a stone-like face the whole time, only giving a few answers to the questions about Laidlaw. "I'll risk it. If you can make the pain quit, do so," Paul told her.

"I'm going to apply a little pressure to your throat for a minute. You'll feel as though you're choking to death, but you're not. Now try to relax." Rachel stroked his throat at first, then squeezed as she located his pulse and measured his respiration. As she applied more pressure, Rachel felt Paul tense and he grabbed her wrist but he didn't hold on. It was instinct to try and free up labored breathing. He released her arm after a few seconds. Rachel could tell he was trying to relax. Gently, she applied more pressure. After a minute or so, Paul was asleep. She had used the method the Guide used to put gold medallion wearers to sleep for members to feed from. Normally, a medallion wearer would sleep eight to ten hours after using this method, but Paul was hurt and weak. He would sleep longer, she figured, if they were left undisturbed. Rachel began with the injuries in the upper body. Each wound she filled with saliva until her mouth was dry. She would then wait a few minutes for the salivary glands in her mouth to produce the needed solution to continue. It took her more than two hours to close all of his wounds. She tried not to get his blood on her. The risk of attacking him for blood grew with each day. The taste might make the difference in her resistance. When Rachel was done, she moved across the cell from him and tried to get some rest herself. She sat there, her back against the stone wall and listened to the restless sleep of Paul Weaver.

Paul woke in quiet darkness, but that was normal of late. No city lights peeking through curtains, nor the sounds of traffic. He was getting used to the cold floor as well. He touched one major injury after another and all were closed over. Most were tender and scabbed up on the edges of the cuts, but there was no real pain. He was glad of that, at least.

"How do you feel?" Rachel asked.

"A lot better. What did you do to me?" Paul asked.

"Nothing. You needed sleep, that's all."

"Sleep didn't stop the bleeding. What did you do?"

"Maybe I just spit on you," Rachel replied.

"You have a strange sense of humor, Rachel."

"Thank you."

"Rachel, will you give me a straight answer about something Nigel said?"

"Probably not, but you can ask."

"He referred to me--"

Rachel cut him off. "As my human friend. Yes, I remember."

"What did he mean, human friend?"

"I don't suppose you'd accept that I'm an animal lover, would you?"

"I'm sure you are, but that answer would have nothing to do with the statement we're discussing," Paul told her.

The overhead lights came to life without warning and Rachel was removed from the cell.

Paul was alone in the dark again. This time, though, his wait wasn't long. In less than an hour, the lights came on again. But instead of Rachel being returned to the cell Paul was greeted by Nigel, and removed. Nigel led Paul through the halls he had seen when taken to lunch.

"I see Rachel worked on your cuts. That almost surprises me. It isn't like you're someone special to her, and she isn't any stronger, so she didn't tend herself after seeing to you. She did good work from the looks of you."

"You can see that, can you?"

"It's noticeable, if you know what you're looking for."

Paul looked down at his scabbed arms. "Well, I heal quickly anyway." Paul stopped walking. "What's going on here? Yesterday you cut me apart like salami and now you're all nice to me. Where is Rachel? What do you people have to do with the killings in my city?"

"That's a lot of questions, Mr. Weaver." Nigel continued walking, giving Paul a slight shove that told him to walk or else. Nigel smiled and walked beside him. He took Paul to a door, opened it, and entered. Inside Nigel and Paul looked down at the table in the center of the room.

Paul stared at Rachel. She said nothing but watched his reaction. "This is what they've been doing to you?"

"It's not important," Rachel replied.

"My God, woman, tell them what they want to know."

Rachel lifted her arm with the I.V. in it. "They would not stop this just because I told them about Eddie. They enjoy this and will kill you and me regardless of what we tell them."

Paul watched the blood slowly drain from Rachel's body into the I.V. and he knew she was right. He swung at Nigel with all of the strength he had in him.

Nigel was fast. He caught Paul's punch, picked him up and tossed him across the room against a far wall. "Now, you were asking what we have been doing to Rachel. You can see that for yourself. What we want is Eddie Laidlaw. The reasons are not for you to know. As for the killings, well, you might say we had something of a hand in it. You see your killer is one of us."

"The rogue mind-touched one of your Followers," Rachel said to Nigel. "And you people let the madness set in."

Paul could see the rage well up in Rachel's face. Her eyes spoke volumes of hatred--hatred Paul thought far worse than the anger she had for the things they had done to her.

Nigel smiled. Her anger pleased him. The door to the room flew open.

"He's here," the guard coming into the room told Nigel.

"Delvar." Nigel said to Rachel, letting her know that the leader of their collection of vampires had arrived.

"No. Laidlaw is here," corrected the guard.

Nigel's head snapped around to the guard.

Rachel smiled and laid her head back, her eyes closed. Her entire body relaxed.

Nigel growled. "How did he know where we are?"

"I don't know," replied the guard.

"Get her back to her cell. Him too." Nigel pointed to Paul and stormed out of the room.

Eddie stood just inside the front door of the house. It was a huge house, although that was an understatement. He looked around the entryway. This piece of Follower property was very nice, he told himself.

"So you're Eddie Laidlaw."

Eddie turned around to find a woman and a man standing behind him.

"You don't look like much. Certainly nothing Partath should have had any trouble handling," the woman said to Eddie. She stepped close to him.

Eddie reached out and grabbed her by the throat before she could move. He grabbed her, squeezed and pushed her down to her knees in one move. "I did not say speak, Follower." Eddie squeezed her throat until he could feel muscles and tendons start to crush. He let the woman hang from his hand, staring straight down at her, letting her pull at his hand. He stood there holding her until she stopped trying to get free. When she did stop, Eddie released her. She collapsed to the floor. Eddie knew the damage he'd done would heal. He hated having to be like this, but he had to keep them off balance and off of him. "Are you Delvar?" Eddie asked the man standing there.

"I'm afraid not--" Eddie stepped over the woman to backhand the man across the face.

"Yes or no. No dialog," Eddie said to the man. He saw the man flex to attack, then force himself to calm.

"If I might explain, Mr. Laidlaw?"

"All right." Eddie stood there waiting.

Nigel rubbed his jaw. "Delvar was delayed in coming here. But he is due to arrive within the day. If you would like to stay, we can make accommodations for you in just a few minutes?"

"Fine. In the meantime, I would like to see Ms. Westchester. Now!"

"Of course." Nigel kicked Augustine in the rib. "Get up you stupid cow and show Mr. Laidlaw to the other guests."

Eddie could see the dislike of this man in the woman's eyes, but she forced herself up and pointed Eddie in the right direction.

She said nothing as they walked, but Eddie figured that had to do with the crushed windpipe, compliments of himself. Augustine showed Eddie to a door.

They were close. Eddie could sense Rachel. Distance seemed to affect his bond somewhat. She was nearby, but not in the room he had been led to. Eddie looked to the woman. "Rachel's not in here," he told her.

The woman looked surprised but opened the door. Inside was a bank of monitors where cameras were set up at different locations around the house. Eddie followed the woman into the room. The two guards at the monitors moved away to give her and Eddie access to the screens. He found the monitor that displayed Rachel's cell. She was sitting in the middle of the cell with Lieutenant Weaver next to her. As Eddie reached out to the monitor, Augustine was delivered a second surprise.

Rachel was sitting, half asleep from the looks of her, but then her eyes snapped open and she looked up into the camera, a smile on her face. Although there was no sound, it was plain to see what she was saying. "I knew you'd come."

Eddie nodded and smiled back at her, even if she couldn't see him. He lost his smile as he turned to the woman. "Show me to my room," Eddie told her.

"How did she know you were here?" the woman asked. Her voice was strained with the effort and not much above a whisper.

"She is Guide, I am Guide," Eddie replied. He knew it was the bonding and their relationship, but he thought it best to put forth a reason to fear the Guide and the abilities unknown to the Followers.

The woman nodded and led from the room.

Before leaving, Eddie gave each guard a scowl to think about as they watched their prisoners.

"Where is Eddie? We have to tell him this plan," Wolf said to Rita Janel and Sebastian.

"I haven't seen him since last night," Rita Janel told him.

Sebastian shrugged his shoulders.

Rita Janel got up from her chair. "I'll try his bedroom."

Dena walked over to Sebastian. "If you're looking for Eddie, you won't find him."

Rita Janel stopped and returned to stand next to Dena.

"He told me to give you this today when you started looking for him." She extracted a slip of paper from her pocket and handed it to Sebastian. "He said not until you started looking for him. He was very clear on that."

Sebastian held the note in his hand. "What does it say?" he asked her.

"I haven't read it, but I can guess," Dena replied.

Sebastian opened the paper. "That foolish boy," he muttered.

Rita Janel took the note from his hand. She read it and

shook her head.

"Well? What?" Gracen demanded.

"He left last night to go after Rachel. He said to give him twenty four hours, then come collect the pieces."

"Of all the boneheaded, arrogant things to do," Wolf said.

Sebastian looked to Gracen.

Gracen stared back. "You taught him well, my old friend. He's running headlong into a fight that just might kill him, much the way you used to."

"When I ran headlong into something, it was usually following you," Sebastian said.

Before Gracen could reply, Rita Janel spoke up. "What is important now, gentlemen, is that Eddie is expecting us to get him and Rachel out. We have lots to see to, so let's get our collective asses in gear. Eddie left specific instructions about what he wants us to use as an attack signal. Wolf, you'll see that this is made ready. It's more your line of work."

Rita Janel had a look on her face that made it clear she wouldn't accept any arguments.

"She's right," Sebastian said, getting up. "Let's go get the children." Sebastian headed off to his room to change into clothes more fitting to fight in. The others followed suit.

"They will not get back to us for a time. They are occupied with Eddie for the afternoon," Rachel told Paul.

"That's fine. We have a lot of things to talk about." Paul sat there next to her. "Why drain your blood?"

"To keep me weak." Rachel told him.

The fact that she replied at all shocked him. To get an answer that wasn't a question surprised him more. "What is this madness you spoke of to Nigel? And what is this about a rogue?"

"A Follower, one of them, is your killer, Lieutenant. But if Eddie is here, that means that the rogue is finished. He like myself, work for a very special group. He was dispatched to your city to stop the rogue. The company I work for will not tell you more. You will not find your killer to arrest him. I can tell you that."

"Are you C.I.A. or some other agency?" Paul asked. He heard about secret teams and about some of the inner workings of those teams. These kidnappings and some of the most bizarre interrogations Paul had ever seen, fit the rumors and official reports he'd heard.

"Something like that," Rachel replied.

Paul knew that was the closest thing to an answer he would get, as to who she worked for. "I'll have to try to find out more about your agency. What did you call yourself? Guide?"

"Did I?" she replied.

Paul continued with his questions, although he received fewer and fewer answers.

Rachel proceeded to talk to Paul about all manner of things that had nothing to do with his case or their situation at hand.

CHAPTER 26

Augustine had been sitting in Laidlaw's room for hours now. She wanted to know what was going on outside, what Nigel was planning. Surely the Guide had not let Laidlaw come alone. Or had they, she wondered. The Followers that returned from the island attack had said that Laidlaw stopped them, that he had killed Partath before Partath could react to defend himself. Reportedly, he had killed three Followers at the priest's brownstone and Laidlaw had fought alone. Was he so powerful that he did not need the others of the Guide to come here and help him? Augustine looked over at Laidlaw.

Eddie looked at the woman he had brought into the room with him. What are you thinking, he wondered. Eddie smiled wickedly at her and saw her shudder as if suddenly cold. Cold with fear, Eddie decided. That was good for now. "What's your name?"

"Augustine, Mr. Laidlaw," she told him.

"Eddie," he told her.

"Yes, sir."

"You now seem to have a more respectful tongue in your head."

"Crushing my throat and not killing me is why. When I was hanging from your hand you could have killed me--entirely killed me. You did not. Thank you. Can I ask you something?"

Eddie nodded, but that was no guarantee he would answer.

"Why didn't you? I would have killed you."

"I didn't want to." Eddie was sitting on the bed, Augustine in a chair across the room. "How long have you been with the Followers?"

"Almost two hundred years. Why did the Guide send only you?"

"There are only fifty or sixty of you Followers here, along with your mercenary guards. There was no need to send more than me," Eddie told her. Eddie could see the look of doubt and fear mixed in her features. She doubted his words, yet feared they were true. Eddie grinned at her. "Come over here," he instructed her.

Augustine got up and walked to the bed.

Eddie took her hand and sat her on the bed. "Who has been torturing Rachel? Which of you?" Eddie moved so he was sitting behind her. "Answer me and I will leave you alive and in one piece when I destroy this place."

"What if the answer were to be me? Will you then still leave me unharmed?"

"Yes. But only if you tell me now." Eddie put a thumbnail to the base of her skull. He pushed gently but penetrated the skin. The blood ran down her back staining her dress.

"I was involved, along with Nigel, the man you met at the door." At that minute, Augustine knew her life in the Followers was over. She twisted her head around. "I will help you, but you must take me out of here with you. Agreed?"

Eddie jammed the nail in a little deeper. "You are mine now. Not Follower, and certainly not Guide. You obey me or you will pay in ways you cannot imagine. No deals or bargains, just my word as your law." Eddie pushed the nail in more.

"Yes, sir," Augustine replied.

"Rachel is hungry. Feed her. Return here after she releases you. Do anything she tells you to, or you will feel my anger." Eddie pushed Augustine from the bed.

She crashed to the floor with a thud but got right up.

Eddie looked at her.

Augustine bowed and left the room.

Eddie got off the bed and went out on the balcony. He had been there for half a day, and there was only an hour or two of sunlight left. Eddie hoped to get his signal soon, before the Followers decided to call his bluff.

Rachel and Paul watched the door open after hearing the locks click.

It was Augustine. She entered the cell, pulled two guards in with her, and closed the door. She walked over to Rachel, stopped in front of her, and said, "I have been instructed to feed you well and obey your commands."

Rachel looked up at the camera.

"I have seen to that already," Augustine told her, and indicated the two unconscious guards.

"Why?" Paul asked.

Augustine ignored him.

"Answer," Rachel told her.

"When this place falls, I will not by crushed beneath it."

Rachel watched the woman's eyes. She could see the fear. Rachel nodded. "Eddie sent her," Rachel told Paul.

"You sure?" Paul asked.

Rachel snapped a punch at Paul's chin. She hated to knock him out, but there would be no way to explain her feeding without revealing her true nature.

"On your knees."

Augustine sank to her knees.

Rachel moved to one side of her. She bent Augustine backward, arching the other woman's back. She then took a secure, if not weakened, grip on Augustine's left arm, twisting it behind her and up. She finished positioning her with a foot on her bent legs and Rachel's right hand at Augustine's throat. The marks from Eddie's hand were still just visible from the morning. With her right thumb, Rachel made ready to cut open the artery in Augustine's neck. "If you move, I'll break your back and neck. Then I'll suck you dry. Are we clear?"

"Yes," Augustine told Rachel.

Rachel cut the artery and drank deeply. She sucked hard on the blood, her hunger being satisfied. She could feel strength pump into her heart and through her, her limbs tingling with renewed power. Augustine's weight went from a burden to being easily managed. After several minutes, Rachel sat up.

Augustine did not move.

Rachel reached to her mouth and wiped the blood away, then licked her fingers clean of the red liquid. She twisted her head to look at Paul's unconscious form. Rachel was not pasty white any more. Her color tone was now almost normal. She picked Augustine up and stood to face the woman. "You have other orders from Eddie?"

"To obey you until you release me. I am then to return to

him." Augustine was light-headed from the feeding.

"Your orders from me are simple. Go to each of your guards and see they do not bother us again. Leave that door unlocked and then return to Eddie." Rachel turned to Paul, dismissing Augustine with a gesture.

Augustine looked at Rachel until Rachel stopped and turned back to her.

"Something else?" Rachel inquired. She lifted one of the guards Augustine had brought in. She offered no niceties like feeding on Guide staff personnel. Rachel opened the jugular vein in the first guard's throat and drained all of his blood in a few strong draws. Then she dropped the corpse.

"No. I guess not." Augustine turned and left the cell.

After Augustine left, Rachel consumed the second guard like the first one. With the guards seen to and her strength restored, she woke Paul.

"We have to stay here until Eddie comes for us, or until we are discovered."

"When Nigel comes in and sees you looking all healthy, we're dead anyway."

"Not necessarily, but much of that will depend on you." Rachel moved close to Paul. "I will explain what you must do in that event."

Eddie was beginning to worry when the door opened and Augustine walked in. He forced himself to stay calm when all he wanted to do was get answers from her about Rachel. The cut on her throat was almost healed, but there was still enough of a cut to see that someone had fed off of her. Eddie grabbed her the instant she was within his reach and took her to the sofa. "Tell me what she had to say."

"She gave me no message for you, but did order me to eliminate as many of the Follower guards, unnoticed, as I could. Then I was to return to you."

"She fed well?" Eddie asked.

"Very well from me, and I left her two guards. I replenished my strength with the first two guards I killed."

Eddie looked to the door. From the look on Augustine's

face, Eddie knew she heard something too.

Augustine looked to Eddie. She reached to her shirt and tore it open. "Backhand me," she told him.

Eddie understood and was on his feet. Just as the door opened Eddie let fly. "Stupid Follower," he growled. "How many times do I need to teach you to hold your tongue?"

"Problem?" Nigel asked from the doorway. The smirk on his face told Eddie this man didn't mind a bit seeing him backhand Augustine.

Eddie wondered if it was just Augustine or if backhanding any woman was fine with him.

"Your woman here has a severe attitude problem," Eddie told Nigel as he walked away from Augustine. "What do you want? Has Delvar arrived?"

"No, I'm afraid not. I thought I'd invite you to dinner this evening though."

"Fine. When?"

"I'll send someone for you in an hour."

"Two would be better," Eddie told him, looking to Augustine.

"Two hours it is. Just yell if you need anything," Nigel told Eddie as he left.

Eddie turned to Augustine. "Scream," he whispered.

She did.

Just beyond the door, Nigel stood listening to the silence. As Augustine started screaming, a smile touched his lips and an evil glitter filled his eyes. After a minute, Nigel walked off.

Eddie sat down next to Augustine. She started to close her shirt, but then stopped. "Do you think he'll be back?"

"Yes, but not for a while."

They didn't get close to dinner before the next interruption. The sun was just down when an explosion sounded in the woods east of the house. Eddie jumped off of the bed and was at the door before the sound faded.

"What is it?" Augustine demanded.

"Reinforcements," Eddie told her.

"You lied."

"Not about killing you if you don't do as you're told," Eddie informed her. "Now take me to Rachel."

They raced through the halls of the house. Everyone was running somewhere. Eddie was with Augustine, so no one looked twice in their direction until they turned a corner into a different hall and came face to face with Nigel and several guards.

"Kill them," Nigel ordered. The two front guards brought their Uzi machine guns up and fired. The bullets hit Eddie in the chest. The impact drove him backward into Augustine. They both crashed to the floor. Nigel smiled with pleasure as he and the guards saw Eddie's body trapping Augustine—he was lying across her legs.

Nigel stepped forward, taking one of the Uzi's away from his guard. He turned the gun on Augustine and Eddie and opened fire. Blood spattered everywhere. "He wasn't that tough." Nigel looked down at his handiwork that had been Augustine. As he did, he realized too late that there was very little blood on Eddie.

Eddie sat up and grabbed Nigel's gun arm. With a firm grip on his forearm, Eddie leaned backward but brought his feet up against Nigel's shoulder and ribs.

Nigel screamed like he never thought he would as Eddie tore his arm off at the shoulder.

In the same move, Eddie pulled the Uzi from Nigel's hand. He came up firing. The guards had no place to scatter to and fired back. In seconds, the hall echoed with the sounds of gunshots and bodies were everywhere. Eddie was on the floor again. Bullets had hit his arms and legs. One had ripped through his throat and a second one had grazed his skull. He lay there stunned by the pain, but he was alive.

Eddie closed his senses to the world around him, the way Rita Janel had taught him, even though it was difficult under these conditions. He focused his vampire magic on his own body and forced the healing to start its repair as rapidly as possible. After a time, Eddie could think clearly and was able to get to his feet. He knew how weak the healing would leave him, but he had no choice. As he opened his senses to the world again, he realized he had been down a long time. The distant fighting was here. "Damn," Eddie cursed, moving again.

Worry about Rachel filled him. He had planned to be there to protect her. Now he was far behind the Followers and the guards that might still reach her. Eddie broke into a dead run.

The door to the cell was ajar so the people moved forward slowly. They reached the entryway and pushed the door open. The cell lights were on. Upon walking in they found several other guards dead on the floor, and then they saw the black man with the machine-gun. Paul had not fought this hard since he was in Vietnam. As he shot, the Follower that had been with this group of guards, ducked back behind the doorframe, catching only one bullet in his left shoulder. Leaping the guards' bodies, Rachel attacked the Follower. Paul watched as the two people went round and round. Their fight went into the hall. Vicious was the only word that came to mind as he watched her fight. The woman tore into men and women alike. She showed no mercy, and why should she after their treatment of her? He sensed that wasn't it, though. She was fighting for Laidlaw. She was not going to be stopped. Paul and Rachel had not made it out of the cell hallway. Rachel didn't want to go far yet, and besides, their cell was defensible. Rachel got through the Follower's guard and landed a solid strike in the form of an eye gouge. The Follower screamed and grabbed his face. Rachel grabbed his head and twisted, breaking bones and cartilage alike.

"There's more coming!" Paul yelled. "And I'm out of ammo." Rachel was tired, but turned to face the next Follower and broke into tears. She raced to Sebastian and jumped into his arms. He was covered in blood but so was she. That was the first good look Paul got of the man, and he could see it was Sebastian. The membership of the Guide moved forward. They were all coated in blood and decimated with injuries, but it was the second best sight Rachel had ever seen. She was looking for Eddie, but couldn't find him. He wasn't far--she could feel that. Paul walked over to the group.

"You ain't New York cops, but I think you just passed the entrance exam," Paul told them.

"Die, all of you!" screamed someone up the hall in the direction Rachel and Paul had just come from. Nigel stood there. He had two grenades in his left hand. His right arm was missing. "Attack the Followers at their home? Who do you think you are? I'm going to kill all of you." Nigel grabbed the two grenade pins with his teeth and pulled. He started laughing as he readied his grenade toss toward the Guide.

At that same instant, Eddie entered the hall behind Nigel. "No!" screamed Eddie. He slammed into Nigel full force. Eddie's speed and their weight carried them forward through the open cell door. The grenades detonated a split second after they passed into the room.

Rachel jerked free of Sebastian and was in the cell almost before the smoke started billowing out. Sebastian and the others were not far behind her. Paul looked into the room and walked away.

Rachel had Eddie in her arms, cradling him to her chest. "I'm here Eddie, hold on," she was crying. She looked into his eyes. He was conscious, but in pain.

Sebastian knelt beside them. The blast had torn Nigel to shreds. They'd have to scrub him off of the walls. Eddie's left arm had been shredded, as well as part of his left leg. The shrapnel from the grenades had ripped through the bulletproof vest Eddie had secured from the policeman in the cruiser back in New York. Even with Eddie's precaution of the vest, there was massive damage to his torso. Deep burns from hot metal covered his chest and face.

Eddie reached for Rachel's hand. He could not talk, but there was nothing to say.

Rachel held him as Rita Janel pushed through the crowd to Eddie and Rachel. "Let me have him Rachel," Rita Janel demanded of her.

"Use your magic," Rachel sobbed.

"Yes, girl, but you must release him to me."

Sebastian took hold of Rachel and pulled her away.

Rita Janel reached deep into the core of her being and drew forth her Vampire Magic. She could not heal him fully--the damage was too great. She knew this as the green light of energy flowed over her and onto Eddie. He jerked, but made no sound. Then the light faded. Rita Janel felt lightheaded, weakened by the magic.

When the light faded, Rachel grabbed Eddie again. He was unconscious now--sleeping, but still badly hurt.

"Will he live?" Sebastian asked Rita Janel.

"His injuries are serious, I've stabilized him but we must move him and the other injured."

"I want him at home," said Rachel. "My home in Vermont. See to it."

Sebastian nodded and left to make the arrangements.

Rachel and Rita Janel sat in the cell and waited for the stretcher that would take Eddie to the helicopter.

Rachel could feel Eddie inside of her. He would sleep for a long time, but she would be there when he woke.

CHAPTER 27

Eddie woke in darkness. He started to try to sit up, but it made his chest pain more excruciating, so he abandoned the effort. He hurt and felt so weak. Eddie rubbed his chest with his hands, surprised to see both of them. He could feel how soft the bones of his sternum, rib cage, and left arm were. Eddie again decided to try to sit up. The effort made him sick to his stomach, and still he couldn't rise.

"If you try again, I'll have you tied down." The voice came out of the darkness but the person there did not surprise him.

"I thought you were asleep," Eddie told Rachel. He had sensed her presence the instant he woke. He had known she was there even in his slumber, watching over him.

"I was. Your pain woke me. You are recovering quickly, but you're too weak to move and far too injured to do more than lie there."

"I could use vampire magic to speed up the process."

"You're weak, Eddie, don't rush things. Heal slowly this time. You're safe, we're home." Rachael came over to the bed and sat down beside him.

"Home?" he questioned.

"My home, our home," Rachel said simply. This answer did little to tell him what he was asking. "More precisely, my bed, in my bedroom, in my house in Vermont. Please feel free to substitute our for my wherever you wish."

Eddie could tell she was smiling, even with the room too dark to see her. He reached his hand up to her cheek. The endeavor was exhausting and the movement was teeth gratingly painful. Even so, the touch of her skin was worth the price of the pain.

Rachel took hold of his hand and held it in place for him. She reached her free hand to his cheek. "You had me so scared, Eddie."

"I'm a Vampire Lord. This was nothing."

"Let me remind you, My Lord, that vampires die, even

Vampire Lords. You came very close this time. You were weak from injury to begin with. You could have easily died, Eddie. You would have if not for Rita Janel's vampire magic, which is all the buzz in the Guide now."

"I know, Sebastian also reminded me the night we stood around planning the attack." He caressed her cheek and then brought his hand down. Rachel still held on to it. They sat there in silence for several minutes. Eddie pulled Rachel's warm body down next to his. It wasn't a painful effort because she didn't resist. Instead, she wrapped him up in her arms. "What finally happened at the Followers' house and the Lieutenant?"

"Gracen sent Delvar a telegram declaring that the house was Guide property and he wants the deeds to be sent to him. Delvar will not object. As far as the City of New York is concerned, Paul is a hero. He stopped the cult killings of their citizens. We made sure he had all the evidence he needed to close his case, and we provided him with a few dead Followers as his cult. He will likely get a commendation of some kind and maybe a promotion. He's convinced that we Members of the Guide are some sort of a secret government intelligence agency. No one has seen fit to correct him."

"What about--"

Rachel laid her fingers on his lips. "Time to rest. I'll tell you more later." She kissed him, and then tucked him in tighter to her body. They did not move for hours and spoke very little. As the sun rose, the room became brighter. Eddie twisted in Rachel's arms until he faced her. He lay there watching her, with Rachel staring back at him.

"All right, what?" Rachel finally asked.

"I'm just watching your face in the morning sun," Eddie told her.

"Why?"

"It's the most wonderful thing in the universe." Eddie slipped his hand gently behind Rachel's neck and drew her closer. Her warm breath caressed his cheek just the instant before he kissed her. "I want to watch it for a thousand lifetimes."

"That's one of the advantages of being a vampire, isn't it?

Once you find that right person, you get the thousand life times to be with them." Rachel kissed Eddie this time.

"Do those doors lead to a patio?" Eddie asked, pointing to the heavy looking doors off to the right side of the room.

"Yes."

"Let's sit out there. I want to watch for dragons."

"You're very weak."

"But with your help--"

Rachel hesitated at first, but then helped Eddie up and outside to a chair on the patio. "I'll get Dena, you must be hungry."

"Later," Eddie told her. "Sit with me."

Rachel nodded and put a second chair beside his. "What are you thinking about?" Rachel asked, seeing the far off look in his eyes, the wondrous expression on his face.

"Marsha. Her, Frank and Debra," Eddie replied. "Marsha must be worried sick by now, not hearing from me." Eddie looked around at Rachel. "How long have I been here?"

"We brought you here from the house. That will be a week tomorrow. But I've been sending telegrams, signed Eddie. I'll show you the notes I mailed. If you feel up to it later, you can call her."

"I should call. I should see if she could get some time off. All three of them."

"Time off, Eddie?" Rachel asked.

"I guess it is presumptuous of me to assume they might want to come."

"Come here?" Rachel asked, still confused. Not that she minded his inviting his family over. The house had plenty of room, but she thought it might be a good idea if he were healed fully first.

"Come out for our wedding," Eddie told her.

Rachel's expression went flat.

"Oh, I guess I should ask you first, huh?" Eddie asked, taking Rachel's hand in his. "Would you please become Mrs. Laidlaw?"

Tears started rolling down her face. Rachel threw her arms around Eddie's neck, kissing him as hard as she could.

Eddie held her, not noticing the pain in his still healing chest.
"Oh yes, Eddie. Yes, I'll marry you."

"Rachel," Eddie said to her. "Do you think our future will be as stormy as our beginnings have been?"

"The future isn't predictable, Eddie, but you'll learn that. We have lots of time. You and I will see a future we can only guess at right now. There will be good times and bad. It's part of life, but we'll have each other, Eddie." Rachel pulled herself in tighter against his chest.

Eddie held her as close as he could, his eyes closed while they sat there enchanted by each other.

High above, snowy white clouds drifted by--clouds that could be described as dragon shaped. Not that even dragons could pull Eddie's attention away from Rachel.

ABOUT THE AUTHORS

Grant's interest in writing developed after high school and continued while serving as an aircraft mechanic in the Air Force. He still works in this capacity for one of the leading aircraft manufactures. This is where he met his future wife and writing counterpart, Mary.

Mary, who also works as an aircraft mechanic, has not only been the consulting writer, but also acts as at-home first-proof editor on their projects.

Together, they have written about swords and magic, adventures in space faring worlds, as well as travelers on worlds less advanced-- seven books at present. They battle the regular problems that any book goes through to come into existence, while building aircraft and maintaining their home with a dog and two cats. Like all writers, there's always one story in the works. See you soon fellow readers.

Printed in the United States
65313LVS00001B/1-48